EVEREST 1153

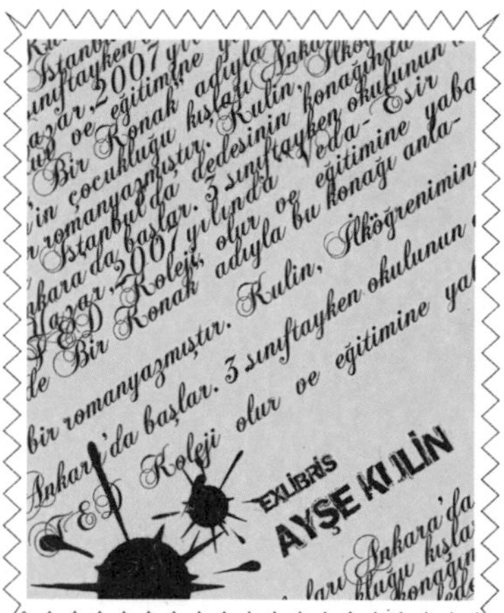

A Collection of Contemporary Turkish Literature

AYŞE KULİN

After graduating from the American College (ACG) of Istanbul, Ayşe Kulin worked many years as editor and writer for newspapers and magazines and also in the cinema industry.

Her first story book won two prestigious literary awards (Haldun Taner & Sait Faik) and her first novel became a best seller. Kulin also holds other literary awards and has been selected the author of the year numerous times. Some of her stories and novels became TV series and motion pictures. Her works have been translated into twenty four languages. She is the Goodwill Ambassador of UNICEF since 2007. Her major novels translated so far:

Face to Face
Farewell

Books in Turkish

1. *Güneşe Dön Yüzünü*
2. *Bir Tatlı Huzur*
3. *Foto Sabah Resimleri*
4. *Adı: Aylin* (Aylin)
5. *Geniş Zamanlar*
6. *Sevdalinka* (Sarajevo of Love and War)
7. *Füreya*
8. *Köprü*
9. *İçimde Kızıl Bir Gül Gibi*
10. *Babama*
11. *Nefes Nefese* (Last Train to Istanbul)
12. *Kardelenler*
13. *Gece Sesleri*
14. *Bir Gün*
15. *Bir Varmış Bir Yokmuş*
16. *Veda* (Farewell)
17. *Sit Nene'nin Masalları*
18. *Umut*
19. *Taş Duvar Açık Pencere*
20. *Türkan-Tek ve Tek Başına*
21. *Veda* (Graphic Novel)
22. *Hayat-Dürbünümde Kırk Sene*
23. *Hüzün-Dürbünümde Kırk Sene*
24. *Gizli Anların Yolcusu*
25. *Saklı Şiirler*
26. *Sessiz Öyküler*
27. *Bora'nın Kitabı*

SARAJEVO
OF LOVE AND WAR

Ayşe Kulin

Translated by
Kenneth Dakan

§

Publication No. **1153**

Contemporary Turkish Literature 16

Sarajevo
of Love and War
Ayşe Kulin

Original Title:
Sevdalinka

Translated by Kenneth Dakan
Cover Design by Utku Lomlu
ex-libris by Eren Üstüner
Page Layout by Bahar Kuru Yerek

First English Edition: December 2012

ISBN: 978 - 605 - 141 - 592 - 5
Certifacate No: 10905

EVEREST PUBLICATIONS
Ticarethane Sokak No: 53 Cağaloğlu/ISTANBUL
Tel: +90 (212) 513 34 20-21 Fax: +90 (212) 512 33 76
e-mail: info@everestyayinlari.com
www.everestyayinlari.com
www.twitter.com/everestkitap

Printed by Melisa Matbaacılık
Çiftehavuzlar Yolu Acar Sanayi Sitesi No: 8
Bayrampaşa/ISTANBUL
Tel: +90 (0212) 674 97 23 Fax: +90 (0212) 674 97 29

Everest is a trademark of Alfa Publishing Group.

To the Undestructible Muslim Bosniaks
whose sufferings lasted eight hundred years
and
to the memory of my beloved father Muhittin Kulin.

This book tells the story of the heroic and honorable people who survived the horrendous war in Bosnia which lasted between 5/4/1992 and 26/2/1996. Sarajevo was held under siege for 1.395 days with electricity, communication and water systems cut. 10.600 Bosniaks of which 1.600 were children lost their lives and the remaining Bosniaks were to accept the Dayton Treaty.

With this treaty, 51% of Bosnia was left to Bosnia-Hersegovina and Serps who formed 34% of the population before the war, gained 49% of the land.

SEVDALINKA*

Sarajevo, September 1986

Nimeta swayed in time to the song on the radio as she washed the dishes, but she was feeling overwhelmed. Even her son had noticed how absentminded she'd been at breakfast.

"Mom, that's the third time I asked you. Are you deaf?" he'd asked.

"I'm a little distracted, dear. I was unable to sleep last night."

"Why?"

"I'm always like this as winter arrives."

"Winter doesn't arrive in september, mom."

"Well, it *is* autumn. An in-between season. Winter will certainly be upon us soon enough."

---

* Love Songs.

Her son gave her a quizzical look, as though wondering whether she'd had too much to drink again, the night before.

For the past three years she'd been drinking far more than any self-respecting woman should, and it was only natural that her son realized as much, along with her husband, her friends and her mother. Fiko was eleven. An alert, quick-witted boy, he'd developed fast, body and mind. At times, under his sharp gaze, she was scared he'd read right through her, straight to her heart. It scared her because she'd made a place in her heart for a love that shouldn't be. When it had taken seed, she'd done everything she could to keep it from growing, but to no end... Perhaps if she and Stefan had been living in the same city it would have been easier to separate. They'd have seen each other every day, at any time, made love until sated and been done with it, and each other. Or perhaps, living now, as they did, in different cities, they'd have been unable to meet at all, and drifted apart...

But circumstances had conspired to snare them in forbidden love, and Nimeta had turned to drink to conquer her helplessness and shame.

"I'm leaving, mom. Hana's not ready yet and I can't wait for her, I've got an exam."

Fiko set their orange tabby, Bozo, down in front of his bowl of milk.

"Run along, Fiko. I'll drop Hana off at school."

Fiko kissed his tired, absent-minded mother on the cheek and hesitated at the door.

"Is Dad coming back today?"

"Yes."

Fiko left. Nimeta slumped onto a chair at the kitchen table and rested her head on her arms. The moment she'd been delaying for years was swiftly approaching. She'd promised

Stefan that she'd tell her husband about their relationship. That had been three years ago. First she'd pleaded that her children were too young. Then her father had fallen ill, and she hadn't wanted to upset him. Next, she'd decided to wait until Hana started school. Well, she'd finally run out of excuses.

"You've got to make a choice," Stefan had told her. "I can't go on like this. It's either me or your husband. I can't stand it anymore, the woman I love being married to someone else."

"I'll tell him I want to divorce. That I'm tired of our life together, of being lonely all the time..."

"No, you won't; you'll tell him the truth, Nimeta. If he doesn't know there's another man he won't agree to a divorce. Don't make him try to find fault with himself. Tell him openly that you're in love with someone else."

"That would kill him."

"In your religion, people die only at the appointed hour, don't they?"

Nimeta had laughed. "Stefan, it's not the angel of death that will kill me, it's our love. And it's my sins that will kill my husband," she'd said.

Tonight, Burhan would come home tired and dirty, as always. Without hugging his wife or children, he'd head straight for the hot bath drawn by Nimeta. He'd recline in the steaming water, trying to recover from those exhausting days spent up in the mountains. Then, as they sipped plum brandy at dinner, he'd outline every excruciating detail of engineering projects in which Nimeta had absolutely no interest. He'd do the talking, as always. It wouldn't occur to him to ask Nimeta what she had been doing, as though she didn't have a career of her own. After dinner, he'd take an interest in the kids, find out how Fiko's lessons were going, appear to listen as Hana insistently sang the new school anthem, cuddle Bozo on his lap as he watched television, drag his wife to the bedroom and, ensuring that the children were locked out, want to make love. That would be the beginning of the most difficult moment of the day.

Nimeta, who'd been madly in love with her husband and had shared his bed since age twenty, would make all sorts of excuses. As it would be impossible to slip free of Burhan, who'd spent the last fifteen days far from home, she'd have to drink enough plum brandy at dinner to send her head spinning.

The only way out was for Nimeta to say she was in love with another man and wanted a divorce. That's what Stefan had told her, repeatedly. Still, how could a woman in her late thirties, with a son growing into manhood and a daughter still so young, simply destroy her marriage of so many years? How could she explain it to a husband who was in no way at fault? How could she tell her children, family and friends of her deception?

"Mom, should I wear the blue blouse or the pink one?"

Her daughter was standing across from her, a blouse in each hand.

"Wear whichever one you like."

"You tell me."

"Wear what you want. You can see I'm busy."

"You're just sitting at the table, mom. What do you mean you're busy?"

"I'm thinking about something I have to write. You're distracting me."

"They're picking kids for the show today. I've got to look my best."

"Wear the pink one."

"Why?"

"Hana! Children usually grow out of questioning everything by the time they turn four. Why are you like this?"

"Why are you like this, Mom?"

"Like what?"

"Like you're always in a hurry or thinking about something."

Her daughter's remonstrance stung. "I'm in love and I'm unhappy and I don't know what to do," was something she couldn't tell her little girl, who stood across from her holding up two blouses, her big blue eyes downcast. Nimeta reached out and gave her a hug.

"Wear the pink one, 'cause you always look pretty in pink. They'll pick you today, Hana. I'm sure of it," she said. God could have the decency to make at least one member of her family happy, she thought to herself.

The phone rang as she was stepping out the door with her daughter. Hana would already be late for school. She hesitated, but when the phone kept ringing she rushed over to answer it.

"What's taking you? Come quick. Incredible things are happening. We're having a meeting in twenty minutes," Sonya said.

She dropped Hana off in front of the school and zoomed down from Alipasina toward the television building on Selimovica Boulevard.

Incredible things were happening! What could be so incredible? Life had been stagnant for so long, everything seemingly predetermined, down to exactly what people would be and do, and even how long they would live. She'd go to work every day, complete the assigned task of writing up news bulletins and collect her salary; as for Burhan, when the construction project finished in Knin he'd start working at another site, somewhere else. The children would continue their studies. They'd take their summer holidays in Split and go skiing in Bjelasnica come winter. Just like his father, their son would grow up to become an engineer; just like her mother, their daughter would marry the boy she loved upon finishing university, bear him children and resign herself to a life of boredom when that great love ran its course a few years later.

How could something "incredible" possibly happen in Nimeta's world?

Tonight, she could tell Burhan that she was in love with another man and wanted to separate. Tonight, she could pack her bags and abandon her home. Tonight, she could fall asleep in Stefan's arms. When she woke up the following morning next to the man she loved, the spell dissipated, she'd remember the reproachful words and stares of her husband and children, and then she could clamber atop the iron railing on the balcony overlooking the vivid autumn garden and plunge downwards.

Now that would be incredible!

"Hey, are you stupid or what? Watch where you're going! How do people like you get licenses anyway?"

She rolled down the window and called out to the man she'd nearly crushed as she'd screeched to a halt:

"I'm sorry. It was my fault. My mind was elsewhere."

"Do your thinking elsewhere, not behind the wheel," the man said. He had a point. For some time now, Nimeta had felt that everyone had a point. Did it have something to do with her crushing sense of guilt? Everyone was always right about everything, except her. She was wicked, a betrayer of husband, family and children. Mirsada was the only person who knew what she was up to, although her mother sensed it. Yet she seemed to be surrounded by accusatory eyes. She couldn't defy those looks, could only resignedly accept that all of them were right.

Just the other day, Ivan, the head of the news-production team, had said, "Something's happened to you, Nimeta, you didn't used to be this meek."

"Is that so bad? You used to complain I was too headstrong," she'd pointed out.

"I have to admit that I sometimes miss the old, fiery Nimeta," he'd responded.

It was Burhan who more than anyone missed the old Nimeta, a woman boisterous and high-spirited, a tenacious defender of strongly held views, gone missing, in her place a woman mute, reluctant and lifeless. Time could do that, could change everything, crumbling all that stood in its path. Who had ever been untouched by time?

While Burhan missed the old Nimeta, he secretly appreciated returning home after long separations to a woman silent and still. He was tired most of the time. He'd grown accustomed to being on his own, and to peace and quiet. In the past, he'd pretended to listen attentively as his wife tried to fill him in on her work in the media. But it bored him. The hectic pace, irregular hours and tumultuous lifestyle were so alien to his world of plans and programs, facts and figures. There was one thing he wanted above all else when he returned home: to feel the smooth, white skin of Nimeta's body, which was a little fuller than it had been fifteen years ago, against his, to bury his head between her breasts, to love her to his heart's content and sleep until morning breathing in her scent. It was Burhan's strongest desire, and it had stood the test of time.

Nimeta parked her car and walked with quick steps toward her office. She shut out the buzz of animated voices in the elevator. Her mind was on other things. Tonight... Things would come to a head tonight.

She wasn't conscious of arriving at the designated floor, turning left as she stepped out of the elevator, pulling out the chair at her desk and hanging her jacket on the back of it. She was on auto-pilot.

"Nimeta, have a look at this."

One of the girls was handing her a faxed newspaper article. She glanced at the page number on the glossy surface and for the first time since she'd awakened that morning the inner workings of Nimeta's private world ground to a stop. The real world was back.

The September 24, 1986 issue of Belgrade's *Vecernje Novosti* newspaper had run an excerpt of a memorandum prepared by Serbian academicians. It claimed that the Serbians residing within the borders of Croatia were in great jeopardy and that the failure to address this issue could lead to a catastrophic outcome for all of Yugoslavia. Journalists had long known a proclamation of this kind was in the making. In fact, the secret police had informed President Ivan Stambolic that the Serbian Academy of Arts and Sciences had initiated such an undertaking. Stambolic, a Serban nationalist accused by the Croatians and Slovenians of being overly partisan and by his fellow Serbs of being insufficiently sensitive to Serbian interests, had expected the memorandum to contain certain socio-economic criticisms of no particular concern. He'd been mistaken. The memorandum went far beyond the incitement of nationalism, asserting that Serbs had been oppressed for centuries and appealing to the long-smoldering grievances buried in the hearts of every Serb.

Nimeta sat down and took a deep breath. She read the excerpt again, from beginning to end. Her instincts were unerring; three years earlier she'd heard the far off rumblings that led to this memorandum. But like the distant patter of footsteps, it was growing louder, drawing nearer and beginning to sound like the heavy tread of marching boots. The Serbs were preparing to play a dangerous game based on ethnicity. They'd begun playing with fire to further their ambition of a Greater Serbia. The first sparks were the lies continuously repeated in the Serbian press, the strident clamor over the supposed threats endured by Serbs everywhere. The voices of unease and suspicion were growing louder and louder all across the land.

She'd first heard them at the funeral of Aleksandar Rankovic. Strangely, a chain of events that would throw both Nimeta's private life and Yugoslovia into upheaval started on the same date, August 20, 1983.

Nimeta had been sent to Belgrade to cover the funeral of Aleksandar Rankovic for Bosnian Television.

A secret police agent expelled from the Communist Party of Yugoslavia in 1966 for bugging the phone of Tito, Rankovic had come to embody Serbian nationalism and the worst nightmares of the Albanians. Once he'd helped ultra-nationalism take root throughout his country, he died, as all mortals do. Tens of thousands of Serbs attended his funeral, on behalf of the ethnic Serbs living in all of the republics of Yugoslavia. A large press contingent watched this racist show of strength from various vantage points. And that's how, on August 20, 1983, Nimeta met Stefan Stefanovic, a journalist from Zagreb.

Reporters from every Yugoslavian republic except Serbia decided after the funeral to send notes of protest to the mayor of Belgrade at the time, Ivan Stambolic, for having failed to keep the crowds under control. Stambolic, who would become the president of Serbia in 1986, had simply looked on that day in 1983.

Along with the other journalists, Stefan and Nimeta had gone to the bar of a large hotel to have a post-funeral drink. Stefan's dark eyes were locked on Nimeta's blue ones all night. They were surrounded by people but she saw only him; among the babble of voices, she heard only his; she could feel the heat of body. It was a sensation she hadn't felt for many years, whose very existence she'd completely forgotten about. For the first time ever, she'd wondered what it would be like to cheat on her husband. And what about Hana, her little girl, her baby; and Fiko, whom she adored… Still, she'd allowed the strange dark man to hold her in conversation, to propel her to the dance floor, to pull her close, to breathe on her neck, to take her captive and to transport her to other shores. At the end of the long night in the bar, when they'd returned to their hotel, she'd been helpless to stop him from guiding her to his room, from unbuttoning her blouse, from brushing her breasts with his lips. She was on fire, and he could do whatever he wanted.

That night, she felt as though she was slipping into sleep not in a hotel room but somewhere by the sea, stretched out on the sand, the waves crashing against the shore, rocking her. A steady stream of stars raining down from the night sky, somewhere on another planet. Never before had her heart raced and her blood pulsed quite like this.

The next morning, when she woke up in Stefan's bed, in tears of shame, regret and joy, she'd said, "Perhaps that demon whose funeral we attended yesterday captured my soul, Stefan. How else could I have done this?"

"Our souls have been captured, Nimeta, but not by Rankovic."

Nimeta was unable to raise her tearful eyes from the floor. Cupping her chin, Stefan had lifted her head until her eyes met his and said, "Darling, it's love that's taken us captive."

Nimeta had left Stefan and returned to Sarajevo. She'd written her articles and prepared her news bulletins. She'd cooked for her husband and children, and scoured the house, from top to bottom, astonishing Milica, who came twice a week to do the cleaning, with her housekeeping skills. She'd taken on extra duties at the television station and hadn't complained when Burhan was sent off to new projects. She'd fully expected to get the better of her heart.

But Mirsada, her friend and confidant since childhood, had said, "You're done for. Just one bite of the forbidden fruit and there's no turning back. You're in for it, Nimeta." Somehow, Mirsada had understood what lay in store for her better than Nimeta herself.

"The meeting's about to start. Better get a move on. What is it with you this morning, anyway?" Sonya was right up in her face. She scooped up her pen and notebook and they walked over to Ivan's office together. An unusually large group had gathered around the conference table.

"There have been some interesting developments, guys," Ivan said. He picked up the pile of newspapers resting in front of him and distributed them to his colleagues. As they scanned the newspapers from all the various republics he lightly coughed as though to clear his throat, and continued.

"Even the Belgrade papers are criticizing that damn memorandum but not a peep from their leader, Milosevic. Doesn't that strike you as a bit odd?"

"Wait a bit," Ibo said. "Milosevic's stooge, Dusan Mitevic, is going to make a speech to the party group. Milosevic will use Mitevic as his mouthpiece."

"Doesn't the guy have a mouth of his own?" Sonya asked.

"Milosevic knows how to play his cards close to his chest. Didn't he rise to his post by dancing to President Stambolic's tune?"

At the meeting that day, they discussed what measures to take if Serbian nationalism morphed into outright racism.

"I think we're being naive," Mate said. "It's already happened, they've pressed the bell. Who could stop the Serbs now?"

"You've got friends in Zagreb, Nimeta. Talk to them and find out that what they think," Ivan said.

After the meeting, Nimeta called Stefan's newspaper. For the first time, they spoke not as lovers, but as colleagues. He sounded grave and worried, and agreed with her that the memorandum signaled disaster. For the first time, he didn't talk about them, and didn't mention about Burhan's return or divorce. He didn't even tell her how much he'd missed her, and wanted to kiss her lips, her neck, her throat. He simply informed her that he would fax the relevant information within an hour and that they would need to talk again the following day. The click of the receiver seemed to shake Nimeta out of a deep three-year sleep; she felt surprised, worried and a little dejected.

The journalists waited. Milosevic's stooge, Dusan Mitevic, delivered a speech in which he proclaimed the memorandum a grave threat to both Yugoslavia and Serbia. Furthermore, a paper reflecting government views published the speech in its entirety. There still hadn't been a peep from Milosevic, but Dusan's words were incorrectly assumed to be his own. Sensible people everywhere heaved a sigh of relief.

That night, Nimeta gave Burhan a typically subdued welcome, but this time they had a long talk about her office. Burhan had heard about the memorandum and was worried. The Croatians in Knin had reacted much more vociferously than the Bosniaks in Bosnia, which had influenced his own reaction.

"What does your journalist friend in Zagreb have to say about all this?" he asked.

"Stefan, you mean?"

"Yes."

"Ivan spoke to him today. Zagreb's more alarmed than Bosnia over this."

"Sometimes I can't help feeling like there's an ill-omened bird gliding over our heads, Nimeta," Burhan said.

"That bird took wing three years ago, at Rankovic's funeral. Let's see when and where it lands." Nimeta said. Her husband gave her an odd look over his eyeglasses, or so it seemed to Nimeta.

When they retired to their room for the night Burhan held his wife, but he didn't make love to her. Nimeta lie frozen in her husband's arms, afraid that if she woke him he would.

Stefan called the following morning after Burhan and the children had left the house.

"I couldn't tell him again, Stefan. I can't tell him that I don't love him, that I love someone else and I want a divorce. I'll never be able to tell him that. Forgive me," she said.

"Nimeta, that's because you love Burhan," Stefan said.

"Oh, no it's not, Stefan. I'm madly in love with you. I think about you and miss you all the time. And you're the only man I want to make love with."

"You're in love with me, but you love your husband."

"What makes you say that?"

"It's clear you don't want to hurt him, even to further your own happiness. How do I know? Because not only am I in love with you, Nimeta, I love you. I love you too much to upset you, which is why I keep forgiving you."

"Try to understand, Stefan," Nimeta said. "When we next meet I'll be able to explain it all face-to-face. When are you coming to Bosnia?"

"Not for a long time. There's a position available in London, for which I applied today."

"Are you serious?" she asked.

Her voice trembled.

"I am."

"I don't believe it, Stefan. Does that mean I'll never see you again?"

"We'll see each other. But if we meet as lovers, we're doing it on my terms. You know what I expect."

"You're a man. You're not attached to anyone. I'm the one in an impossible position. You want me to break up my family."

"I can't share your love, Nimeta."

"You're not! I… I…"

"I asked you to make a choice. You've made it."

"It's not a choice I wanted to make. I had to. I've got responsibilities."

"You choose the way you prioritize your responsibilities."

"And you, you're really going to punish me by going off to London?"

"I'm not doing it to punish you."

"Then why are you going?"

"To forget you."

"Will you be able to forget me? Is this possible?"

"I'm going to try."

"Well I don't need to try to forget you to know I never could."

"I have to try."

"Why?"

"Because the woman I love is unable to share her life with me."

"I'm doing everything I can, you know that. I do everything I can to see you every chance I get. I make excuses and create opportunities by lying to my family and friends."

"It's not enough for me, Nimeta. This is no way to live. Either you walk with me or I end the relationship."

"Do whatever you want, Stefan," Nimeta said drily.

She didn't get up when she hung up the phone. She sat motionless, her arms and legs paralyzed.

She knew she'd never forget Stefan for as long as she lived. But apparently he thought that by putting some distance between them he might forget her! The man she'd loved for three years thought a few thousand kilometers would take care of everything.

So intense had their love been that she had no idea what she'd do without it or him. Memories of their time together, from the day they met to the present, flashed before her eyes. Tears streamed down her cheeks.

For three years, each time the phone on her desk rang something would catch in her throat. What if it was him? If it was, the world would recede. In his voice was birdsong.

Stefan would frequently come to Sarajevo. They'd meet in the bar of the Hotel Evropa. There might be there with colleagues but they heard and saw nothing but each other, just like that first day.

Stefan had rented a flat in Ali Pasino Polye, near Nimeta's workplace. It was easy for them to meet since Burhan was so often out of the city. Nimeta would stop at Stefan's for a few hours on the way home from work. There, with him, she was transformed from a mother of two careening towards middle age to a woman of joy and passion. At the touch of Stefan's hand her breasts seemed to firm, her curves to grow more rounded.

Nimeta had gone to Zagreb twice on business and once, during a national holiday, she'd claimed to be doing so. They were more carefree in Zagreb, where nobody knew her. Nimeta had reveled in being able to go out for candle-lit dinners and hand-in-hand walks in the streets and parks.

After a while, though, their relationship began hitting some road bumps. They weren't spending enough time together for Stefan. Nimeta felt the same way, but it was Stefan who made an issue of it. Finally, he forced her to make a choice and dismissed her protestations about not being able to abandon her children. "You don't have to leave them behind," he'd said. "I'll move to Sarajevo. My work allows me that flexibility."

For the first time in her life, Nimeta had rebelled that day. She could be stubborn and capricious, and demanding of her husband, in particular, but she'd always hesitated to do anything that would cause upheaval in her ordered life, even when she was an impetuous teenager.

At the beginning of the 1970s, she and her family had gone to Istanbul to visit relatives her parents hadn't seen for years. Nimeta was about fifteen or sixteen, a willowy, fair-skinned girl with wheat-colored hair. Istanbul so enchanted her and her family that they visited at several times years in a year, staying at the summer-house of relatives in Erenköy.

Even today, she still treasured her memories of those wonderful holidays spent giggling and cavorting with cousins in the cafes on Bağdat Avenue, eating ice cream, meeting with local boys at the open-air summer cinemas, renting rowboats at the seaside…

During one of those summers she'd flirted with a neighbor boy from the next house over. Back in Bosnia, she found herself counting the days until summer and started learning Turkish to better decipher letters from her first love.

Near the end of one summer, not long before her family planned to return to Bosnia, the family next-door had paid a visit to ask her parents for her hand. Her father had looked favorably on the proposal, but not so her mother, Raziyanım.

"You said you were going to send her to university," she'd said to her husband, who'd approved their daughter's marriage to a young Turkish man.

"Istanbul has universities."

"She doesn't even know proper Turkish," said Raziyanım.

"She'll learn."

"But Nimeta's my only daughter."

"That's all the more reason to make sure she has the best of everything."

"What's so good about that boy?"

"He has a degree, he's well-mannered and good-looking."

"Sarajevo is swarming with well-mannered, good-looking boys with degrees."

"That's true, but who can predict what'll happen to Sarajevo the very day Tito dies. Istanbul is Turkish, and has been Ottoman for five centuries. She can put down roots and feel secure in her future. Don't be selfish."

"If we're going to marry her off to a Turk then we might as well pack up everything and migrate to Istanbul ourselves," Raziyanım said.

Nimeta was as in love as only an eighteen-year-old who has given her heart for the first time can be. Even so, she was unable to rebel against her mother, to insist, "I'm staying here." She'd cried all during the hastily arranged trip back home, not once looking at her mother's face. She'd kept the roses he'd presented that day, dried and hidden away. Months passed before she smiled at anyone in her family. They didn't go back to Istanbul, not the next year, nor ever again.

Raziyanım had her reasons for disliking Istanbul.

The end of the sultans' four-hundred-year reign in the Balkans had led to an exodus of Ottoman administrators and their families. Bosniaks have been migrating ever since. Every time the winds of war blow -and they rage through the Balkans all too often- Bosniaks gather up their worldly possessions and set off for strange lands.

Istanbul came to mean separation for mothers and sons, husbands and wives, brothers and sisters, fiances and loved ones. It meant lost homes and lands. These journeys along a road of no return meant unrelenting homesickness in a foreign land. Each person leaving Bosnia for Istanbul would carry with him an abiding sense of loss and pain.

Istanbul was the city of flight. The point past hope. The place of last resort. It was to Istanbul that those who had lost all hope were swept on a flood of tears.

Migration 1878

It was in 1878, the Ottomans relinquished their rule of Bosnia, with that the Bosniaks suffered their most heart-rending separations. The administration of Bosnia and Herzegovina was transferred from the Ottomans to the Austro-Hungarian Empire. The Ottomans had resigned themselves to the inevitable. A great empire was fragmenting piece by piece. At each turn another bit of territory was wrenched from its bosom. Without the firing of a single bullet, without a single skirmish, without the shedding of a single drop of martyr's blood, the Vilayet of Bosna was surrendered to the unbelievers through signatures at a conference table. The Ottoman Empire was dissolving.

Raziyanım's great grandfather was shedding tears of blood, his heart in the clench of a fist of flame... Desperation... Indecision... Either he would spend the rest of his life bowed and dishonored in "the shadow of the cross", or he would be uprooted from his land and deprived of his home and livelihood... He would be among the hundreds making their way to Stamboul among the bundles, packages, sacks and pack trains... to a place with no prospects for jobs or homes.

Once Husrev Agha had made the decision to migrate he immediately set about preparing a turquoise necklace and matching earrings. The client was a man of great esteem. Salih Zeki Bey had admired a necklace painstakingly crafted by Husrev Bey that he'd glimpsed around the neck of his sister, and had ordered a similar one for his wife. No matter what, Husrev Agha would have to surrender the order before he went anywhere. Salih Zeki Bey's family also had a claim on him. His mother had been reared on a farm in Travnik belonging to Zeki Bey's father. They'd given his mother a fine trousseau and assisted her children once they were born. Husrev even owed his shop in Bascarsı market to that family of benefactors. Fehim Bey had not only helped Husrev to open the shop, but had had him craft all the silver found at the family country estate in Travnik and home in Sarajevo, from trays, plates and jugs right down to the girdle encircling the waist of his daughter, Reside, and the tobacco box in the pocket of his son, Salih Zeki.

Having decided to migrate, Husrev Agha had pushed his apprentice to set the stones in the jewelry as quickly as possible. At last, there it was: a turquoise necklace gleaming sky blue, delicately coiled on the workbench.

The pendant earrings and necklace were carefully packaged and a pair of horses stood at the ready to ensure their speedy arrival in Travnik. As luck would have it, however, they had received word that Salih Zeki Bey was in Sarajevo, at the family manor in Vratnik. Husrev would be able to rush over with the delivery and still have time left over to meet some of his other orders, return payments for those he couldn't, and prepare for the journey that lay ahead.

The wait in the inner courtyard of the manor was brief. He'd soon slipped his feet into one of the many pairs of fine, soft goat leather slippers in rows before the door and been ushered into the sun-washed *selamlık* where male guests are received. He was presented with a chilled glass of morello cherry sherbet and an assortment of rose and mastic lokum sent from Istanbul. He observed that the silver ewer from which the sherbet was poured and the silver platter on which the lokum was arranged were both his handiwork from seventeen years earlier. His breast swelled with pride. In his youth he hadn't relied on apprentices, preferring to craft his pieces with his own two hands. Now, however, those once sure hands trembled and his eyes, too, were not up to the task of high precision work. A few moments later, a tall man with piercing blue eyes dressed in a freshly pressed shirt of raw silk strode through the door. Salih Zeki Bey greeted Husrev Agha with the deference due a man his age and enquired about his health.

Husrev Agha opened the package and laid the necklace and earrings out on the low, backless couch. Salih Zeki Bey gazed appreciatively at the stones, which were a slightly lighter shade of blue than his own eyes.

"My wife greatly admired the jewels you crafted for my sister. I wished to present her with a remembrance from Bosnia before we left. I now understand why your work caught Gül Hanım's eyes. God bless your skilled hands, Husrev Agha."

"May she wear it on many days of joy, sir," said Husrev Agha, gazing one last time upon his handiwork.

Salih Bey made a wordless sign with his eye and brow to the manservant he'd summoned with a clap of his hands. The manservant returned in moments with a dusty rose purse of velvet. Salih Zeki took the purse and handed it to Husrev Agha.

"May God bless you with abundance, sir," Husrev Agha said, before working up his courage to ask a question.

"You mentioned that you were leaving these parts. Are you considering moving to Istanbul?"

"I'm thinking about it, Husrev Agha. This place will go downhill once it's under the administration of the giaours. Half of my family has already migrated. I wish for my children to be born in Muslim lands. My elders have often told me of the cruelties they suffered under the unbelievers."

"I myself feel the same way. I'm thinking it's best to take my family and leave. But how are we to earn our daily bread in a strange land?"

"You're a skilled artist, Husrev Agha. They say Stambol is a much larger city than this one. I haven't see it myself, but so I've heard. Fear not, you'll be able to make a living wherever you go," Salih Zeki said. "It is we who must fear migration. Unless these lands and properties are registered to us, how are we to subsist in a strange country? Unlike you, we have no craft or trade."

"Mercy me, sir," Husrev Agha said respectfully, "how can gentlemen be engaged in trade?"

"We may not be granted lands to administer but we have made up our minds. Those of our relatives who have already migrated do not regret their decision. My nephew, Fehim Bey, is the deputy for Bosnia in the first Parliament. They've sent word that they await us. If you too decide one day to migrate to Stambol, Husrev Agha, find either Fehim Bey, who lives in the district of Rami, or Senate member Halilbasıc Rıdvan Bey. They'll know where we are," said Salih Zeki Bey.

Husrev Agha was in high spirits when he left the manor. He'd stuck the purse in his waistcloth and made his final decision. It augured well that even the esteemed Kulinovic Salih Zeki was prepared to leave behind his villages and vast properties and move to Stambol. Tonight, he would most certainly broach the subject to his wife. They would have to prepare immediately. They must set out without delay. Without even realizing it, he broke out into a folk song. He felt the hot sun on his back and felt the urge to stretch like a cat. For the first time in days, he felt at ease.

He walked along with a sense of inner peace. He didn't yet know that his son-in-law would oppose migration, and that he would have to leave his beloved grandson, Memo, behind. He didn't know that the decision to migrate meant that his daughter would separate from her child, never to be reunited.

Raziyanım grew up listening to this tale of the grandmother who abandoned her son and moved to Istanbul. She had grown to hate this woman, who'd died in Istanbul and deprived her son of a mother's warmth and love.

Istanbul meant the separation of children from their mothers.

Memo, the boy Faika left behind when she moved to Istanbul with her family, the boy grew up unloved and with dim memories of his absent mother, would develop an antipathy towards the female sex. That's why he didn't marry until he was well into his fifties, and only then to ensure a male heir. What a mockery it seemed when his young wife placed their twin girls in his arms. Black fate had decreed that he would dandle two girls on his knees at an age when his contemporaries were playing their grandchildren. He never grew to love the girls and departed this world a peeved a distant figure for them.

Istanbul meant fathers who didn't love their daughters.

Fortunately, the twins had a young and jolly maternal uncle who doted on them, acted as a pseudo father and took them under his wing. A much loved uncle whose family had been torn apart by Istanbul, and was now all alone...

Years later, Raziye's twin sister had gone off as a bride to Istanbul, with the pledge that they would meet at last once a year. The sister was terribly homesick and missed her twin. Then she fell ill.

By the time Raziye got to Istanbul it was too late. Clutching a bouquet of violets and a handful of soil brought from Sarajevo, she'd knelt in front of a marble slab and run her fingers along the inscription of her sister's name. She'd watered the soil. Tears had streamed like rain down her cheeks.

Istanbul meant broken families and yearning for one's sister.

Back home in Bosnia, troubles were never-ending, and as the globe was ravaged by World War II, the Bosniaks once again endured some of the worst suffering in the Balkans.

It wasn't the Bosniaks who had started the war, nor had they taken sides. They reached for their weapons only to defend their homeland and their lives. They'd imagined that only the invading forces comprised the enemy, but soon found their enemies multiplying. Their own neighbors turned on them. The trials and tribulations of the Bosniaks were without end.

In pursuit of the dream of Greater Serbia, the paramilitary Chetnik organization had slaughtered Bosniaks in 1942. Then, in 1943, the Chetniks had killed 9000 elderly Muslims and children.

Next, the Bosniaks found themselves battling with the fascist Croats known as the Ustase... More wounded, more dead, more extinguished hearths... Famine... Misery and poverty. In a desperate bid to save their lives, they even ended up joining Hitler's 13th SS Division. In order to stay alive, Bosniaks fought with the Germans against the Partisans, with the Croatians against the Serbs, with the Serbs against the Croations, with the Chetniks against the Ustase, with the Ustase against the Chetniks, and with the Partisans against all the others. They were unable to ingratiate themselves with anyone. They always suffered the highest fatalities. In April of 1945, when Sarajevo was liberated, 75,000 Muslims had died in the Balkans, a number higher than that of either the Croatians or the Serbs.

Thanks to a relative who'd fought in the 13th SS Division, her maternal uncle was granted special permission by the Germans and arranged for his family to flee to Istanbul. He wanted to educate his sons in a country that wasn't at war. He wanted to live without fear, work hard and spend his earnings on pleasure.

On the morning of the day their day was to depart for Istanbul, he'd asked his wife to prepare an early breakfast. He'd tapped on the bedroom doors of their sleeping sons, first the elder, who'd turned eighteen the previous day, then the younger. He'd gone to the kitchen and brewed some tea, calling out to his older son, who was still in bed. When the boy still failed to appear, he'd gone back up to his bedroom and, this time, banged quite hard on the door. There was still no response. When he opened the door and lit a lamp he found a letter resting on a bed that hadn't been slept in. With shaking hands, he read:

> Dear mom and dad,
>
> I can't go with you. I'm following my ideals by going up to the mountains. Don't worry about me, wait for me or try to find me. By the time you read this letter I'll be in the mountains. If we succeed in our cause I'll find you wherever you are. Forgive me.
>
> Your devoted son,
> Fikret

The morning still was shattered by the heartrending scream of a mother.

Fikret had gone up to the mountains and joined Tito's forces. When the revolution was successful, he'd stayed in the army, been promoted and become a respected and admired officer in the Yugoslavian Armed Forces. Years later, he'd arrived in Turkey in an official capacity. His brother, who'd been a boy of twelve when the family left Yugoslavia, had graduated from the Harbiye Military Academy and was now a handsome staff officer in the Turkish Armed Forces. He'd been granted leave to see his big brother and had come to Istanbul to that end. Reunited for the first time after so many years, the two brothers strolled the length of Beyoğlu arm-in-arm, one in Yugoslavian uniform, the other in Turkish. Then they'd visited their mother's house, changed into civilian clothes and returned to Beyoğlu, where they'd gone to a *meyhane* in the Balık Pazarı. Speaking half Bosnian and half Turkish, with the odd word in German and English, when necessary, they'd caught up with each other. Rakı was knocked back, and Rumeli folksongs and *sevdalinka* sung. They went from tipsy to plastered, and Hikmet had begun loudly criticizing the Turkish government, becoming more and more enthused, with the criticism soon turning into a string of denunciations and curses. Fikret had tried to silence his brother. He was terrified. He quickly paid the bill and propelled his brother out of the *meyhane*. They'd hailed a cab and continued on to Kumkapı, in whose *meyhane* they watched dancing girls and listed to the *saz*. Just as dawn was breaking they'd stopped in Arnavutköy for a bowl of tripe soup and, as the sun cleared the horizon, a glass of tea in the Cınaraltı tea garden in Emirgan. But it was only after Hikmet stripped, plunged into the waters of the Bosphorus in the chill of morning, was caught up in a strong current and was mercifully returned to shore by clutching the line of a small sailing boat that he finally sobered up. On their way home they bought a newspaper. Fikret was astonished to see that *Sabah* newspaper was full of the same denunciations given voice by his brother at the *meyhane*. The next day, after visiting his father's grave and kissing his mother's hand, Fikret returned to Belgrade.

His beloved niece, Raziye, had traveled all the way from Sarajevo to Belgrade to see her uncle and accept any gifts he'd brought her from Istanbul. She immediately noticed an uncharacteristic moodiness on the part of her uncle.

"What's wrong, uncle. You seem glum," Raziye had said.

Her uncle said nothing at first. When he was ready to confide to her in a low, disillusioned voice, he'd said, "I understand now that I've missed out on life. A life wasted due to a youthful mistake. And it's too late to do anything about it."

"Uncle, you're a man of high standing in this country. You shouldn't have a problem in the world..."

"I'd never plunged into the flowing waters of a city at dawn. I'd never lambasted the government, either drunk or sober. I've missed out on life... It's passed me by."

Never again would Uncle Fikret be the man whose loud guffaws could be heard three houses away. Nobody knew what had happened but they all agreed that he was a changed man after his visit to Istanbul.

Fikret never expressed his disappointment to his family. He watched in silence as Muslim cemeteries were bulldozed over to become parks and high-rises, without even the courtesy of notifying the families. He never told anyone how aggrieved he was when Tito converted mosques into museums, storehouses and cowsheds. Nor did he let on that he could never accept the closure of Muslim associations, schools and, worst of all, the Gazi Husrev Bey Charitable Foundation, which had been operating since 1530.

He never pointed out that Tito began currying favor with Muslims only after he became Secretary General of the Non-Aligned Movement, and never mentioned how transparent he found the practice of appointing Yugoslavians with names like Ahmet, Mehmet and Mustafa to posts in Arab countries. The fervor that had burned in his heart had turned to ashes in his mouth.

Except for that bout of depression when get got back from Istanbul, Raziyanım dimply perceived her uncle's heartbreak on only one occasion. The father of her son-in-law, Burhan, had got to chatting with her uncle at a family dinner one day, and conversation had turned to Tito's nationalization of private property. The father had said:

"I felt so sorry when I became unable to send our relatives in Istanbul their fair share of the property. For years, I'd been sending a share of the revenues and provisions, not once neglecting to ship off canisters of Travnik cheese. What did they do, how did they manage to scrape by once those shipments were cut? How can you possible explain to someone unfamiliar with a regime like ours that Tito has seized lands that have been in our family for centuries, and that they no longer belong to us?"

Knowing how fond her uncle was of Tito, Raziyanım braced herself for yet another one of those endless political debates between those who supported Tito to the death and those who smeared Tito, ignoring his many services to their country.

"Don't worry about the relatives in Istanbul. If you're going to feel sorry, feel sorry for us," her uncle had said in a deeply disappointed voice. Raziyanım was astounded.

According to her, Istanbul was a city that saddened and crushed loved ones. It was a city that sowed discord.

When she'd seen her daughter falling for that Turkish boy she'd whisked her straight back to Sarajevo from Istanbul. She wasn't going to allow her family to be scattered; she'd keep them together and intact. "Unity and Solidarity": that was the slogan of Yugoslavia and it applied just as aptly to her own family.

A year later, Nimeta had started university. That's where she'd met Burhan. She'd quickly got over her first love. Burhan was handsome and from an old Bosniak family. Two years later, he'd become an engineer. This time, Raziyanım had no reason to object.

They married right after Burhan graduated and for the first few years Nimeta doted on her husband and was happy. After their life had settled into a routine, however, it dawned on Nimeta that up until the day she died she would occupy herself with nothing but work, running a household and raising children.

She felt as though she were stumbling through a thick, grey fog. And it was as she fighting for breath in that fog that she met Stefan, breaking though like a ray of light. Now, plunged into the mist once again, she felt that he'd been nothing more like a roman candle, flaring up and engulfing her with light, only to fizzle out...The eternal, endless fog was back.

When the children returned from school Nimeta was still sitting straight-backed in the chair by the phone, staring at the wall and unconscious of Bozo rubbing up against her legs.

As Burhan drove his wife to the clinic that evening it was with a terrible sense of guilt that he opened up to the doctor sitting next to him in the car. He was guilty of neglecting his wife for work. Having to look after the children on her own while holding down a demanding career had driven her to depression. He was going to organize his work so that he could stay in Sarajevo with his family. He'd been running himself ragged to give them a better life but he now realized that happiness didn't necessarily lie not in earning more money. He'd brought prosperity to his home but this time true happiness had slipped through his fingers. Now his wife was depressed, his children were adrift and he was confused. Each member of the family was unhappy, and he, Burhan, acknowledged his role in that.

What he didn't know was that as his wife was going through her personal hell, his country, too, was sliding into a hell of its own.

As Nimeta recovered in a clinic bed, the scene was being set to turn Yugoslovia into a bloodbath.

April 1987

As the leader of the Serbian communists, Slobodan Milosevic, was sent off to Kosovo by his dear friend, President Stambolic, to pacify yet another incident of Serbian minority unrest, he was planning to tip the scales in his own favor but had no idea of the extent to which destiny was working on his behalf.

Slobodan Milesovic and Ivan Stambolic had been close friends ever since they were students at Belgrade Law School. Because Ivan Stambolic had devoted himself to the party throughout his university years, his rise through the ranks happened earlier than Milosevic's. But he had always looked out for his friend. Milosevic even owed his first Party assignment to Stambolic. After twenty-five years of sharing a common fate the two friends were inseparable, with Milosevic becoming both the leader of the Communist Party and Stambolic's right-hand man.

Stambolic had visited Kosovo for the first time on April 6, 1986. In Kosovo, where ethnic Albanians comprised 90% of the population, the Serbs had collected ten thousand signatures to protest the arrest of the separatist activist Bulatovic. Stambolic had been forced to go to Kosovo to try to alleviate the mounting tensions.

A year later, the Serbs were once again up in arms and it was necessary for an official from Belgrade to pay a visit and calm them down. Stambolic assigned the person he most trusted to take on this mission, his good friend Milosevic. It had never occurred to him that this same friend would stab him in the back in a bid to emerge as the leader of the Serbs.

But Milosevic has his own plans, ambitions and abettors. His leading follower/disciple was the head of Belgrade Television, Dusan Mitevic, who would so abuse the power of television, so inflame the Serbs, so incite the people with false scenarios, that all would be helpless to prevent Yugoslavia's dismemberment under the guidance of Milosevic.

On April 24, 1987, thousands of Serbs turned out to welcome Milesovic at the door to the Cultural Center in Kosovo Polye. The police had taken all precautions to prevent a riot. Television cameramen, press corps and journalists from all of the other republics leaned out from the balconies and windows of apartments in the vicinity.

Nimeta had gone back to work three or four months earlier. She'd been discharged after two months in the clinic but had stayed at home for a time. Ivan had sent Nimeta some writing assignments and translations that she could handle at home. By the new year she was back at her desk in the office. At first they'd hesitated to send her on assignments outside the city but she now appeared to have made a complete recovery and would slowly have to reassume the responsibilities of her profession.

Stefan was in London when he heard of her illness. He'd sent flowers and a card, clearly reluctant to upset any further the woman whose life he'd sent into such upheaval.

In order to look after the children while his wife was in the clinic, Burhan had stayed at home and sent a fellow engineer to take his place at the construction site in Knin. Raziyanım had also come to live with them and had stayed on even after Nimeta was discharged from the clinic, determined to guard against Nimeta's unsavory friends and drinking habit.

Nimeta hadn't objected, even though she knew that her mother would constantly stick her nose into her business. She had no intention of succumbing to another affair of the heart. In any case, Stefan was in London and other than a call or two to wish her a speedy recovery they weren't speaking. She was so heartbroken she assumed it was over. She would never see Stefan again. Nor would she think about him.

And yet, as Nimeta set off for Kosovo with a cameraman, a little voice kept telling her that she would run into Stefan.

There was no sign of him among the journalists from Zagreb arriving at the hotel and she didn't dare to ask anyone.

In this overwhelmingly Albanian province, the tens of thousands of Serbs had appeared out of nowhere, gathering in front of the Cultural Center where Milosevic was scheduled to make a speech. It was as though they'd been lowered from the sky in baskets. The Serbs pressed against the door of the Cultural Center as police with truncheons tried to force them back in order to protect Milesovic from enraged protestors. There simply wasn't enough room in the center for a crowd of this size. The police called for calm on their megaphones. Out of nowhere, stones began raining down on the police from a truck parked in the street. As the police attempted to respond to both the Serbs and the hail of stones, chanted shouts of, "Killers! Killers!" broke out...

The doors to the center had been secured and the members of the media were jammed into the lobby of the building, where they could hear the uproar outside but had no idea what was going on.

After looking on for a time from his perch on the balcony, Milosevic would come down and make the speech that would change the course of his life. At the first glimpse of him, the Serbs who had been chanting, "Killers! Killers!" at the police and government would begin chanting, "Slobo! Slobo!"

The president had dispatched Milesovic to Kosovo not to inflame the Serbs, but to placate them. Furthermore, there were no incidents of Serbs being beaten and such. However,

Milosevic had already determined how far the winds of Kosovo Serbian nationalism could take him if properly harnessed. Ultimately, it didn't matter that the words leaving Milosevic's mouth that were fabrication designed to inflame.

Nimeta was among the journalists packed into the lobby so tightly they were in danger of suffocating. It was the speech being delivered by Milosevic, however, that left them breathless and stunned. They could easily see where fiery rhetoric of this kind would take the already enraged Serbs.

Ironically, even as Milosevic was assuring the Serbs that "on these lands nobody can dare to mistreat you," each and every Kosovon policeman on duty that day was being pummeled, stoned and abused by Serbs.

Not to be outdone by Milosevic, the other attendees at the rally delivered speeches demanding the autonomous status be revoked immediately and leveling accusations against the Albanian leaders. A dramatic appeal for help was made to Belgrade and Serbs were said to be in mortal danger from their neighbors of Albanian descent. The journalists on the ground floor of the Cultural Center fought for a glimpse through the windows of the events taking place outside, but had already heard enough to know that something momentous had happened.

"This has gotten completely out of hand, Nimeta. Let's try to go up to the next floor and get some footage from the balcony," Mate said.

"What? I can't hear you!" Nimeta shouted.

"Let's go up one floor. I want to shoot from the balcony."

"You go ahead. I'll follow."

Nimeta pushed her way through the crowd towards the stairs but couldn't see Mate anywhere. Perhaps he took the elevator, she thought to herself. By the time she reached the stairs she felt as though she'd been torn to pieces. The stairwell was relatively empty. She could take a deep breath at last. Someone came running down the stairs. Thinking it might be Mate, she craned her neck for a better view and found herself unable to breathe once again.

"Nimeta!"

"Stefan! What are you doing here?"

"I'm a journalist, aren't I?"

"I thought you were in London."

"I came back two months ago."

"Two months ago?" The hurt in Nimeta's voice was clear.

"I didn't call you because…"

"You don't have to explain anything to me."

"I'm not explaining, I'm just saying I didn't call you because…"

"Stefan, I'm not interested in why."

"Aren't we friends, Nimeta?"

"We'll always be friends."

"I'm glad to hear that," Stefan said. "Are you alright now? Have you completely recovered?"

"Recovered from what? Are you asking about the alcohol, the insomnia or the depression?"

"Was I so bad for you, Nimeta?"

"Don't worry about it, Stefan. Anything good comes with a steep price tag. I don't have a drinking problem anymore. I've come out of my depression. If I have trouble sleeping, I take a pill."

"I'm so happy you're healthy again. Is your husband okay?"

"He's fine."

"And Hana?"

"She's fine too."

"How's Fiko?"

"Fiko's fine... so is my mother. Mirsada, Ivan and Sonya are all fine. Even Bozo's fine. Bozo's our cat, remember?"

Stefan hesitated, uncertain for a moment what to say next.

"Do you want to go get something to eat and drink when this horrible demonstration is over?"

"Why are you asking me this? Weren't you the one who didn't want to see me?"

"A friendly drink in memory of old times..."

"Let's not have a drink, Stefan. The happiness of everyone at home, including the cat, depends on my staying away from you."

Stefan stopped two steps down and looked up at Nimeta. He reached out his arms and pulled her towards him. He rested his head against her stomach. They stayed like that for a moment.

Then he slowly said, "I understand. Goodbye, Nimeta." He raced down the stairs and was gone.

Nimeta sank down onto the stairs, too weak to continue climbing them. "Whenever these damn Serbs go on a rampage a storm also breaks out inside me," she thought to herself. The wound in her heart started seeping blood again.

A week later, as she was preparing the following day's program in the news room, Milos called over to her from his desk:

"Nimeta, your call's been mistakenly put through to me. They're calling from Zagreb."

Nimeta went weak at the knees. Struggling to control her voice, she asked, "Who is it?"

"I have no idea. I've put it through to you."

Nimeta let the phone ring a few times as she composed herself. Then she reached over and picked up.

"Hello."

"Nimeta, it's me, Stefan."

The quaver in her voice got the best of her: "Ah, how are you, Stefan?"

"I wanted to share some information with you."

"What information?"

"It's about Milosevic's speech in Kosovo."

Nimeta sat upright on her chair.

"I'm listening, Stefan."

"I don't want to bother you, but I thought you'd want to hear this."

"I'm listening."

"That speech we all thought he'd ad-libbed… Everything had been planned four or five days before, Nimeta, from the crowd and the truck full of stones to the assaults on the police force. The whole thing was carefully orchestrated, Nimeta."

"Who… who planned it?"

"Milosevic, of course. Who do you think benefitted most from the events of that day? I just wanted to let you know. You can use this information any way you choose. If they ask for a source, say it's from Belgrade. I can vouch that it's trustworthy."

"Thanks, Stefan," Nimeta said. "I'll talk to Ivan."

"Good-bye. If I come across anything else juicy I'll let you know," Stefan said.

After she hung up, Nimeta felt a sense of disappointment. He'd addressed her as he would any colleague. She lit a cigarette and waited until she'd smoked it all. Then she went to Ivan's office.

"A reporter friend of mine just passed on some information from Belgrade that he'd heard on the grape line," she said to Ivan.

"What is it? Why'd he tell you?" Ivan asked.

"I'll tell you what he said. As for why, let's just say he owes me one," Nimeta replied.

September 1987

In 1974, Tito granted certain rights to the ethnic Albanians who made up the overwhelming majority of the population of Kosovo. As a result of these rights, a number of Albanian held important posts in the national government. Kosovo wasn't a federal republic, but it was an autonomous area within the Yugoslavian republic of Serbia.

After Tito's death, the Serbian populace of Yugoslavia grew restive. They maintained that Kosovo belonged to the Serbs, even though they accounted for only 10% of its population.

Serbs who subscribed to this view developed an insidious plan to deprive the majority Albanians of rights and to treat them even worse than a minority. To this end, Serbian television broadcast a constant stream of propaganda alleging that the Serbs were under threat from the Albanians, that their lives were in danger, and that their wives and daughters were being raped. The main actor in the broadcast of these false accounts was Dusan Mitevic, a flunkey of Milosevic.

On September 1, 1987, the news agencies in the Yugoslavia Republics received a faxed message from Belgrade.

At the Paracin Barracks in central Serbia, a private of Albanian origin had shot and killed privates of Serbian origin as they slept, with his own body later discovered about half a mile from the barracks. Aziz, the Albanian soldier, had most likely committed suicide.

That same day, Mirsada rang her colleagues from Belgrade.

"Do you have any idea what's really behind this so-called massacre of Serbs?" she asked, her voice shaking with emotion.

"Why do you think we sent you there? Tell us, Mirsada," Ivan had said.

"The private who shot the four soldiers is an ethnic Albanian. That much is true. But of the four soldiers, two were Muslim, one Croatian and one Serbian."

"Are you sure?" Ivan asked in a strangled voice.

"Of course I am. I'm calling from Military Headquarters," Mirsada said. "And there's one more thing, the body of the assailant was reportedly discovered half a mile from the barracks. A suicide, apparently."

"What are your sources?"

"Military officials. The army won't give us permission to see the body."

"So we'll never know if it was suicide or if they had him eliminated."

"We'll never know. But I can confirm that the Albanian had some kind of nervous breakdown and killed his fellow soldiers."

"Anything else, Mirsada?"

"There is, Ivan. The other families came to claim the bodies and have already buried their sons. But the Serb's funeral is being held tomorrow. Let's see what they get up to," Mirsada said.

Mirsada had been living as a correspondent in Belgrade for ten months. After separating from her husband she'd taken Nimeta's advice to get a change of scenery and applied for a transfer outside of Bosnia. A system of rotating posts had already been in place and she was soon sent to Belgrade. She'd settled into a flat near work and found herself a lover who was a fellow journalist. Relationships with non-journalists tended to fall apart, so it was just as well. While irregular hours and chaotic schedules were acceptable for a man, there was much less tolerance for women who worked in media. A man from the same field was more likely to forego a homemade dinner and spotless home for a woman racing from location to location with a camera dangling from her shoulder. Mirsada's career had ended her marriage. Her husband wanted an orderly life and children. Having suffered three miscarriages and being at a critical juncture in her career, Mirsada wasn't prepared to risk another pregnancy. Finally, they'd separated, with the husband keeping their home and Mirsada squeezing a few possessions into a suitcase and embarking on a new life in Belgrade, where she soon met Petar.

Petar was a good-looking Serb from a political family. Thanks to him, Mirsada had acquired a group of Serbian friends who would tip her off on political developments. Life was good.

She was feeling good as she went off to attend the funeral of the slain Serbian private. It was a great opportunity for a political analyst. Her mood would soon sour due to the events at the funeral.

While the other bodies had been transported to their hometowns and buried without fuss, this funeral was as crowded as one held for a prime minister. A throng of thousands pushed and shoved, prayed as one and heaped curses upon their enemies, transforming the ceremony into a show of force. The young man's weeping parents tried to speak to the crowd, begging them to disperse out of respect for their son.

This ceremony no longer centered on the tragic death of a private who'd been randomly shot and killed. This ceremony had turned into a demonstration against Albanians by enraged Serbs who rejected the Albanian presence and the Albanian leadership in Kosovo. Milosevic's flunkey, Mitevic, ensured that incendiary footage from the funeral aired for days, further whipping the Serbs into a fury.

Petar had proposed to Mirsada shortly after moving in with her. She'd only recently been divorced and was enjoying her freedom. They had a wonderful life together. Weekdays, they'd worked until all hours of the night; at weekends, they'd play until all hours of the night and sleep in till evening. They shared similar views and tastes; they both enjoyed a drink, travel and raucous good fun; neither of them had any tolerance for racists and ultra-nationalists. Petar's elderly father was a huge fan of Tito and Petar had grown up being told that all Yugoslavs owed him a debt of gratitude. In his eyes, Yugoslavia was a colorful mosaic and must always stay that way. It was with great alarm that Petar and Mirsada watched events unfold in their country. Like all reasonable Serbs, they had much to concern them.

Fifteen days after the funeral Mirsada called Ivan on his private line to tell him she had obtained some leads through highly confidential sources.

Belgrade Party General Chairman Dragisa Pavlovic had summoned the owners of Belgrade's newspapers to a meeting fifteen days after the funeral and requested they tone down their coverage. Events were spiraling out of control. Far from easing tensions over Kosovo, the press was playing with fire. The architects of recent developments were inflaming nationalist and racist sentiments, plunging Yugoslavia into a game fraught with peril. It was past time to stamp out the flames they had ignited.

While the General Chairman hadn't named names, it was clear to everyone that he was referring to Milosevic.

"You recall Dragisa Pavlovic's sternly worded warning, Ivan?" Mirsada said.

"Yes, what of it?"

"Two days later one of the papers ran an item lambasting Pavlovic... He was portrayed as an enemy of Serbs and the Yugoslavian Federation. You remember it? Even President Stambolic was said to have thought it went overboard."

"Yes, I remember."

"Do you know who wrote that piece?"

"One of the paper's columnists. It was signed."

"That's what you think," Mirsada said. "That piece was written by none other than Milosevic's wife, Mira."

"You're kidding! How did you find that out?"

"I can't reveal my sources. But I can verify its authenticity."

"So you're saying Milosevic is launching an offensive against Stambolic?"

"He's already done it," Mirsada said. "And if I what I hear is true, he'll maneuver behind the scenes as always and emerge victorious. You'll soon see."

Milosevic gradually implemented his plan by using his team to plant misinformation and disinformation, and by relying on the television network under Mitevic's control to gain him supporters. In a two-day, september session of parliament he emerged with a stunning political victory. He'd managed to plunge a knife into the back of Stambolic, the old friend who had engineered his own rise.

A short time late Mirsada, too, felt as though she'd been stabbed in the back. Petar was deeply troubled by the shifting balance of power in Belgrade. He'd begun fearing Milosevic's swift ascent and objectives. Right around that time, he'd rented a house with a garden outside the city, and announced that he'd like them to settle there. Mirsada thought it was ridiculous to give up a home so close to work and move out to the sticks. She linked Petar's desire to move house to his distress over the political climate and general need a change, expecting he'd soon change his mind. But Petar grew even more insistent and the house he'd found was so spacious, with such a large garden, that she'd finally given in.

There were other ways in which he began acting strangely. He'd started calling Mirsada, "Miza".

"Why are you changing my name?" she asked one day.

"Miza's short for Mirsada," he said.

"No, it's not."

"What's wrong with my calling you Miza?"

"There must be a reason for it. Has my being Muslim started bothering you?"

"Mirsada," Petar protested, "you know me better than that. I just want to protect you."

"Protect me from whom?"

"Don't put me in a difficult position, Mirsada."

"Protect me from whom?" Mirsada insisted. "If I'm in danger, I need to know."

"I'm just taking measures. Those damn racists won't listen to reason. I'm not talking about our close friends or colleagues, of course. But in our new neighborhood it might be better to introduce you as Miza."

"What are you going to do about my surname?"

"You can use mine. Anyway, it's not like anybody's going to ask for your ID."

"So I'll be Miza in the neighborhood and Mirsada at work?"

"Just so nobody bothers you, Mirsada."

"And who are they, these people who would bother me?"

"Darling, Yugoslavia is changing fast. I have no way of knowing how people will be acting a few weeks or months from now. I'm not asking you to change your name. It's your safety I'm worried about."

"We've been living openly with our different backgrounds for all these years in this country. There's never been a problem. Do you think people are going to change overnight just because a madman is taking the reins of government?"

"Nobody could have predicted that reasonable Germans would stand by as their Jewish neighbors were rounded up and exterminated. But when madman came to power everything changed and reasonable people did nothing to stop it. They all tried to save their own skin first and foremost."

"That's very sensitive of you, but I'm prepared to resist to the end. Besides, since you bring up Germany, do you really think humanity would allow a new genocide? You've become paranoid."

Defiant though her words had been, something started gnawing at Mirsada. Was Petar hiding anything from her? Was she ignorant of new developments in Belgrade? She was too excited about the move to brood on these and other questions, and they were both relaxed and happy as they picked out new furniture and gardening equipment. For a moment, Mirsada even regretted having turned down Petar's offer of marriage. But it was too late now. He was unlikely to propose again after such an unequivocal "no". He'd never brought it up and Mirsada was too proud to tell him she had changed her mind.

Mirsada and Nimeta spoke on the phone several times a week. They'd been confiding in each other since childhood, and when they were unable to phone they'd write long letters. This baring of their deepest secrets was a form of confession, of therapy. When Nimeta was in the clinic Mirsada had called her every day and come to Sarajevo a number of times to see her friend. She did all she could to offer her support, even though Raziyanım was there.

Raziyanım had always resented Mirsada's access to the inner world of her daughter. If anything bad happened to Nimeta, she tended to blame it on her best friend. Mirsada knew this. In her eyes, Raziyanım was an oppressive, tyrannical mother who discouraged her daughter's talents and narrowed her horizons. Raziyanım knew this. And yet, nobody could come between these two women who had shared so much in childhood and as teenagers.

In her most recent letter Mirsada had written:

"I don't know how everyone else celebrated on the day of Milosevic's victory, but Petar and I certainly had a wild night. We were so worried about that Serbian madman we drank ourselves silly. Some might have reached for the bottle to toast him but we drank out of sheer terror. We must have visited every night club in Belgrade… It was great while we were actually knocking it back and, of course, afterwards in bed together, but the next morning was a disaster. That was days ago, and I'm still feeling muddleheaded. You're such a slip of a thing, how ever did you manage to put away so much plum brandy back in the day? Milos brought me the sweater and scarf you sent. Thanks, sweetie. You picked out the most beautiful color. I'm told you're feeling really good these days. You've gained weight, cut your hair and grown even prettier. Whatever you do, don't go and fall in love again. At our age, it can only mean trouble."

Nimeta folded the letter and put it in the drawer. Ah, to be in Mirsada's shoes. She'd put an end to an unhappy marriage and gone off on her own. God had created the same opportunity for her, but she'd chosen depression over a new life.

Yes, she'd gained weight and cut her hair. But for who? For what?

She studied her face in the mirror. There were fine lines above her lips, where her face was pressed into the pillow every night. And there was another new line in her chin and the dark circles under eyes she could only conceal with lots of powder.

"Your drink and cigarettes will turn you into a crone before you reach forty," her mother had always said, as though she herself hadn't become quite the crone without the benefit of either vice.

"Mother, my piano instructor sent you a letter."

Her daughter was at the door waving an envelope.

"What does he want? Did you go to your lesson without practicing again?"

"How can you say that, mom? I'm one of the five students chosen to give a recital at the end of the term."

Nimeta was ashamed of herself. First she'd been so busy she'd neglected Hana, and then she'd been too depressed to take much of an interest.

"Come here you little squirrel," she said. She pressed Hana against her bosom. Her blonde head of hair smelled like lemons.

"Your hair smells wonderful."

"Grandma washed it with lemon shampoo."

She felt ashamed again. She was all better now, but Raziyanım was still looking after the kids. Wasn't it time she sent her mother home and shampooed her little girl's hair herself?"

"You've got such pretty hair, Hana, just like your grandmother. She had thick, blonde hair just like you."

"Did she wear a headscarf?"

"No, she never did."

"Are you sure, mom?"

"Of course I'm sure. What's all this about headscarves?"

"Saliha's mother wears one. She says everyone did in the old days."

"Not everyone. The ones who wanted to, just like now."

"Why not everyone?"

Nimeta cleared her throat and swallowed hard.

"Mom, didn't Allah say to cover our heads with a long, long scarf?"

"What makes you think Allah takes an interest in women's fashion?"

"But that's what our God says in that book over there."

Hana was pointing to the embroidered blue purse housing the *Koran* that was hanging next to the bed.

"Hana, what do you mean by 'our' God? There's only one God."

"But doesn't Mirka have a different one?"

"Dear, the prophets might be different, but God is one."

"Mom, are you sure?"

"Of course I am."

"I'm going to tell that to Saliha's nana. You know what else she says, the piano is the devil's plaything."

"Who?"

"Saliha's nana."

"Who's Saliha?

"A classmate."

Nimeta took the envelope from her daughter. Long after Hana was gone, she continued staring at the doorway.

She didn't even know her daughter's friends. She'd made a choice. She'd chosen her husband and children over love. Well then, it was high time she followed up on that decision. She'd put in a request to work part-time starting at the end of the year, or she'd quit her job. Hana was growing up. She had no intention of leaving her little girl under the influence of Saliha's grandmother. She'd speak to Ivan first thing tomorrow.

1988 Spring

The first thing Nimeta did when she stepped into the lobby of the television building was to ask information if Ivan had arrived yet.

"Yes, he has. He's expecting all of you in his office. You'd better go up straight," said the girl at the information desk.

Nimeta ran into Milos in the elevator. "Do you know Ivan's called a meeting?" she asked.

"No, but if he's calling us in at this hour of the morning it must be something important." Routine evaluation meetings tended to be held toward noon, once everyone had finished their own assignments and bulletins.

"Every time I've got a personal matter I need to discuss something more important comes up," Nimeta grumbled.

She'd made up her mind months ago but had never found the opportunity to inform her boss. Every time she attempted to do so there a major incident, she was sent off on location or there was a staffing issue. Today, however, she was determined to cut to the chase and inform Ivan before she was given an assignment she couldn't refuse.

The section of the office where she worked at her desk was empty. She hung up her jacket and raced to Ivan's office.

Everyone had gathered around the oval conference table. "You'll never guess what's happening in Slovenia," Sonya said.

"What could possibly happen in Slovenia? Catholic villagers are making Alpine yogurt from fat cows and their red-cheeked, big-breasted daughters are making cheese," Milos said. They all laughed.

"You all remember the *Mladina* incident?" Ivan said. "The war of words between the Slovenian political magazine and the army?"

"Didn't that happen way back in january?"

"Yes, but the altercation between the army and press has been raging ever since, as you all know."

"So what's the latest?" Nimeta asked.

"They've arrested the editor, Franci Zavrl, and the supervisor, Janez Jansa."

"On what charges?"

"For the crime of publishing stolen military documents."

"But who authorized it?" Nimeta asked. Her mind was on the conversation she planned to have with Ivan later.

"Don't ask silly questions. Our federal army, of course. Our own glorious Yugoslav National Force."

"Get ready to go to Slovenia, guys. You'll be attending hearings and monitoring developments."

Nobody moved.

"Have you called our Slovenian correspondent? Surely he'd be the best man for the job," Milos said.

"Go to your desk and give him a call," Ivan said. "Pack a bag, Nimeta. You'll have a cameraman. Take a backup reporter if you like, but leave me Milos. I'll try to schedule an appointment with the Slovenian party leader, Kucan. With any luck, you'll be able to meet with him before you return. Your travel expenses are ready at accounting."

Back in her own department, as Nimeta waited for a call to put through to Burhan, she turned to Sonya and said, "I was getting ready to send mother home and take care of my kids myself. What's going to happen to my life if we go on like this? Yet again, I have to tell my husband I won't be home tonight. And on a day when he was expecting me to come home with the good news about working part-time."

"This is a really interesting assignment. Cover it, and then you can get back to thinking about life," Sonya said.

When Nimeta reached Lubliyana the city was abuzz with rumors of a military coup. It's the only thing anyone was talking about, from pedestrians and shoppers, to students and businessmen.

Meanwhile, Defense Minister Admiral Mamula had been hastily retired and Colonel Vasilevic, the officer credited with suppressing the Albanian rebellion in Kosovo in 1981, was being dispatched to Lubliyana to bring Slovenia to heel. Confronted by the sight of Janez Jansa's worn, unshaven face behind the glass partitions in the city prison Nimeta realized just how trivial her own worries were. Even pain should be suffered in freedom. The man across from her was so close, and yet she couldn't reach out her hand and touch him. The expression on his face was a kind of despair she'd have found impossible to put into words. Reflected in his eyes was helplessness of a person who doesn't know where or what he'll be in a week, a month, a year, or even an hour.

Any sense of security in Yugoslavia was being obliterated. Anything could happen to anyone at any time.

"Did they torture you?" she asked him, barely hearing her own voice.

Jansa shook his head "no".

"Who interrogated you?"

"Vasilevic himself. All he wanted was who in the army had passed along the document. Unfortunately, that's something I don't know."

Nimeta knew they were being listened to but she hoped that Jansa would be able to give her hints even if he was unable to answer her questions directly. She also wanted to give the ghostly man behind the glass some hope.

"Jansa, there's an incredible sense of solidarity on the outside. Everyone's collecting signatures petitioning for your release and that of Franci."

"Vasilevic told me that even were all of Yugoslavia to take to the streets it would make no difference. He said that in the interests of the state I could be held for fifteen years or executed on the spot. He even said they could destroy my family and kill my children. You know what..." Before he could finish his sentence an official stepped between the prisoner and Nimeta. Standing right in front of Jansa he scowled, "The interview is over."

"But fifteen minutes haven't passed yet," Nimeta objected.

"The interview is over."

Nimeta hunched over to try to get glimpse of Jansa. "Goodbye, Jansa. I'll let the others know that you're fine, that they're treating you well, that I didn't see any evidence of torture," she shouted as he was being led away.

Despite having received permission just the day before, she was denied an interview with Franci Zavrl. It was obvious that the members of the armed forces detested those members of the press who weren't from Serbia or of Serbian descent.

That afternoon she found herself in airy office sitting across from Kucan, the leader of the League of Communists of Slovenia, in morocco leather chairs.

"It's very gracious of you to see me, sir. I know how busy party leaders are, but the people of Bosnia are closely following events here," Nimeta began.

They sipped coffee and made small talk for a few moments.

"It's being said that you were given prior notice of the arrests made by Vasilevic..."

Kucan interrupted Nimeta with a scowl.

"The army and its intelligence agency are responsible for these arrests. The government of Slovenia knew nothing about it."

"But according to the briefing I received..."

He cut off Nimeta a second time.

"How could we possibly be connected to these arrests? Do you have any further questions?"

"General Kadijevic told me himself that the government of Slovenia has been informed of all developments."

"And I am telling you otherwise. Young lady, I have an important meeting to attend in five minutes. Now if you'll excuse me." His tone was as harsh as the expression on his face.

Nimeta got up to leave and was accompanied as far as the door, where Kucan shook her hand, gave her a gentle push and immediately shut the door behind her.

When she left the party building she encountered a large march. A woman came up and handed her a sheet of paper on which was written: Petition to free the prisoners."

Nimeta signed it. The streets of Lubliyana, the most conservative city in Slovenia, were staging their first demonstration. Nimeta joined the crowd and tried to take the pulse of the people as she walked as far as her hotel with them. Journalists, professors and intellectuals had turned out for the event. Slovenia seemed to be transforming these arrests into a banner of freedom for its own future.

She called Sonya as soon she got to the hotel.

"Ivan strongly opposed the idea that Kucan had cooperated with the army, but he seemed overly defensive when I spoke to him," she said.

Next, she sat at her desk to write the fax she would send to Bosnia.

> "Huge crowds have gathered in front of the building where the hearings taking place. People are dropping everything to gather there and demonstrate. They carry placards strongly condemning the court, which is closed to the public and which has refused to grant the defendants their right to an attorney and to a defense in their mother tongue. Those inside can't see the placards and the crowds but they must be able to hear their chants and slogans. The uproar is unnerving the military and uplifting the spirits of the prisoners. The military continues to make mistake after mistake. Under the command of Milosevic, the people of Yugoslavia have lost their affection and respect for the Republic. I'm afraid our country has begun to unravel, Ivan.
>
> Best wishes to all. See you soon.
>
> Nimeta

Nimeta called home after she sent the fax. Her mother answered. She asked after Fiko and Hana. Fiko hadn't come home yet. Hana wanted to go to the home of her friend, Saliha, but Raziyanım wouldn't let her. Nimeta asked to speak to Hana.

"How you are, my lamb?" she asked.

"Mom, when are you coming home? Grandma keeps poking her nose into my life," Hana said.

"You need to learn to listen to your elders. Why are you picking a fight with your grandmother?"

"I want to go to Saliha's, but she won't let me."

"What business have you got in a house where they think a piano is the devil's plaything?"

"Because they make the tastiest zucchini fritters."

"I'll be home tomorrow, Hana. Hang on for another day. And don't upset your grandmother."

That was it. She'd speak to Ivan when she got back. She didn't care if the republics all sank together or went to war with each other. She wasn't going to leave home again for a faraway assignment. Her decision was final.

Gazimestan-28 June 1989

"Who's going to go to Pristina, Nimeta," Mate asked.

"Ibo wants to go," Nimeta replied.

"Don't you want to? This isn't to be missed," Mate said.

"It's not right for me to take on every assignment, Mate," Nimeta said. "I might be our senior correspondent but it's not right for me to go everywhere."

"Not right for whom?"

"Not right for my colleagues and, even worse, for my husband."

"Are you saying that Burhan still hasn't got used to the tempo of the media?"

"Burhan has, but the same can't be expected of the children. Hana is going through such a sensitive phase right now, Mate, that I'd hate to neglect her. I want to be a mother. Sometimes I feel like handing in my resignation."

"There's no way in the world you could do that, Nimeta. Take it from me, you'd get into a depression. The thrill of chasing a lead isn't so easy to give up."

"I know that," Nimeta said. "I know that as well as you. I'll even admit that a part of me is secretly praying Ivan will send me. But staying here would be the right thing to do."

"Do what's right, but don't regret it later," Mate said. "We've been planning this celebration for months. It's going to be a blast, believe me."

The time had finally come for the Serbs to avenge the ethnic Croatian Tito for all the years he had suppressed Serbian nationalism.

Mate's voice shook as he reviewed the Gazimestan incident in detail for Nimeta.

"...the images on TV just don't get it across, Nimeta. You had to be there to feel that incredible electricity. A million people had fallen under his spell," he was saying. Milesovic seemed to have possesses the very souls of his listeners. You'd have believed that the Serbs were in grave danger. As though a phantom army was on the march to destroy them. As though Serbs were being crushed and slaughtered. Milosevic gave the performance of his life, trembling and thundering. He's an amazing actor. The Serbs were enraptured. It was horrifying. It was there, on that day, that Milosevic ignited Serbian nationalism."

"No, that's what Milosevic did on June 28, 1987," said Nimeta.

"That's true in a sense. But the spark he ignited would turn into a blazing torch two years later, on June 28, 1989." Her face was lined with anxiety.

DISINTEGRATION

The Knin Incidents (1990-1991)

Reporters were left reeling by the dizzying series of events that took place in the first months of 1990.

Burhan had often been to Knin and had worked on some municipal road contracts, so he was well aware of the rising tensions in the town. The region was ripe for strife and the local Serbs hadn't decided what they wanted. Some of them favored taking up arms and seceding from Croatia, as supported and planned by Babic; others thought they should secure their rights through peaceful means.

The company Burhan worked for had initially been controlled by Croatian administrators. With the shifting political winds had come the purging of Serbs, in particular, as well as other "foreigners". Tenders were cancelled, payments were made and business relations were severed until the majority of the employees were of Croatian origin.

Then the tables suddenly turned. With Babic emerging victorious in municipal elections, ultra-nationalist Serbs took over and not a single Croation engineer remained at the company. Burhan knew that he would be next, along with all the other non-Serbian contractors and subcontractors. However, he and his team were working so quickly and productively that the powers that be never quite got to him. He kept his anxiety from his wife. Nimeta was under a lot of stress at work, and he didn't wish to add his burden to hers... In any case, they both sensed that their lives would be caught up in sweeping changes beyond their control.

Near the end of april, Burhan went to Knin to inspect some road works washed out by heavy rains. When Nimeta called she was in the office. She didn't tend to call him from her workplace unless it was an emergency. He was alarmed to hear her voice. "Is everything alright, Nimeta? I hope nothing's happened?" he asked.

"Actually, I'd like you to let me know what's going on out there, Burhan," she said. Something's happened concerning the Knin police force. We've heard some rumors but I was hoping to get a true account from you. Do you think we can do that?"

"What happened?"

"The policemen of Knin refuse to wear their new uniforms."

Burhan guffawed. "Why not?" he asked.

"Apparently the new uniforms remind them of the Ustashe. And the shields they've distributed supposedly bear swastikas. The ethnic Serbs refuse to put them on. We've learned that someone has written a letter of complaint to Belgrade. There must be someone at the Municipality who can get to the bottom of this."

"You've got to be kidding," Burhan said. "This is all too ridiculous. What are they, a bunch of kids?"

"I know it's funny, but we need to confirm the veracity of these reports."

"I'll see what I can find out at lunch. I'll give you a call if I learn anything," Burhan said.

Nimeta's phone rang that afternoon.

"You're right. Knin Police Inspector Martic has bypassed Zagreb and written directly to the Ministry of the Interior in Belgrade in order to avoid wearing the new uniform. What you said is true. The uniforms are black and the emblem on the shield does resemble a stylized swastika. These guys are nuts, they've got no idea what they're doing," Burhan said. "And if that wasn't enough, Nimeta, they've refused to meet with the delegation Tudjman sent all the way to Knin to handle this matter. Just imagine if a spat over uniforms led to war."

"It would be the first fashion war," Nimeta said. She was still laughing when she hung up the phone.

On May 5th the Croatian Ministry of the Interior sent a three-person delegation to Knin to investigate the headstrong policemen. They returned full of regret for having bothered in the first place. The Serbs had presented the delegation with a long list of demands. They didn't want the Croatian flag to wave within the municipal limits. The insisted that all the street signs written in Latin letters be replaced with ones in Cyrillic. Meanwhile, Babic did all he could to spread rumors that the Croatians had begun rekindling their ambitions from for which reason they were even designing police uniforms in the fascist colors.

The Serbs of Krajina decided to hold a referendum in august to the legitimize their control of the region. If they won the referendum a separate Serbian entity would be established within the borders of Croatia.

The rumor spread that Zagreb would not permit the referendum to take place, so the Serbian police begun distributing arms to the Serbs of Krajina.

When Nimeta heard on the 17th of August that the Croatians were sending heavy vehicles loaded with arms to Knin, she gave thanks that her husband was home in Sarajevo. There were also reports that helicopters transporting policemen from Zagreb to Knin were intercepted and forced to return by YNA jets sent from Belgrade.

The wrong order by a restless madman could lead to full-scale war. Knin radio had been calling on the public to be prepared ever since dawn. The shops and workplaces were closed and the people took to the streets. When the radio announced that Babic had declared a state of war panic broke out. Bells clanged in the towers of all the Orthodox churches as the people took to the hills and fled to the mountains. Politicians full of mutual hatred and distrust accused each other on opposite ends of the phone in Zagreb and Belgrade.

The following day, the interior minister of the Republic of Croatia announced that he had averted bloodshed by calling back the police forces making their way towards Knin. The Serbs indulged in yet another example of televised theater, frequently rebroadcasting the claim that it was only their own heroism that had saved them from this most recent Croation attempt at massacre.

At first, it was a cold war. All of the media organs continuously propagated allegations of the mortal threat posed to the Serbs of Knin and Krajina. They searched for and found fascist terror behind every step taken by Tudjman, created artificial terrorist incidents, frightened the public with bogus news accounts, trafficked guns to the villagers and townsmen, and, when the police arrived and found a heavily armed local populace, even Serbs who had never so much has imagined joining in a popular revolt found themselves in opposition to Croatian police whether they wished to be or not.

Five months later, in January of 1991, the area was declared to be "The Krajina Serb Autonomous Region".

As if that weren't enough, an armed group from Krajina surrounded Plitvice Park, one of Croatia's most popular tourism attractions. Croatia could no longer look the other way. Soon, bullets would be fired and the cold war would become very hot indeed.

Intrigue in Slovenia and Croatia (April 1990-January 1991)

"I need you guys to write up a report with specific examples," Ivan said. "It's time we finally revealed what the YNA is really up to."

"Which guys are you referring to?" Ibo asked.

"You know who you are," Ivan laughed.

"I'm telling you, Ivan," Nimeta said, "I'm tired of doing all this research and writing up all these reports. It's time the men did some work. Ibo hasn't sat down at a computer for two weeks."

"Yeah but I'm been out in the field chasing down a story," Ibo said.

"Sit down at a desk for a bit while we chase down stories," Sonya said.

"In that case, travel through Slovenia and Croatia and see the cunning of the YNA with your own eyes, like I have. The army is stealthily confiscating all the weaponry of the local defense forces in these two republics."

"And that's exactly why I want a comprehensive news program on this very issue," Ivan said. He was getting unbearable. Even though he knew their hands were tied and that he'd be unable to use any hard news they did find, he still demanded the most of his team.

YNA, the Federal Army, was an army created by the communist revolution and owed its very existence to that revolution. Were the regime in Yugoslavia to be toppled, it was only natural that the army would be toppled with it. Not only would the officers lose their power, they'd also lose all the attendant privileges they'd accumulated over the years. The transition to a multi-party democracy would bring about the end of the power of both the state and the army. Who would wish to saw off the branch on which they were sitting pretty?

The moment elections ended in Slovenia, just two days after the new government was formed, the YNA began disarming Slovenia's Local Defense Force.

The Slovenian government didn't become aware of this for quite some time. How could it? The commanders of the YNA concealed everything from Slovenia's minister of defense, who was none other than Janez Jansa, the man they'd imprisoned two years earlier for leaking confidential military documents.

When Sonya burst upon Nimeta she had a funny look on her face. "Nimeta, you won't believe what I'm going to tell you," she said. "Slovenian President Milan Kucan has finally found out about something that Ivan's known about for ages. That's how formidable the YNA is. Can you believe it!"

"Journalists across the world always get the first whiff of news," Nimeta said. "And Ivan hears about things before they even become news."

"Kucan has ordered the Local Forces not to surrender a single weapon to the YNA. The arms depots are now being guarded by the police."

"Well, they're too late," Ibo said, joining the conversation. "Jansa's already admitted that over half of the weapons in Slovenia had been turned over to the YNA by the time the defense ministry woke up to what was going on."

"How'd you find out about that?" Nimeta asked.

"Where do you think I was the other day? Huh?"

"You weren't in Lubliyana, weren't you?" Sonya asked.

"That's right. While you sat here on your bottoms I was chasing after intelligence. There's something else I learned. You'll love this."

"But we were the ones assigned this report, weren't we?" Sonya asked.

"Well, I'm a few steps ahead of you girls," Ivan said. "Jansa wants to set up his own Defense Force, completely independent of the YNA. If it were up to him, he'd sever all ties with the Federal Army within a day. Kucan wants to be a bit more cautious. The lack of a consensus between the President and the Defense Minister is making it difficult for the government."

"Those two haven't been on good terms ever since Jansa was imprisoned. Jansa has always suspected Kucan of playing a role in that," Nimeta said. "If Jansa weren't so widely admired and supported by the public Kucan would never have appointed him defense minister."

And because Jansa didn't trust Milan Kucan he really had begun slowly procuring weapons and smuggling them into Slovenia without informing the president.

The day would come when he had his own armed forces. That is, when the citizenry voted in a referendum to secede from Yugoslavia and declare independence.

Nimeta followed the events in Croatia with her heart in her mouth. If war broke out, Stefan would be out on the battlefield, either as a conscript or a journalist. She hadn't had any news of him for such a long time. She hadn't called him even to learn about the political climate in Zagreb. The pace of life had accelerated so much, and the winds of war were blowing so hard, that nobody had the time to lift their heads from their work and listen to their heart. Nimeta was grateful for this. Despite her heavy workload, she'd been able to form stronger bonds with her family. Burhan was home more often, almost never going to Knin and finding plenty of time to spend with the children. When they gathered around the dinner table they were the close knit family they'd once been.

Hana wasn't entirely happy with these family dinners. Unlike the old days, her elders didn't listen to her stories about school. Even her grandmother, who'd once seem transfixed by her every utterance, would tell her granddaughter to hush so she could listen to Hana's parents discuss politics. They were always talking about the latest developments... This just happened in Slovenia, that just happened in Croatia...Bozo was the only one left at home who paid her any attention. Because the cat was an unable to catch anyone's attention as Hana, he was forever weaving patterns between her feet.

They were all seated around the dinner table again. For the first time in ages, her grandmother had made a persimmon dessert that day. RazIyanım had put the dessert dish on the sideboard and kept a vigilant eye on it.

"It's unavoidable," her father said. "There's going to be a showdown between Croatia and Yugoslavia. When Kadijevic wanted to seize all the weapons in the possession of the Croatian police, Croatia refused. Am I right, Nimeta?"

"That was the doing of America, not the Croatians. When the deadline for turning over the weapons passed, Milosevic put his army on high alert and was poised to seize all of the police weapons in Croatia by force. It was the American ambassador who warned the Serbs in the strongest possible terms not to use military force. The Serbs have retreated, at least for the moment," her mother said.

Fiko ran over and turned on the TV so they wouldn't miss the news. Except for Hana, the entire family eagerly waited for the news to start.

"Mom, since you already know what'd going to be on the news why do you have to watch it again?" Hana asked. There was no answer.

"Mom. Mom! Why aren't you presenting the news anymore? You used to be so good at it."

"Because your mother wants to be at home with her family in the evening," her father said.

"But I love watching mom on the TV."

"Stop it, Hana!" Fiko said. "Shut up so we can hear the news."

"You think you're real special just cause you got tall of a sudden," Hana said. She lifted the cat off her lap and tossed him at Fiko.

"Whoever got you a cat… You kids don't know what it is to love animals!" Raziyanım scolded.

"Please be quiet while the news is on!"

They held their breaths and watched.

Afterwards, Nimeta said, "Actually, Milosevic doesn't favor the army using armed force. Unlike the generals, he wants to divide Yugoslovia, not unite it. The Serbs wants to break away. That's why he informed Kucan that he wouldn't object if Slovenia declared its independence."

"He couldn't care less what Slovenia does," Burhan weighed in. "There's no Serbian minority in Slovenia!"

"They've reached an understanding. If Slovenia is allowed to go its own way, Kucan will vote the way Milosevic wants him to on Croatia."

"And why not? Kucan's not interested in Croatia's internal affairs. He's only interested in saving his own republic."

"But Tudjman's gone berserk," Nimeta said. "Because of Milosevic and Kucan cutting deals without bothering to consult him."

"Dad, can you explain what's going on? I don't get it."

Fiko always asked for a personal summary of the day's news. Hana thought him a bit thick. The beanpole! He was always asking silly questions.

"Serbs are the majority in Knin and Krajina, which are both regions in Croatia. If Tudjman demands autonomy for Croatia he'll have to sacrifice those two regions. Milosevic has been hatching plans for a Serbian Republic for years now," Burhan explained.

"And that's why he's prepared to reach an agreement with Kucan. You scratch my back, I'll scratch yours."

Hana was so fed up with all this talk of Croatia and the Croatians. Dinner was no fun anymore. When was the last time they'd joked around and talked about things she was interested in? They wouldn't even let her sing any of her new songs.

"Come on, talk to me too," Hana said, tugging on Fiko's arm.

"You're too young to understand."

"No I'm not. I understand everything. Go on."

"Kucan's bargaining with Milosevic in order to save his own ass," Fiko said. "Do you understand?"

"Go to your room this instant!" Burhan shouted. "Is that any way to talk in front of your elders? What kind of example are you setting for your little sister?"

Fiko flushed beet-red. Raziyanım shook her head resignedly, as though to say, "Let the boy be." Hana decided to fan the flames with an impromptu chorus of, "Kucan's ass... Kucan's ass."

"If I catch you using that word again I'll rub red pepper on your mouth. Off to your room. The two of you, get out of my sight," Nimeta said.

"And take your insolent cat with you," Raziyanım called after the two children scuffling as they left the room. "Pissst... pissst... get away from my feet. I've already got a run in my stocking because of you."

Burhan stifled his laughter. "This house's cat is as ill-mannered as its children," he said.

"It's only natural for children whose mothers work outside the house to grow up ill-bred," Raziyanım. Nimeta bit her lip. She wondered if her mother envied her the luxury of a world where she was completely independent and free of Ranziyanım.

There were three different takes on career women in this house, she thought to herself: My husband, who respects working women but wishes I wasn't one of them; my mother, who hates the very idea; and me, who has no idea of what I really want!

There were also three different takes on Yugoslavia in those days: The army, which insisted on remaining a single nation; Milosevic, who was determined that the Serbs living in other republics have their territories annexed to Serbia; and Slovenia and Croatia, who would settle for nothing less than full independence. And then there was Bosnia, which didn't know what it wanted but was prepared to do whatever it took to prevent a civil war. Milosevic, who very much knew his own mind, had just given Croatia a ten-day deadline to surrender all its weapons to the YNA.

On the 25th of January Nimeta called Burhan at his office. She was extremely worried.

"Burhan, do you know what's just happened? Milosevic has ordered the Army into Knin to protect the Serbs there. Kadijevic then announced that the army wouldn't be mobilized without the necessary authorization from the federal republics. Milosevic has summoned all the delegates to Belgrade. They're meeting at two o'clock to vote on whether or not to approve an army operation to disarm the Croatian police."

"I'll be home by about three, Nimeta. If anything important happens let me know," Burhan said. The entire country, and especially the Croatians, held their collective breath and waited.

The delegates from Slovenia, Bosnia, Serbia, Kosovo, Voyvodina and Montenegro all arrived at the hastily called meeting.

The Serbs knew they could count on the votes of Kosovo, Voyvodina and Montenegro. All of them would vote for the army to sweep into Croatia and Slovenia and disband the local forces. The Slovenian delegate had had his hands tied by his own president's secret agreement with Milosevic. In order to save his skin, he instigated a quarrel and stormed off without voting. The Bosnian delegate voted no. Milosevic was stunned. His cunning plan had come to naught. The failure to gain five votes allowed Kadijevic to reject the mobilization. The meeting ended in disappointment for the Serbs.

March-June 1991

Fax in hand, Nimeta raced down the hallway. She burst into Ivan's office without knocking.

"Anything wrong?" Ivan asked.

Nimeta handed him the fax without a word.

"It's from Mirsada," she said, after a moment.

The fax encrypted certain codes they'd agreed on previously.

"Get the team together in the conference room and give me a few minutes," Ivan said.

Belgrade was up in arms. Students were protesting the government clampdown on the press and television, as well as its racist and fascistic stances. Revolucije Boulevard had filled with mounted police, police dogs and tanks. The cries of students clubbed by the police mingled with the sounds of gunshot. Teargas had penetrated every corner. A seventeen-year-old student lay in a pool of blood.

Four years earlier, Milosevic had bellowed to the Serbs of Kosovo that nobody would ever dare to beat them. Now, unable to bear criticism, he had unleashed tanks, batons and bullets on his own people.

When the television correspondents had gathered around the conference table Ivan said, "This was inevitable. Mate Milosevic has completely taken over Belgrade Television to use for his own purposes. Serbs were continuously incited to hate first the Albanians of Kosovo, then the Slovenians and finally the Croatians. Within the borders of his own republic, Milosevic will not tolerate dissent or opposition of any kind."

"When he tried to use the television station against the opposition it backfired. He's only just begun to realize that he's been playing with fire," Mate said.

"Are than any deaths or injuries?" Sonya asked.

"One death so far. But just think about it, Sonya, they've killed aboy seventeen-year-old," Ibo said.

"Keep the line with Mirsada open," Ivan said. "Do I have any volunteers to enter that hell?"

There wasn't a peep from Nimeta, who used to jump at assignments outside Bosnia, especially in Croatia.

"Shall I get my camera ready?" Mate asked.

"Wait a little longer," Ivan said. "Let's see how things develop. The students have demanded that opposition leader Draskovic be released, that Dusan Mitevic be relieved of his post at Belgrade Television and that the minister of the interior resign."

"Milosevic would die before he served up Mitevic's head," Nimeta said. "Theirs is an alliance of devils. Milosevic would never have got to where he was today if Belgrade Television hadn't been in his pocket."

"Oh, Mitevic will be handed over all right. Milosevic would sell his own mother."

As the demonstrations continued throughout the rest of the week the students set up camp around the 19th century fountain in Terazije and announced they were staging a sit-in until their demands were met. The liberal intellectuals of Belgrade kept the students supplied with food, drinks and blankets. Writers, professors, actors and artists joined hands and sang peace songs. On a platform temporarily erected over the fountain, speeches were delivered and telegraphs and messages of support from the other republics were read out.

On the 11th of March, another fax arrived from Mirsada. Fearful that the student protests would spread throughout Serbia, Milosevic had agreed to meet with student representatives.

Ivan and his team excitedly awaited the next phone call from Mirsada. Finally, it came.

"Tell us quick," Ivan said.

"Ah, Ivan. You won't believe it. Milosevic really does deserve an award for best actor," Mirsada said.

The young leader of the student uprising had been received. Milosevic sat at one end of the table, the student and his companions at the other. Milosevic shouted across the expense of table about the dangers posed by the Ustashe, the separatist Albanians and numerous other unsavory elements.

Unimpressed, the students listed their demands. Milosevic claimed that it was not in his power to grant them. Mirsada began laughing as she summarized the meeting. "Do you know what happened next, Ivan?"

"No, what?"

"A student asked permission to open the window to air out the smoke-filled room, and the moment he did, the room filled with chants of, "Slobo Saddam! Slobo Saddam!"

Mirsada fell silent.

"What'll happen next?" Ivan asked.

"They're trying to assemble all of the Federal Chairmen to vote on the imposition of martial law," Mirsada said. "I'll keep you updated, minute by minute."

"You see that?" Raziyanım said to Nimeta. "You and your husband worried for nothing. Slovenia's declaration of independence hasn't led to war. Your generation has never known war. Do you think it's easy? I wouldn't wish it even on my enemies. Nobody with a lick of sense favors war. I know, I've been through it. It's not the fear of death, the hunger and the privation that scares me, it's what people are capable of doing to each other when they're at war. Even worse, we're all brothers and relatives in Yugoslavia. We've been marrying with each other for at least seventy years. How can you expect people to shoot their relatives and neighbors? You've been worrying for nothing."

July-December 1991

Nimeta reread the report, this time with the radio turned down, Bozo fed and the dishes washed. As hard as she tried to concentrate, she couldn't make sense of it. Croatia was in turmoil, and even though Nimeta kept her eyes trained on the printed words her mind was elsewhere.

If war broke out, would Stefan be conscripted? War meant casualties and fatalities. She hadn't heard from him for so long. There must be a woman in his life. Perhaps he'd got married. A man that loved and wanted children so badly… But wouldn't he have told her? Of course not. Why would he feel the need to give an account to a former lover who'd let him down?

"He can do whatever he wants, but I hope he doesn't join the army and die in the war," she thought to herself. Burhan noticed his wife was feeling down.

"Nimeta, you've been rustling those sheets of paper for half an hour now," he said. "Is something wrong?"

"I need to summarize something but I just can't concentrate."

"What's the problem?"

"I don't know. Perhaps I'm a little upset about Fiko joining the football team. Couldn't a boy with such high marks and all the options in the world choose a better pastime than football?"

"Don't even try to understand the values of kids these days. You'll never get it. Just let him do what he wants."

"Is it really that simple?"

"Yes. You can't force anyone to do anything. You want him to play the violin; he wants to play football. Just be happy Hana plays the piano and let the boy be, Nimeta."

"You've got a real knack for problem-solving, Burhan."

"Give me those notes of yours and I'll see if I can help," her husband said in a bid to change the conversation. He took the dossier, scanned it, peered at it over his glasses and began speaking in soothing tones.

"You really must be bothered by the thought of Fiko out on the field. There's nothing complicated here, Nimeta. It's clear that Croatian President Tudjman and Defense Minister Spegeli have been unable to reach an agreement. Spegeli wants to arrest the YNA members in Croatia, seize their weapons and win a military victory. Tudjman prefers to seek freedom for their country on an international platform. He thinks that if they reach for their weapons they'll miss out on that opportunity. It's that simple."

"Well what do you think," Nimeta asked.

"After the Slovenia fiasco, the Serbs are looking to boost their morale. Whether Tudjman wants to or not, he's going to have to fight. Belgrade is itching for a new battle."

"So you expect war to break out in Croatia, Burhan?"

"Definitely. That's why I'll need to go to Knin to make final payment to the engineers and close the office."

"I'd thought you'd done that a long time ago."

"I've got to sign a few papers. I wish I'd sold the office furniture. Who'd be interested in furniture now on the eve of war?" Burhan said.

"You've already pushed the button. Nobody got hurt in Slovenia. Perhaps they'll fire a few shots and reach agreement with Zagreb."

"I doubt it," her husband said. "That so-called war was a bit of theater staged by the Serbs and Slovenians to make it easier for Slovenia to secede, to disgrace the YNA, which had become a nuisance to the Serbs, and to prove how worthless the Federal Republic is."

Nimeta couldn't help feeling strangely envious of her husband, who, even though he didn't follow politics on a daily basis, had proven to be remarkably forward looking and astute. She had no doubt that if Burhan had chosen politics or the media he'd be more successful than most people she knew, and even herself.

All through july and august the Serbs expanded their checkpoints on the border with Croatia. Serbian youths organized by the Interior Ministry in Belgrade had formed the group, "Serbian Voluntary Guards" and received training from a mafia figure known as Arkan and a former torturer with the secret service. The forces of the YNA had finally decided that if war were to break out they would fight on the side of the Serbs. "Arkan's Tigers" went on a one-night rampage in Croatia, forcing people from their homes, looting and burning houses and workplaces. Latin script street signs were torn down and replaced by Cyrillic ones.

The Croatian forces were a pitiful sight in comparison to the Serbian army. Tudjman had launched an operation in may to raise a standing army mainly comprised of policemen. In contrast to the tanks, armored vehicles and heavy artillery of the Serbs, the Croatians relied on a ragtag army of inexperienced volunteers and military vehicles fashioned out of delivery vans and tourism coaches. It was enough to make their supporters laugh through their tears. The army was ill-equipped for the onslaught of the Serbs. In any case, Tudjman had opted to win the war at the negotiating table, not on the field, just as Burhan had predicted.

The problem was, the Serbs of Krajina and the YNA would eventually embroil Trudjman in a hot war regardless of what he wanted; again, just as Burhan had predicted.

Burhan kept delaying his visit to Knin until august. First, he was unable to locate the engineers. They'd all disappeared, having migrated to escape an attack by the Serbs. What were their outstanding payments compared to everything else they had left behind? In this area now completely dominated by Serbs, the Municipality objected to the presence of any more foreigners and made it difficult for Burhan to hand the company over to anyone else. Burhan fixated on the term "foreigner", joking to the Serb on the other end of the line that it was quite a feat to remain a foreigner in one's homeland of 500 centuries. "If Bosniaks are foreigners," he said, "what on earth do you call people who aren't from Yugoslavia? Martians?"

"It's interesting," Nimeta said to Ivan. "My husband's been right all along about what would happen."

"Don't take offence, but if he's so smart what's he doing in Knin?" Sonya said.

"He had to go. It was now or never. They've set up roadblocks, as you know," Nimeta said in defense of her husband. She might have had her complaints about Burhan but she wasn't going to let anyone else criticize him, not her mother and most certainly not a colleague.

"But now he won't be able to get back."

"Ivan, please send me to Kijevo!" Nimeta pleaded.

"The situation is truly serious this time. I think it would be better if we sent a man."

"I've gone anywhere you've asked me, Ivan. You never had a problem with sending me to Kosovo and God knows where else."

"That was different. War is about to break out."

"Are you telling me that you're practicing sexual discrimination, Ivan?"

"Don't be ridiculous, Nimeta. Now leave me alone. Why don't you go check the afternoon bulletin."

"I'm begging you, Ivan."

"This isn't a domestic matter."

"Ivan... please."

It was a dejected Nimeta who left Ivan's office. As she walked to Studio 2 to check the bulletin as instructed, she turned over in mind a way she might be able to go to Knin.

Kijevo was a Croatian village right next to Knin, and surrounded by towns taken over by the Serbs. Ever since the armed conflict in Plitvice, the Croatians had surrounded the village with barricades and refused to leave. The Serbs refused to allow this Croatian boil to fester within the borders of the newly declared Republic of Krajina. If Croats were living in Kijevo, Kijevo would be wiped off the map, and that was that!

Nimeta ran her eyes over the bulletin. The Croatian police had been given an ultimatum to clear out Kijevo within 48 hours. The grace period would run out that very day, the 20th of August. Her husband had been in Knin for three days and she hadn't heard from him at all. Her hand trembled as she held the bulletin. The words were swimming in her tears.

"What on earth's wrong?" Sonya asked.

"I haven't heard from Burhan," Nimeta said.

"Haven't you got a house in Knin."

"We emptied it out a long time ago. Burhan was going to stay at a hotel. All he had to do was sign a few documents to shut his business down."

"Didn't you call the hotel?"

"Of course I did. He wasn't at the hotel where he always stays. Even worse, he hasn't called me. He always calls as soon as he arrives, just to hear my voice and those of the kids."

"Who knows who bagged him," Mate said.

"Why would they shoot an innocent man?"

Tears streamed down her cheeks.

"What happened to your sense of humor? I was talking about a Serbian wench, not a hunter," Mate said.

"Burhan would never do something like that," Nimeta said.

"That's what you think," Mate said in a low voice. "You never know where a man's organ will lead him."

Nimeta was too engrossed in the bulletin to hear Mate. There was something about Lieutenant Colonel Ratko Mladic. It was as though her female intuition was trying to tell her that this man would play a pivotal role in her life one day.

Ratko Mladic was a Serb born and raised in Bosnia. He'd been transferred to Knin from Pristina. Like so many soldiers his age, he'd been a brainwashed communist. When communism collapsed, he'd found another obsession to stave off his own psychological collapse: this time, he was going to defend his country against Croatian fascism. By "country" he was now referring not to Yugoslavia, but to Serbia.

During one of those days when there was still no word from Burhan, Nimeta was making up a soothing story to tell the kids when the phone rang. An old friend in Knin told her not to worry about Burhan, who'd been forced to hide out for a couple of days. He'd be unable to return to Bosnia by the usual route, but was well and would call his family at the first opportunity.

"Please, Boris, tell me where and how to find him," Nimeta said.

"Don't risk it, Nimeta. I'll keep you posted. Burhan's fine but he's got to stay in hiding for a while. Only Serbs are allowed to stay in Knin and the vicinity. He's trying to find a way to get home," he said, and hung up the phone.

The following day, on the 29th of August, a full week after the Croatians had been ordered to abandon their homes, Kijevo was razed to the ground. Ratko Mladic led the operation, backed by Belgrade.

Tudjman was now forced to rule out a peaceful resolution. If the people of Croatia heard the word "peace" one more time, they were liable to topple their president.

On the day Kijevo was cleansed -the term favored by the Serbs- Croatia mobilized its forces and declared its war of independence.

Burhan was stranded in a country where balconies and windows were sealed with sandbags, roads were barricaded with barbed wire, a single lane remained open to traffic on the highways and the telephone lines were down. He had no idea that his wife had done all she could to reach him and tried to get an assignment to Croatia. In his most recent communication to Boris he'd said he would try to make it to Zagreb, even though it was in the opposite direction to home. You'd have had to be a sorcerer to get from one town to another in those days. The people of Croatia flooded the streets, frenzied. Not a single shot had been fired but hundreds of thousands of panicked people rushed about in circles with no idea of what to do or where to go.

Nimeta reached Croatia the same day Vlado Trifunovic, the commander of the encampment in Varazdin, surrendered with his arms in order to save his young soldiers from being slaughtered by the Croatians.

"You just kept blinking those blue eyes until you got what you wanted," Mate had said. "I did everything I could not to get sent, but to no effect. Ah, to live on this earth as a woman! Why did God have to endow me with these useless bits." He pointed to his crotch.

"If you think I 'want' to be sent to a warzone you're even stupider than I thought, Mate."

"Then why did you keep begging Ivan to send you?"

"I'm the only person who can get my husband out of there. International organizations are extremely responsive when it comes to journalists."

"So, you're some kind of guardian angel?"

I wish I were, Nimeta thought. With her white skin, honey-colored hair and large blue eyes she bore more than a passing resemblance to Renaissance depictions of angels, but she'd been unable to guard either her husband or her lover from the ravages of war. All she could do was find out where Burhan was and try to ensure their safe passage back to Bosnia. She sent an appeal to every NGO and television station she knew. She'd and Burhan had agreed before she set out that if anything went wrong they would try to communicate via the media. She expected to hear from him within a few days.

Stefan was very much alive in Nimeta's heart. She hadn't called him. She had no idea where he was. But she was certain to run into him again one day. She'd see him and they might exchange a few words. She'd touch his arm, squeeze his hand and give him a kiss on the cheek. They'd spend no more than ten or fifteen minutes together. They'd be a bit stiff and distant with each other, if for very different reasons. "Did you get married?" she'd ask, or perhaps she'd phrase it, "Is there a woman in your life?" She'd wish him joy. Then, like so many times before, she'd turn round and walk off, trying not to stumble. For a long time, a very long time, his voice would remain in her ear, his face in her memory, the warmth of his touch on her hand.

After the Croatians seized Trifunovic's weapons they'd sent his forces home after making them exchange their YNA uniforms for civilian clothes. They hadn't yet realized that they'd given the Serbs yet another excuse to whip themselves into a fury.

On the morning of the 19th of September, journalists awoke in their hotel rooms to a bombshell of a news item. A convoy of Serbs nearly ten kilometers long was headed for Croatia. The convoy, which included at least 100 tanks, trucks carrying troops and heavy artillery, was seen off by an enthusiastic crowd of well-wishers, just as the one leaving for Slovenia had been two months earlier. Serbian women lined the streets and hung out of windows and balconies, tossing cigarettes, food and flowers to the soldiers.

This time, the army would not return empty-handed.

The journalists gathered in the courtyard of the Ministry of Defense. Everyone was talking at once, firing off questions, and pushing and shoving as they awaited the arrival of the press spokesman. Nimeta lost Mate in the crowd. She tried to help an English journalist by translating for him. At the touch of a hand on her shoulder she spun round to greet Meta and was confronted by the sight of Stefan.

"What are you doing here, Nimeta? Are you the only war correspondent they could find?" Stefan asked.

"Ah, Stefan!" She realized she was beaming. Nimeta was unable to prevent her feelings from shining through her eyes.

Stefan took her hand and gave her a peck on the cheek.

"You're looking good. You're a tasty little thing, Nimeta, as always."

"How are you, Stefan?

"What do you think? We're going to war and I'm joining the army in two days. We were unable to stop the Serbian butcher, as you see."

"Are you volunteering?"

"Anyone Croat able to stand on two feet is expected to grab a weapon. As you know, we don't have a regular army. Until recently, our army was the YNA. But the Serbs stole it. Anyway, that's how I am. What are you doing in this hellhole?"

"My husband," Nimeta said.

"I'm sorry?"

"Burhan had no choice but to turn over the building site in Knin. He went to Croatia to handle some business for the last time..." Her voice trailed off. Knin wasn't in Croatia anymore. "He was in Knin when the trouble in Kijevo exploded. I didn't have any news from him. He sent word through a friend that he was going to Zagreb. I was going to wait for him here so we could go back together, but now this has happened..."

"You'd better go back to Bosnia, Nimeta. Croatia's going to be a mess. Burhan will find a way to return."

"I insisted they send me here. I can't leave just because war broke out. I'll stay here until things calm down, and then I'll send word to Sarajevo."

The press spokesman appeared on the balcony. The roar of voices died down somewhat. As the press spokesman's voice blared from the speakers, Stefan said, "Nimeta, come to the hotel for lunch. Let's have a bite together." The English journalist was tugging at Nimeta's arm.

"Just wait a moment. They'll be repeating everything in English," Nimeta told him. By the time she'd translated a couple of lines at the journalist's insistence and turned back to Stefan, he was walking off.

Stefan had gone before she'd had the chance to tell him she couldn't have lunch.

Nimeta didn't go to the hotel for lunch. All the journalists and television crews were up to their necks in work. They followed the press releases on the hour, did their best to gather information through unofficial channels, tried to get a sense of the general atmosphere and prepared their own commentary for immediate transmission to their television channels and newspapers. Nobody had time to scratch their heads, let alone lunch with friends. Nimeta was out of breath. She'd been too busy to reflect on her meeting with Stefan. This time, God was certainly determined to protect her from him!

After running around all day, writing up her final bulletin and dispatching it to Ivan, and fending off Mate's entreaties for her to join him and some of their colleagues for a drink at the hotel bar to wind down, she finally closed the door to her hotel room some time after midnight. Nimeta was barely able to stand. She dragged herself over to the shower, waited in vain for hot water, settled for a cold bath, wrapped herself in a towel and stretched out on the bed. She picked up the receiver and called home, even though she knew her mother would be asleep. The voice on the other end of the line was sleepy and worried.

"How are you? Where are you? Are you okay?" Raziyanım asked.

"I'm sorry, mother, I thought you were sleeping but I wanted you to pass on some news to the children first thing tomorrow morning. I might not have time to call tomorrow. I got some news about Burhan. When some skirmishes broke out where he was he went on to Zadar and got in touch with some colleagues of mine. I was even able to speak to him. When things settle down he'll come to Zagreb and we'll return together. Don't worry about us," she said.

"Why are you waiting for him in the middle of all that chaos? Come home to your kids. Burhan will find his own way home."

"Ivan won't be able to replace me. I have to stay here a bit longer, mother."

"Do you have to? You could have called your husband from home."

"It's too late to argue. Don't worry about me. Take care," Nimeta said. She was eager to ring off before her mother launched into another diatribe.

"I'm exhausted, mother. You're nagging at me as always. I've got to hang up now. God bless," Nimeta said.

"Did you wake me up just to give me a scolding?" Raziyanım said.

"I woke you up to tell you I've located Burhan," Nimeta said, putting down the phone. Her mother had worn her out yet again. She slipped out of the damp towel and under the covers. Just as she was falling asleep there was a knock on the door. Springing from the bed, she retrieved the coverlet that had fallen to the floor and raced to the door.

"Who is it? What do you want?" she asked.

"Open the door, Nimeta," Stefan said. Nimeta opened the door a crack, caught a glimpse of Stefan's pale, drawn face and unlatched the chain. Walking to the middle of the room, Stefan asked, "Why didn't you come?"

"Come where?"

"To lunch at the hotel."

"I was busy Stefan. I couldn't leave the press center."

"Don't lie."

"I swear it's true. I didn't get back to the hotel until about half an hour ago. I was so tired I was just nodding off."

"Would you have come if you hadn't had to work?"

Nimeta didn't answer.

"Why are you scared of me? I won't force you to do anything."

Stefan sat down at the foot of the bed. Neither of them spoke for a moment, Nimeta, standing, wrapped in a coverlet, and Stefan, sitting on the end of the bed.

"Come here, Nimeta," Stefan said. Nimeta didn't move.

Come sit beside me. I suspect this really will be the last time we see each other. There's a war raging outside, bloodier than you can possibly imagine. Everyone's turned into monsters. Both the Serbs and us. Soon it will be your turn. But I was meant to die. I'll be in the army in two days. The Serbs are strong. They'll come with heavy artillery, tanks and a professional army. We'll fight back with hunting rifles, pots and pans. None of us are soldiers; we're just men trying to defend their country. We'll all die, have no doubt of that.

The Serbs are going to win this war. But at least we're willing to die so they can't do it without a fight."

Nimeta walked toward the foot of the bed, her feet tangled in the coverlet.

"Nimeta, be with me before I go off to die. Let me make love to you one last time."

Stefan reached out and tugged at a corner of the coverlet. Nimeta's skin gleamed mother-of-pearl in the dim light. Tears ran down her cheeks and dropped onto her breasts. Stefan touched his lips to one of those teardrops. His hot lips.

"Love me, Stefan," Nimeta cried. "Love me without stopping… until you go."

Nimeta awoke first as the the first rays of morning light struck the bed. She glanced at the man next to her. She'd succumbed to her emotions, as always. Mirsada had been right. "You'll always find a reason not to refuse him, a good reason, Nimeta. Because you're still in love with him," she'd said. Just when Nimeta thought she had run out of excuses and established self-control, she found herself with him again for reasons she'd never imagined. "One last time" before she sent Stefan off to die. One last time to be held in his arms and feel the touch of his hands and his lips, again and again.

For two days, she'd believed that this expression of their love would last her for the rest of her life. She'd sent Mate a note to silence his persistent calls: "Mate, don't call me for a couple of days. I've got some personal business to attend to. You understand."

She was certain Mate would think she was spending her time trying to track down her husband, or had found him and wanted to spend some time alone. Everyone knew why she'd been so insistent about going to Croatia. As she wrote those few lines she'd reddened with shame. Her hands had trembled. She was using her husband even as she deceived him. She wasn't aware of it at that moment, but she instinctively sough to protect Burhan from gossip. To protect the husband she was unable to leave.

Spent from love, she and Stefan would eat, dream and laugh together.

"If you'd agreed to marry me we'd have had children that look like you. You'd have chosen our girl's name and our boy would have been named Stefan," he said. "My father's name…"

"Was your father named Stefan, too?

"Yes."

"And your grandfather?"

"Him too."

"Why were you all named Stefan? Don't you Croatians have any other names?

"According to family legend," Stefan said, "it was the last wish of a dying ancestor. It's been passed down from generation to generation and become a family tradition. We're all Stefans."

"If I have another son I'd like to name him after my father."

"Fikret was your father's name, wasn't it?

"We named our son after my mother's beloved uncle," Nimeta said.

Stefan clasped Nimeta's hands, looked into her eyes and said, "I'm serious, Nimeta. If this war ends, and I survive…"

"No, Stefan. I can't leave Burhan. He's the father of my children. You made me a promise: 'the last time'. I beg you, survive the war and live a long life, but keep your word and never call me again. If you love me at all, don't call. Every time we meet, every time we make love, I feel as though I've just been through twenty wars. I feel wounded. I die. The shame and regret kills me. I'm separating from you, and this time I'm dying inside. It's so hard to pull myself together again, Stefan. Please!"

"All right, Nimeta," Stefan said, just as he'd done so many times before.

This time really was the last time. Nimeta felt it in her heart. When Stefan woke up this morning he would get dressed and go off to join the army, and, probably by the end of the day, die in a bomb raid.

She silently got out of bed and went to the bathroom. She stayed under the cold water for several minutes, as though to cleanse both body and spirit. She took her time brushing her teeth. She brushed her hair. She tried to conceal the dark rings under her eyes with powder. She applied lipstick to her lips, and then she put a dab on each cheek and smoothed it into her skin to put some color in her pale face. When she returned to the room, the bed was empty. Stefan had left a note on the bedside table: "Goodbye, darling. You sent me off to my death a happy mean. But if I do survive I'll keep my promise."

With war breaking out everywhere, Burhan and Nimeta were stranded in Zagreb. Nimeta was struggling to get press credentials for her husband so they could leave Croatia alive and well. She also scanned the list of fallen soldiers every day looking for Stefan's name. She didn't know where he was but she felt certain he was in Vukovar, a city under siege, fighting for survival against a much more powerful army. Most volunteers and recent recruits to the Croatian forces were deployed to defend Vukovar.

In Zagreb, everyone was calculating how long irregulars could hold out against a professional army. The ever hopeful Tudjman was still waiting for someone to say "stop" to the Serbs, whether it was the UN, the EU, the US.

YNA, the fourth biggest army in Europe, was in a truly sorry state. Deserters left in droves. None of the non-Serbian soldiers wanted to fight. Among the deserters were Serbs who weren't ultra-nationalists. Discipline was virtually non-existent and the chain of command was broken. It was not clear who was leading and who was following. That's how the people of Vukovar had been able to continue to resist an army that was far more formidable on paper than on the battlefield.

After this display of heroism engaging the enemy in hand-to-hand battle, Vukova finally fell. The Vukovar police identified the bodies of at least five hundred civilians alone. The hospitals were overflowing with the wounded. The Croatians living in Vukovar accused Zagreb of failing to come to their aid. They suspected Tudjman of sacrificing them to sway international opinion.

Nimeta studied the latest list of casualties and fatalities. Stefan Stefanovic had been lightly wounded, treated at Vukovar Hospital and discharged.

Dubrovnik was under Serbian fire. Artillery had riddled the picturesque city. When the handful of Croatian National Guards charged with defending Dubrovnik and its outskirts turned tail and fled, YNA swept into the area unopposed, pillaging villages and towns one by one, and burning down the houses they'd pillaged as they advanced.

The defense of Dubrovnik fell to the small group of National Guards. Taking up positions in the old city fortress, the guards were determined to fight to the end.

Ivan had wanted asked Nimeta to travel over to Dubrovnik, where interesting things were taking place. The Hotel Argentina, which had become famous during the war, was full of foreign correspondents and delegates from the EU. And it was at that hotel that Ivan wanted Nimeta to stay. Burhan didn't normally get involved in his wife's business affairs, but he finally exploded.

"We're going home, Nimeta. Ivan can find himself a new war correspondent."

"He didn't want to send me to Croatia, Burhan. In order to find you I..."

"Alright. But we have been away from home for months. It's time we returned. Mate can go to Dubrovnik."

Nimeta was taken aback by how decisive Burhan was, but she didn't push him. They prepared for their return to Sarajevo and, two days later, were to travel to Bosnia with a group of journalists...

As they were having a drink at the bar on their last night in Zagreb, Burhan leaned toward his wife, whose back was to the door, and said, "Look at that guy who just came in. Isn't he a journalist friend of yours? Nimeta turned round and looked. There were a few men standing at the entrance to bar talking to the waiter, and one of them was Stefan. Her husband had stood over and was beckoning to Stefan to join them. Stefan left his friend and limped over to their table. He shook Burhan's hand before he greeted Nimeta, who was riveted to her seat. Stefan leant over and gave her a kiss on the cheek.

"Won't you have a drink with us?" Burhan asked.

Stefan pulled out a chair and sat down. "How's it going, Burhan?" he asked. Nimeta was worried about you, but I can see that everything's alright now." He'd lost weight. He looked at least ten years older.

"Yes, we're finally going home tomorrow," Burhan said.

"Stefan, how are *you*? Nimeta asked, a slight quaver in her voice. "I heard you were wounded."

"Who would make up gossip like that?" Stefan laughed. "After what I've seen I'd be ashamed to say I was wounded."

"Were you fighting?" Burhan asked.

"I was in Vukovar. Believe me, when that was over I was completely done, in the full sense of the word. I'm going back to Dubrovnik tomorrow."

"Back to battle?" Burhan asked, a note of respect creeping into his voice.

"Yes," Stefan said. He downed the glass placed before him and turned to Nimeta: "I've escaped death this time, but there will still be plenty of opportunities."

Nimeta didn't respond. Burhan jumped in and said, "God forbid."

"There are moments when death is preferable to life," Stefan said. "War is the most vile and horrific thing that can happen to a man." Thanking them for the drink, he got up.

As he shook Burhan's hand and made his farewells he said, "You're a lucky man." Nimeta kept her eyes on the floor. Burhan laughed bitterly and said, "My luck won't last long. Our turn's coming up."

Nimeta summoned the strength to stand up and take Stefan's hand.

"Godspeed, Stefan," she said in a low voice. "May God watch over you." She kissed him on his sallow cheek. The corner of her eye glistened. After Stefan left, they ordered another drink.

"Nimeta, I can see how upsetting that must be," Burhan said. "It can't be easy to send a colleague off to war." When Nimeta didn't say anything, Burhan continued. "Your friend said I was lucky but, like I told him, it'll be our turn soon enough!"

And it soon was. The Serbian and Croatian leaders had agreed on just one thing: Bosnia-Herzegovina would be partitioned between them. Burhan couldn't have known that, but his instincts were sound.

SHIRT OF FLAME

September 1991-March 1992

As war raged in Croatia, Nimeta and Burhan returned safely to Sarajevo, a city helplessly awaiting its fate like a sacrificial lamb. The people of Bosnia were tense but calm. With a fatalism that might be peculiar to Islam, they gravely and patiently waited for disaster to strike.

President Alija Izetbegovic was doing everything in his power to delay the international recognition of the separatist republics of Croatia and Slovenia. The Bosnian president was well aware that such premature recognition would put Bosnia in a difficult spot. Bosnia would have no choice but to secede from Yugoslavia the second Croatian and Slovenian independence was recognized, thereby risking civil war with the ethnic Serbs living within the borders of Bosnia. The only other option would be to remain a part of the Yugoslavia federation and under the Serbian fist, like Kosovo, Voyvodina and Montenegro.

There was only one other person who shared Izetbegovic's concern: Lord Carrington, the man charged with bringing peace to Yugoslavia. The first foreign minister in Margaret Thatcher's cabinet, Lord Carrington had a record of successful diplomatic operations. When Hans van den Broek, then chairman of the EU Council of Foreign Ministers, asked Lord Carrington to develop a formula for achieving peace in Yugoslavia within two months, the British Foreign Minister chuckled to himself. Only a fool would believe that peace was possible within two months, and Lord Carrington was no fool. Furthermore, at his first meeting with Tudjman and Milosevic he'd immediately seen the map taking shape in their minds.

Neither the Serbs nor the Croats were particularly fussed by the separation of Slovenia from Yugoslavia. They were too busy calculating the division of territory in what remained of Yugoslavia once they themselves declared independence. Carrington knew that without careful consideration, planning and mutual approval from the remaining republics, official recognition for Croatia and Slovenia on an international platform would lead to all of Yugoslavia being divided between Croatia and Serbia, as well as to an end to the aspirations of the other peoples of Yugoslavia. The only republic able to evade disaster would be a Slovenia populated exclusively by Slovenians.

Meanwhile, Radovan Karadzic, who realized that Bosnia-Herzegovina would have no choice but to eventually declare its independence, had begun the systematic implementation in Bosnia-Herzegovina of the tactics being used in Croatia. The Serb Volunteer Guard under his control, Arkan's Tigers, were now battle hardened. Karadzic had also learned something from his experiences: the stronger side always struck first and won. Some things never changed, even in the twentieth century!

At the beginning of September the Bosnian Serbs asked the Federal Army to protect the four "autonomous" regions they themselves had declared. This time, they apparently feared not the fascist Croats but the fanatic Muslim Bosnians. The army wasted no time in responding to this dubious request. By the end of september troops armed with heavy artillery had surrounded the regions in Bosnia and Herzegovina designated "Serbian" by the Serbs, not only effectively creating a state within a state but using these same territories as a base from which to attack Croatia.

The "Tank Training Unit" in Banya Luka has in fact been used for this purpose for quite some time.

Fed up with these Serbian games, Aliye Izetbegovic called on parliament to declare Bosnia's neutrality in the war on September 14th, upon which Radovan Karadzic accused the Bosnian President of assisting the "blood-sucking Croats", and the Serbian delegates walked out of parliament and boycotted the vote. Karadzic was now busily lining up all the pawns that would transform Croatia into a bloodbath. Ever more inflammatory propaganda was being broadcast non-stop in the Serbian autonomous regions within Bosnia, ludicrous conflicts were being deliberately provoked and then quelled with the help of the Federal Army, and Serbian civilians were openly being armed to the teeth... The Serbs had done their homework.

But they weren't finished yet.

Izetbegovic and all of the other republics had approved the plan drawn up by Lord Carrington to offer equal protection to all of the republics, with full recognition of their ethnic groups, languages, religions, education and flags. At first, Milosevic had appeared to favor the plan as well, but he was merely winning time until he emphatically rejected it on October 18th. Even the Republic of Montenegro, which always followed Milosevic's lead, had approved of the Carrington Plan.

Milosevic faced something of a dilemma. He wanted all of the ethnic Serbs living in the various republics to be consolidated in a single Serbian state and he did not want any Serb anywhere to be relegated to minority status. Milosevic had risen to power by securing rights for the Kosovo Serbs. Now, under the Carrington Plan, the same rights he had demanded for the Serbs would be extended to the Albanians. He rejected the plan.

Time was passing, but there had been no progress in securing peace for Yugoslavia. Milosevic had found an excuse to turn down every proposal put before him. Finally, former US Secretary of State Cyrus Vance joined the commission attempting to hammer out a deal. Vance put a new proposal on the table: a UN Peace Force. Serbia, which had rejected the idea of a peace force out of hand, seemed to be warming to the idea when another obstacle emerged: Germany!

At the beginning of december Tudjman had travelled to Germany and met with Prime Minister Kohl and Foreign Minister Genscher. Germany, whose antipathy toward the Serbs has been an open secret since World War II, ignored Carrington and threw its full support behind Tudjman. While Britain and America were being cautious about recognizing Croatian independence, Germany guaranteed that it would recognize this new state.

In the first week of december, Ivan did some research into countries supporting Bosnia and came up with the idea of preparing a program designed to lift the spirits of the Bosnians. Nimeta was presented with an offer she couldn't refuse.

She was to visit Ankara for three days, where she'd meet with the Turkish prime minister and foreign minister, as well as travel to major cities to sound out the public.

Nimeta was full of joy when she went home that day. "Something amazing has happened, Burhan," she told her husband when he got home. "Ivan wants to send me to Turkey. You haven't got much work these days. And the children will soon be out of school for the New Year's break."

Burhan really did have a lot of time on his hands. Construction, along with all the other sectors, had crawled to a standstill in Bosnia. Other than getting the basics at the corner store and butcher's, nobody was doing any shopping. Nothing was bought, sold or produced. Hearts in their mouths, the Bosnians waited under a heavy fog, for the first bullet or bomb. Burhan, who occasionally dropped by the office out of habit, like so many of his colleagues, immediately said, "Alright, let's go."

Nimeta clapped her hands like a delighted child. Her delight spread to Fiko and Hana. The children were unable to contain their joy over going to this fairytale land they'd heard tales of from their elders, fantasized about and where half of their family now lived.

"I'll be coming too," Ranziyanım announced. "I haven't been to Istanbul for nearly twenty years."

"But Grandma, who'll look after Bozo?" Hana asked.

"Am I your cat-sitter?" Raziyanım retorted.

"We'll leave Bozo with Azra," Nimeta said. "I've looked after her dog so many times when she's been travelling."

"Good then. Now that you've found a nanny for Bozo I'm coming too."

"Mother, keep in mind that I've got to be in Ankara for a few days. You'll have to stay in Istanbul with Burhan and the kids."

"I'm going to find my relatives and stay with them," Raziyanım said.

"How can you possibly expect to find any of your relatives? God only knows where they've been scattered to after all this time. And they'll be too busy anyway."

"Unfortunately, your generation has forgotten the meaning of family," Raziyanım said. "It used to be that a relative was a relative, even if you hadn't seen them for forty years. Blood really was thicker than water. And let me tell you something else, Nimeta: If I find my great aunt's children I plan to visit Bursa this time as well."

"Visit where?"

"Bursa. It was the first city my relatives settled in when they migrated. They say it's a lot like Sarajevo. At the foot of a snow-capped mountain, the same marketplaces, the same domes..."

"Mother, don't be silly. Even if you manage to track down their addresses, the cities, the houses and the marketplaces have all changed. People change too. How do you expect to just show up at the door of complete strangers."

"They're family."

"How will you talk to them? Do you expect them to understand your Turkish, or to know Bosnian?"

Raziyanım ignored the question. "I'm not staying in a hotel in Istanbul; I'm staying with my relatives. In the mansion in Erenköy."

Nimeta was happy to leave behind, if only for a brief time, her anxious countrymen and their dispirited conversations in this gloomy country fatalistically awaiting war. Her family hadn't gone on a trip together for a long time. Even just a short week traveling with the kids would be a return to the old days of happy holidays... those carefree times! But how could she expect a return to the old days? Nothing was the same. Nothing would ever be the same. Yugoslavia, Bosnia and Sarajevo were changing fast.

Even Istanbul wasn't the old Istanbul. Raziyanım looked in vain for the car ferries in which they'd waited in line for hours the last time they'd visited the city, this fairytale city stretching out in all its grandeur along the shimmering blue waters of the Bosphorus, down below the pair of imposing bridges linking Europe to Anatolia.

When Nimeta had first arrived in Istanbul as a girl they'd been able to fish in the Bosphorus by casting their lines directly from the balcony of their relative's home in Arnavutköy. She wanted Fiko and Hana to see this house perched on the water, but it was no longer on the coast. The sea was gone. The cool indigo seawater that had seemed to shatter into pieces of crystal when you jumped into it was gone, replaced by the kind of murky, dirty water you'd find in any port city anywhere in the world. When they went to Erenköy there was no trace of the leafy gardens and mansion where they'd spent their summers. The houses, the pines and the plane trees had been displaced by towering apartment blocks of concrete. Raziyanım's relatives had moved from the many-roomed mansion with hand-carved decorations on the high wooden ceilings to a housing estate in one of the newly developed neighborhoods springing up across the city – to an apartment that didn't have guest rooms. Young people spent hours in frenzied traffic to reach offices where they worked at a frenzied pace. Too timid to plunge into the chaotic daily life of the city, the very elderly watched from the windows of their homes as life streamed on by. As for Raziyanım's peers, the hosting of guests, which had once been one of life's greatest pleasures, had turned into a chore.

Nimeta and Burhan checked into a newly restored hotel located on the site of a former mansion in the historic district of Sultanahmet so that their children would be able to see the nearby Ottoman monuments and architectural masterpieces.

"Salih Zeki and Gül Hanım had a mansion surrounded by a garden somewhere around here," Raziyanım said.

"Mother, if Salih Zeki and Gül Hanım are still alive they've probably celebrated their 130th birthdays by now," Nimeta said. "I'm sure they'd be overjoyed to see you if they could recognize you, though."

"Stop talking nonsense. They've got children and grandchildren. At least one of their descendants must be living in that house."

Nimeta followed her mother and looked for the old mansion in the street behind Ibrahim Pasha Palace. Raziyanım stopped in front of the derelict building on the corner, its facade still bearing traces of pink paint. "It was here," she said. A few birds took wing from their perches on the eaves of the gutted building. Raziyanım marched into the small grocery store on the opposite corner. She enquired first in English, then in German.

"Tourist? You want carpet? Coca-Cola?" the grocer asked.

"Mother, please; just let it go," Nimeta pleaded. Gesturing toward the ruined house, Raziyanım produced a few words in broken, heavily accented Turkish: "Bosnian family here? That house? Salih Zeki Bey and Gül Hanım from Sarajevo... Saadet Hanım?"

"Ah," said the grocer. "You're asking about the old owners of that house. They died a long, long time ago." He repeatedly wagged his cupped hand back and forth to indicate just how many years had passed. "Their daughter, Saadet Hanım, is dead too. The grandchildren sold the house. The new owner was going to turn it into a hotel, but couldn't. Seems there's an antique city under the foundation or something."

"Let's get going, Mother," Nimeta said. "We'll check the phone book back in the hotel. We'll call all the Kulins we find, all right?"

That evening they found two Kulins listed in the directory, but Raziyanım changed her mind at the last minute, saying, "I've never met the grandchildren. I don't know how they'd welcome me."

"We can't just spring in on them," Burhan said. "People have got lives. We'll let them know in advance the next we come. That way they'll be expecting us. I'll jot down those phone numbers."

"Do that," Raziyanım said. "After all, they're *your* relatives."

What a funny world we live in, Burhan thought to himself. He shared a surname and a bloodline with people living in this city, people he'd never met or seen. Everyone had gone their own way, and their homelands, languages and customs were different. And yet they were still bound together, the way all the strands in a thickly woven braid belong to the same head of hair. They might be very different from each other or they might have a lot in common.

The day after they arrived, Nimeta left her family in Istanbul and went to Ankara. She had an appointment with the Prime Minister and the Foreign Minister. She also wanted to find out what the man on the street thought about UN Forces being sent to Bosnia. The state television channel, TRT, had provided her with a cameraman and a young female translator. They began stopping people scurrying through snow flurries in Kızılay Square so Nimeta could ask her questions. The first person was an elderly woman.

"Bosnia? Ah, Bosnia… Of course it's very important to us. We have a lot of Bosnians around here. The place is full of them. My neighbor's son-in-law is a Bosnian." As she walked off she added, "God help them."

"Bosnians and Turks are one and the same. Aren't we all Muslims? They're our brothers," said the next person, flashing a gold tooth and waving at the camera.

An elderly man in spectacles said, "Ottoman troops used to come from Bosnia. And there was that grand vizier from Bosnia… Sokullu something or other. We like Bosnians. I think our soldiers should go and protect them."

A young man spit his cigarette butt onto the ground. "That's all we need right now; Bosnians!" he snorted. "As if the Cyprus problem isn't bad enough, now we've got to go and get mixed up in the Balkans. Then we'll be blamed for anything that goes wrong in Bosnia for the next fifty years."

"Are you saying you oppose the participation of Turkish troops in a UN Peace Force?" Nimeta asked him.

"I'm against it, yeah. Turkish soldiers should protect Turkey. What business have they got over there?" He lit a fresh cigarette as he strode off.

A girl rushing to catch her bus paused just long enough to say, "Who? Bosnians? What do I care! They can do what they want."

Raziyanım's hoped-for visit to Bursa, one of the former Ottoman capitals, was not to be. Burhan and Nimeta had hastily packed their bags and arranged the family's return to Sarajevo, promising the kids that they would one day return to this chaotic, muddy, noisy, vibrant, inscrutable and enchanting city where the well-dressed and impoverished rub shoulders, where timeless beauty is being disfigured by ramshackle development.

They'd planned to have a dinner for two on the shores of the Bosphorus, just husband and wife. They hadn't even been able to do that. Ivan had called Nimeta back to Sarajevo.

Something major was happening. This wasn't the time for holidays; it was time to make some critical decisions.

At a meeting in Brussels, German Foreign Minister Genscher had informed his shocked EU counterparts that he would recognize Croatia's independence whether they chose to or not. Even though Carrington repeatedly pointed out that such recognition would lead to disaster and torpedo his peacemaking efforts, Germany stood firm. America, for its part, shared Carrington's view but thought the issue should be resolved by the countries of Europe.

On the 17th of December the EU announced that any republics wishing to break away from Yugoslavia should apply to do so by the 24th of December.

On the day after Nimeta returned to work, Slovenia, Croatia, Macedonia and Bosnia-Herzegovina all applied to have their independence recognized.

Nimeta was handing round the pistachios and *lokum* she'd brought back from Istanbul. She put two bottles of *rakı* on Ivan's desk.

"Let's open those up and toast our application," Ivan said.

"Are you crazy? Drink *rakı* at this hour?"

"People can do anything they want today. The moment of reckoning is approaching," he handed round glasses of *rakı* filled to four fingers.

"Wait! You can't drink it like that. You need to add water," Nimeta darted round the room with a pitcher of water. Then she made a phone call. "Burhan, we're having a celebration with the *rakı* I brought. Why don't you come over?"

"Don't drink on an empty stomach, especially at this time of time," he warned her. As soon as he was free he jumped into the car and raced to Nimeta's office. By the time he got there everyone was completely plastered and singing *sevdalinkas* at the top of their lungs.

"Hey, so you decided to join us, Burhan!" Ivan shouted. "This might be the last time we enjoy getting drunk. Get over here, man."

Everyone knew that the Bosnian bid for independence would carry a heavy price, with the Serb -and Croat- majority regions certain to insist on forming their own Serbian and Croatian states.

Milosevic had long since drawn up a map partitioning not only Bosnia but Sarajevo as well. Tudjman had also completed his own set of calculation. To make matters even worse, there was Milan Babic, a loose cannon and the leader of the Krajina Serbs, a self-proclaimed entity within Croatia. A monster created by Milosevic but no longer under his control, Milan Babic had his eye on Bosnia. If Bosnia succeeded in gaining independence, there would be a state between Krajina and Serbia, the rump Yugoslavia. Babic wanted Krajina and Serbia to share a common border.

The European Union recognized the independence of Croatia and Slovenia on January 15, 1992, thereby bringing to an end the war in Croatia.

On the evening of the same day, the news presenter on Sarajevo Television looked decidedly grim.

"Is he crazy or what?" Ivan asked. "He looks like he's reading off a list of the dead, not news about independence. Send him a note, would you?"

"How do you expect him to look?" Mate replied. "He knows as well as we do what's going to happen next. Now that the army's finished in Croatia they've started deploying in Bosnia. In line with UN orders, troops, artillery units and heavy weapons are being withdrawn from Croatia and sent to Bosnia."

"Even worse," added Sonya, "we've turned over the weapons of our local forces as a sign of goodwill. Our president thinks that by proving he supports peace he can stop war."

"Don't keep blaming İzetbegovic," Ivan said. "Didn't the Federal Army respond by confiscating the weapons of the Serbian paramilitary?"

"Did you really fall for that?" Sonya asked.

"What does it matter if Ivan fell for it or not?" Mate chimed in. "İzetbegovic fell for it, and that's all that matters!"

"What you idiots don't seem to understand is that the president had no choice but to believe it," Ivan said. "He's a statesman. His primary duty is to avoid war, and that's that!"

Izetbegovic was indeed doing his best to avert war, but there was no way to avoid a referendum. The vote on Bosnian independence was held on the 29th of February and the 1th of March. Radovan Karadzic ordered the Bosnian Serbs to boycott it. For good measure, he also set up barricades at all points of entry to the self-declared autonomous Serb regions to ensure that no ballot boxes got in. For two days, planes belonging to the Federal Army buzzed the skies above

Bosnia, raining down pamphlets urging the populace to boycott the referendum. Despite this overwhelming pressure, many of the Serbs in the big cities were known to have voted for independence anyway.

When Radovan Karadzic learned that Bosnia-Herzegovina had applied to the EU for independence he remarked, "It'll be a stillbirth. There's no way we'll let a Muslim bastard of a country be born in these lands."

This infant marked for death was about to be born. With the referendum, the wheel of fortune would now spin for the Bosnians, and everyone expected it to point to "war".

And that's exactly what happened one cold march day. A hoodlum upset by all the Serbian flags hanging at the main marketplace had one drink too many, burst into a church wedding ceremony and fired his gun, killing the father of the Serbian bride and wounding a priest.

It was a tragic but isolated incident. A lengthy prison sentence or execution could have been the end of it, but Karadzic smelled an opportunity and wasted no time taking advantage of it.

Some of them wore black ski masks, others had pulled nylon stockings over their heads. Other than their gleaming eyes, their features were completely concealed. All of them were armed. They looked like a bunch of gangsters on the way to a robbery. In fact, they were a group of highly-trained soldiers acting with incredible discipline and speed. On March 2, 1992, in less than a half a day, they'd transformed Sarajevo into a labyrinth of barricades.

General Kukanjak, the commander of the Sarajevo Army units, watched in horror from the barracks in Bistrik. Even he was opposed to using the JNA forces under his command to partition Sarajevo. Kukanjak tried to arrange a meeting between Karadzic and Izetbegovic so they could hammer out an agreement. Karadzic refused to visit the presidential residence; Izetbegovic naturally objected to the Holiday Inn. They finally came together at the Television Station. This meeting, during which both sides heaped accusations upon the other, succeeded in postponing for just one month the outbreak of war in divided Sarajevo.

April 5, 1992

It wasn't just Muslims, but members of all of the various religious and ethnic groups living in the Bosnia, that turned out for the "DON'T DIVIDE BOSNIA" protest march.

The peace rally began with a few people in the western part of Sarajevo. As this small group worked its way toward the city center, people from every neighborhood, street and building joined the swelling throng.

Carrying photos of Tito and Yugoslavian flags, their numbers and their conviction growing with each step as they protested the shameful partitioning of their beautiful city, they turned out in force that day, the men and women, the Bosniaks, Serbs and Croats, the Muslims, Orthodox Christians, Catholics and Jews who had been living together in harmony, side-by-side, just as their ancestors had done for centuries.

They marched along, these Bosnians of all ages, swept along and away by this show of unity, believing at that moment, deep in their hearts, that war would never break out in their tiny country.

These people had been living together for 500 years. They had never separated their neighborhoods, workplaces and schools. By the end of the Tito era, this intermingling had become such a part of daily life that it was as though all ethnic and religious differences had been erased. A child became best friends with the child living next door, no matter his or her background. Aliya and Boris and Janko played together in the same gardens and courtyards and went to the same schools; Serbian women married Muslim men and Muslims married Catholics without a second thought; friendships, collegial relationships and partnerships formed across all religious and ethnic lines. The people of Bosnia and their country were enriched by their multitude of faiths and races.

Were there no objections to this effortless commingling? Yes, of course there were. No country is completely free of those who would divide. Countries with even the most homogenous of populations have people who condemn, envy and attack those who merely belong to a different political party or support a rival football club.

But Bosnia had, from the beginning, been perhaps the only district in Europe whose varied inhabitants had managed to coexist more or less peacefully even in times of war. It was a distinction that made Bosnians proud.

And so they marched, these people of Bosnia, in a spirit of proud solidarity, determined to show a certain Montenegrin peasant that they wouldn't stand for the barricades he'd thrown up across Sarajevo.

Nimeta and Serbian Sonya were arm-in-arm; Ibo and his Jewish colleague were shoulder-to-shoulder. Unable to join them was Milos, who was responsible for covering the demonstration on the evening news and was up in front of the convoy. Except for the skeleton staff manning the office, everyone from the television station was there, marching.

None of them took Radovan Karadzic's threats seriously. Those Bosnians old enough to remember Karadzic's arrival in Sarajevo still regarded him as an awkward villager with a rustic accent and pointy shoes. Among Bosniak families who had been attending universities for generations, Karadzic enjoyed a modicum of respect for being the first person in his family to get a higher education but was still considered to be too much of a peasant to be taken seriously.

However, a lot of water had flowed under the bridge since Karadzic's arrival in Bosnia. He was now ready to avenge all those years in which he'd been scorned, ridiculed and -worst of all- ignored.

As the crowd in front of Parliament chanted "Don't divide Bosnia" and sang peace songs, they had begun surging towards the barricade on the other side of the Vrbyana Bridge. They intended to cross the bridge, reach Grbavika and show that all the districts and corners of their city still belonged to all of them.

Their intentions pure, armed with nothing but flags and banners, they were unwittingly edging closer and closer to the Police Academy surrounded by heavily armed Serbian militants the night before. That is, they were marching straight into the arms of those who hated them most.

A gunshot rang out. They kept marching. Nobody believed that a group of unarmed civilians would be fired upon. A few more shots rang out, and this time all hell broke loose. A hand grenade had been tossed right into the middle of the marchers. Suada, a twenty-one-year-old medical student, was struck in the chest and collapsed to the ground.

Because her hometown was under siege by the Serbs, Suada had come to Sarajevo to study medicine as a teenage girl. She would have graduated as a doctor that may. She could have chosen not to join the rally that day. Suada was from Dubrovnik, but she, too, couldn't bear for the city she'd grown to love to be divided. She'd been singing, her blonde hair blowing in the wind, when that red carnation burst forth on her breast.

April 8, 1992

"If the EU hadn't recognized Croatia's independence in January, Izetbegovic wouldn't be struggling so hard now," Burhan said, taking another gulp of whiskey. "Now he's in such a bind. You know the saying: 'If he spits downwards, he'll hit his beard; upwards, he'll hit his moustache.' If he hadn't declared Bosnian independence we'd all be under the Serbian fist."

"Do you remember what that guy said?" Raif asked. "He said that if the EU recognized an independent Bosnia he'd make sure our country was stillborn. He's gone on a killing rampage just to make good on his word."

"Of course I remember," Burhan said. "I was furious. He said he wouldn't allow a 'Muslim bastard of a country' to be born in the lands of his Serbian ancestors."

"Who said that?" Raziyanım asked.

"Radovan did, mother," Nimeta told her.

"Are you talking about Radovan Karadzic? That Montenegrin peasant?"

"That's the one."

"He should spend more time tending to his own craziness," Raziyanım said, referring to Karadzic's education as a psychiatrist. "And since when has Sarajevo been considered the lands of his ancestors?"

"Mother, if everyone starts pointing their family trees this city really will be torn apart."

"It already has."

"He suggested dividing up the city without going to war but Izetbegovic wouldn't hear of it," Nimeta said. "It's going to end up divided anyway... At least a young woman would still be alive today."

"How could you say that?" Raif said. "A divided Sarajevo! It's unthinkable!"

"Well, when Karadzic decided to declare the Serbian Republic of Bosnia-Herzegovina did he bother to ask our opinion? Well, did he? Did he say he'd consult Bosniaks and Croats first? Maybe there weren't many, but there were some Muslims and Croats living in those regions claimed by the Serbs," Burhan said.

They could hear shouting and gunfire outside. Hana appeared in a flannel nightgown at the end of the corridor, the cat in her arms.

"Dad, is there going to be a war?" she asked.

"God forbid. What makes you say that?" Burhan said, ignoring the sound of gunfire.

"That's what everyone at school says," Hana insisted.

"Do you think a few idiots firing off their guns could start a war?" Nimeta said.

"Those Serbs have always been hotheaded," Raziyanım muttered. "They're always looking for trouble."

"That's not true," Fiko said. "My best friends are Serbs: Janis, Milos, Konrad."

"I've got nothing against your friends," Raif said. "It's their fathers who are throwing up barricades across the city." Nimeta motioned for Raif not to talk in front of the children.

"Come on, Hana. Back to bed you go. There's won't be a war but you will have to go to school tomorrow," Nimeta said.

"Your nightgown's covered in cat hair. How many times have I told you not to pick him up," Raziyanım said. "Be sure to brush yourself off before you get in bed."

"We're on the brink of war and Mother's still worrying about cat hair," Nimeta whispered to Raif.

"Fiko, you should go to your room too," Burhan said. "It's late."

"But Dad, I want to learn what's going on."

"Nothing's going on, son. You watched the news tonight. People were out on the streets saying they didn't want Bosnia divided, and trouble broke out. That's all."

"You still treat me like a child. All the other dads are teaching their sons my age how to use a gun," Fiko said.

"It's solving problems without resorting to guns that takes real skill," Raif said. "I'll tell you exactly what's going on, but you better not mention guns again. Do we have a deal?"

"It's a deal, Uncle."

"Let the children go to bed," Nimeta said.

"He's not a child, he's a young man," Raif said.

"Even you're still a child in my eyes," Raziyanım said to her son.

"Uncle, pay no mind to the women. Go on, I'm listening."

"The main point," Raif began, "is that Serbs, Croats and Bosniaks have lived together in these lands for centuries…"

"Uncle, by Bosniaks do you mean Muslims?"

"Up until the time of Tito Bosnian Muslims were called Bosniaks. Being a Muslim is one thing, being a Bosniak is another. Muslims live all over the world. Turks, Iranians, Arbs, Indonesians and many many others are Muslim, just like us. Why do they insist on calling us 'Muslims', but the Croats aren't called 'Catholics', nor the Serbs 'Orthodox Christians'?"

"It's perfectly obvious," Burhan said. "They're changing the definition of the word 'Bosniak', slowly and stealthily. They'll eliminate our ethnic identity so we're left with only our religious identity. That way they can claim the homeland we've lived in for nine centuries. Once we're branded 'Muslims' it will be easier to kick us out of Europe."

"But we are Muslims," Fiko pointed out.

"Of course we're Muslims," Raif said, "and we'll always be Muslims. But we're also Bosniaks. We're called Bosniaks, and Bosniaks are also Muslim. Never forget that."

"Alright, Uncle. Go on."

"So we had all these different groups, living together but preserving their own ethnic and religious distinctions under an ideal formula in which the chairman of the presidency was elected on a rotating basis, and then a madman named Milosevic pops up in Serbia and decides that all the Serbs living all across Yugoslavia have to be a part of Serbia. Why did fighting break out in Kosovo and Croatia was about? Because of what I just told you. And now he's provoking the Serbs living in Bosnia to set up a Serbian state of their own."

"But the Serbs are already a part of our republic, aren't they?"

"They were, son. A parliamentary election was held in Bosnia-Herzegovina. The party of Muslims won 87 seats, of Serbs 71 and of Croats 41. This coalition fell apart after only a year, and a new government was formed with the same parties. This time, the Serbs found they couldn't stomach Izetbegovic in the office of the presidency."

"Why not, uncle?"

"Izetbegovic was accused of siding with the Slovenians and the Croats in their bid for independence. This was just an excuse for the Serbs to make trouble."

"There's another, little-known reason Serbs had a problem with Izetbegovic," Burhan added. "When Izetbegovic attended the Organization of the Islamic Conference Summit in Turkey in July of 1991 the Serbs' blood ran cold. They've always been afraid he was planning to set up an Islamist state."

"That's utter nonsense!" Raziyanım exploded.

"Well why do you think they made him rot in prison all those years?" Burhan asked.

"I don't understand why he attended that conference at a time when tensions were running so high. He was kind of asking for it."

"He attended the conference so that he could show those who were really 'asking it' that the Bosniaks also had friends backing them up," Burhan said. "The ethnic Croats could depend on Croatia, the ethnic Serbs on Serbia. What was wrong with Izetbegovic trying to drum up some support among Muslim countries?"

"You remember what that scoundrel Vojislav Seselj said, don't you?" Raif asked.

"What'd he say, Uncle?"

"He said that unless the Bosniaks admitted that they were nothing more than Serbs forcibly converted to Islam, he'd kick their butts all the way to Anatolia."

"Raif! Please! That's enough! He'll be sitting in class with his Serbian friends tomorrow." Nimeta was looking increasingly upset. Raif ignored his big sister.

"Look, Fiko, we're having a man-to-man talk so you can learn the facts. In March of '91, Milosevic and Tudjman met in Tito's old hunting lodge, of all places, and hashed out a plan to divide Bosnia up between them. As the two leaders sat there, all brotherly, trying to figure out the best way to wipe out the Bosniaks, their own people were slaughtering each other. But that's another story."

"Raif, isn't this a bit much for a boy his age? When he goes to school tomorrow..."

Raif cut Nimeta off with, "When he goes to school he'll know who's a friend and who's an enemy!"

"Uncle, why do they keep plotting against us behind out backs?"

"Because they don't believe there's such a thing as Bosniaks. If you ask the Serbs, we're fellow Serbs who converted to Islam under pressure from the Ottomans. If you ask the Croats, we're Croats who turned our backs on the Catholic Church. They've repeated this lie so many times they've started to believe it. And now they've got their eyes on our land."

"Look, everyone's at each other's throats as it is. Don't go filling the boy up with separatist ideas."

"Nimeta, it's too late. Darling, the Serbs announced they were setting up their own parliament way back on October 25th. The boy, as you call him, is living in a divided country. It's time he learned the truth," Burhan said.

"Well, since April 6th we've also been living in a free country liberated from the repression of Milosevic. It's known as the autonomous Republic of Bosnia-Herzegovina."

Raif tipped the bottle of plum brandy over his glass and waited for a moment. "We've run out of booze," he said. "Haven't you got any more?"

"I'll go get it," Fiko said, springing to his feet.

"You sit right back down," Raziyanım said. "You've all had enough to drink."

"But we're celebrating, Mother," Raif said.

"That's all you ever do. I remember the last time you celebrated."

"Let me say something while Fiko's gone," Nimeta said. "Let's stop talking politics, Raif. We have to live with those damned Serbs, whether we like it or not. I don't want you encouraging Fiko to see every Serb as an enemy."

"I need to say one more thing and then I'll shut my mouth," Raif said.

"And what's that?"

"Fiko needs to know this: Under Milosevic's orders, all Bosnian-born soldiers in the Bosnian Army, regardless of rank, are being recalled to Belgrade. Meanwhile, all Bosnian-born soldiers of Serbian origin anywhere in Yugoslavia are being deployed to units in Bosnia. Do you know what that means?"

"Is that really true?" Burhan asked. "Nimeta, do you know anything about this?"

"Yes. We received the same information some time ago," Nimeta said.

Silence descended on the table.

"Does the president still believe that the Bosnian units would never fire on us?" Burhan wearily asked.

"Aliya Izetbegovic has always been an incurable optimist. Do you remember the speech he gave on TV in October of '91?" Raif asked, standing up to do his best impersonation of the president's speech that day: "The Yugoslovia envisioned by Karadzic is unacceptable to everyone but the Serbs. The Yugoslavia he seeks to create is abhorred by one and all! I wish to assure you, the people of Bosnia-Herzegovina, that there is nothing to fear and there will not be a war! Fear not and sleep in peace!"

Raif sat back down and, lips twisted in a wry smile, began tapping his spoon on the table in time to a well-known Balkan folk song:

"The end is nigh, Aliya. The end is nigh, Aliya."

"Your humor's a bit too dark for me," Nimeta scowled.

"Don't be mad at him," Burhan said. "Milosevic and Tudjman really did sing that sone when they met in March of '91 to plot the partition of Bosnia. Someone who was there leaked that little tidbit to the press. You told me all about it, remember?"

Raziyanım's lips had begun to tremble. Nimeta was staring daggers at her husband and brother.

"Why are you looking at us like that? You mean you never heard about that song? What kind of journalist are you anyway, my dear?"

"I'd suggest you stop digging at me, put down your drink and pack your bags," Nimeta said. "Remember, you're got to leave first thing in the morning."

Raziyanım cut in with, "I'm a little worried. Who's going to look after Hana while you're at work? If only you were able to get along with housekeepers."

"Mother, it's not like there's a abundance of housekeepers these days. And is it my fault if Milica left us just because she's Serbian?"

"After all those years in this house, what an ingrate she turned out to be," Raziyanım said.

"She was a good person. I never had any complaints. Besides, it was her brother who made her quit," Nimeta said.

"They think we're just like them," Raziyanım said. "What harm have we ever done anyone? I'm just sorry Hana will be coming home to an empty house."

"Don't worry, Mother. Hana won't be left alone. I'll be working part time as of this week. Ivan promised me a long time ago but something always came up. It's time I insisted."

"If I didn't have any other grandchildren I'd stay here but..."

"Mother, you act as if I haven't managed on my own all these years. You've hardly ever stayed with us but you still act as though we'd all die of starvation and neglect without you."

"I don't know about the others, but now that I'm used to your cooking I really might die of starvation once Nimeta's back in the kitchen," Burhan said. Raziyanım's eyes sparkled.

"Mom, I can go home alone if you like. You stay here," Raif said.

"If it weren't for Muho..."

"Muho needs his grandmother. Don't make such a big deal about being apart for a few months," Nimeta said.

Nimeta badly missed being the lady of the house. She was fed up with the disapproving glances every time she smoked a cigarette or sipped a drink, as well as with the disturbingly neat and tidy state of her home. Sometimes she felt like knocking the books lined up biggest to smallest from their dust-free shelves, flicking her cigarette ashes into every corner and tossing onto the floor the cushions stiffly arranged on the sofa. She sometimes thought back to growing up like a soldiers in her mother's tightly run barracks, all the times she was ordered out of bed to screw the cap back onto to the tube of toothpaste or to pick her clothes up off the floor and hang them in the wardrobe. She could almost hear her father saying, "She's still a little girl, Raziye, leave the poor thing alone."

"I made Hana a big jar of jam. Be sure she has some every morning at breakfast."

"OK, mother. Nimeta gathered up the dishes in front of her husband and brother and carted them off to the kitchen. A moment later Raif came in with a stack of dishes.

"Where's the cognac?"

"You're going to drink cognac after all that plum brandy?"

"With coffee. Just a finger."

"Don't, Raif. You've got to get up early tomorrow and drive all the way to Bijelina."

"If you don't give me cognac I won't take Mother away tomorrow."

Nimeta pulled a bottle of cognac out from under the cupboard and said, "Ok then, poison yourselves until you pop."

"Sis, has Mother gotten on your nerves?"

"I just want to be home on my own for a while, Raif. She's been a great help. I don't know what I'd have done without her. But when she's around I feel like I'm living in boarding school."

"She is something of a retired school mistress. A real disciplinarian."

"Thank God she's missing her other grandchild. I was at the end of my rope. I'm a little worried, though. Serbian commandos have begun patrolling Zvornik. I hope nothing happens while she's there."

"We can't let the Serbs stop us from living out our lives. We've got to get used to their threats even as we ignore them. Relax; I promise not to bring Mother back before autumn. She might even decide to stay in Zvornik for good."

"I'm ashamed to say it, but I really do need some time on my own."

"Are you two talking about me behind my back," Raziyanım said from the door to the kitchen.

"Yeah, that's our one and only past-time. We talk about you every time we meet," Raif said. "How could there possibly be anything more important in our lives than you?"

"Ingrates," Raziyanım said. "But anytime you get yourselves into trouble it's me you come running to. Ah, is that a bottle of cognac in your hand? You're getting up…"

"You're getting up early tomorrow, and you'll be driving," Raif said, mimicking his mother's voice. "Don't drink, son. Be a good Muslim and perform your prayers five times a day."

"Do whatever you want. I'm going to bed," Raziyanım said.

"It'll be a brand new day for you tomorrow when we walk out your front door," Raif said, winking at his sister.

"It'll be a brand new day for us all," Nimeta said. "Let's see what another dawn brings us."

April 9, 1992

Raif whistled all during the trip but he was feeling glum. His head was all in a muddle and he knew things would only get worse. Like all Bosniaks, his heart wanted to believe war wouldn't break out, but a nagging voice deep inside kept telling him otherwise. Still, he kept whistling.

"I expect you'll give up whistling completely after today. You've been tooting every song you ever learned right in my ear ever since we got in the car," Raziyanım said.

"Mother, you're already against cigarettes, booze and cursing. Are you telling me whistling is forbidden as well?"

"I've never been able to understand why our people are so fond of drink, tobacco and swearing. Why are you unable to talk without resorting to profanity and expletives?"

"Don't try to change the subject. I ask you if whistling was forbidden."

"And I asked you why you all love cursing so much."

"Who do you mean by 'you all'?"

"You, the Bosniaks."

"Well aren't you a Bosniak, too?"

"I can't stand vulgarity."

"So does that mean you're not a Bosniak? Have you decided to become a Turk? Believe me, they're even worse than us when it comes to cursing."

"How would you know?"

"Don't you remember how we'd spend our summer holidays in Istanbul? We'd visit relatives and buy all our winter clothes there. You'd bring back box after box of nylon stockings for your friends. If Nimeta hadn't fallen for that guy we'd have gone to Istanbul more often. But you didn't want to give up your daughter."

"Of course I didn't. I was against her moving all the way to Istanbul."

"You're a selfish woman. You took her away from her first love and she ended up marrying the Burhan the following year."

"At least she stayed where I could see her."

"That's right, you've got to keep your kids in your sight forever so you can keep taking care of them."

"When you're a father you'll know how I feel."

"Mother, just listen to yourself! I *am* a father."

"You've been one for only three months. Your fatherly instincts haven't developed yet. You'll get more attached with each passing day. Do you think you'll be able to leave Muho when he turns one?"

"I adore him already but I'll never smother him with attention."

"Are you trying to say I smothered you? You're impossible. There's no point in trying to talk to an ingrate like you. You can go back to your whistling now."

They drove along through the green countryside in silence. As they were approaching Zvornik Raif noticed a strange shimmer of color on the right hand side of the road, way off in the distance. He started driving faster.

"Ah, look Raif, there's a big crowd of people over there," Raziyanım said, forgetting for a moment that she and her son weren't speaking.

As they got closer they heard the buzz of voices.

Raif decided to park some distance away from the crowd and investigate on foot.

"Whatever you do, don't get out of the car, Mother. Lock the door, roll up the windows and wait here for me," he said. Ignoring his mother's repeated calls, he broke into a run.

Five thousand people! Thousands of men, women and children, wounded and dying. Piles of corpses. People slowly bleeding to death form bullet shots to the leg. Women with flesh sliced to ribbons. Men, disemboweled, entrails trailing. Infants in shock. Young girls, repeatedly raped and seeping blood. Elderly men, who escaped the bullets but died of heart attacks... dumb-stricken... deranged.

About half of the inhabitants of the town of Zvornik were there – the Muslim half.

Raif ran through the crowd, trying to understand what they were saying, what had happened. Trying to find a familiar face. The overpowering stench of blood and feces stung his nostrils.

"Arkan's Tigers! Arkan's Tigers!" That was the only comprehensible thing he heard. Arkan, the fascist commander of the terrorist Serbs! His blood froze and he felt faint. He struggled to pull himself together. He'd realized something else: There were no young or middle-aged men among the crowd. All of the wounded, mutilated men he saw were in their sixties, at least. The ragged screams of the women made it impossible for him to understand what anyone was saying. As he got used to the horrible din, he found he was able to pick out the odd word.

They'd come at night, broken down doors, forced people out into the street. They'd given everyone an hour to leave behind their homes. They'd killed all the young men. They'd raped women and girls. They'd skewered babies. Nobody had been allowed to take anything from their homes. They'd stamped on *Korans* and shredded family portraits.

Raif searched for his wife and son among the five thousand people, turning over women and babies lying face down in the field, never giving up hope.

"Raif... Raif... It's me, Mijda."

Raif straightened up from the corpse he was bent over.

"Mijda, have you seen my wife? My son, my aunt?"

"I'm so sorry, Raif." Mijda started sobbing.

"Don't cry. Talk to me."

"Raif, they're dead."

"Dead? How? How did they die?"

"Some commandos raped Bianka. We were in the same house. Bianka came to our flat when the looting started. She brought the baby with her. We locked the door and hid in the bedding cupboard. They kicked the door down. They might not have found us, but the baby started crying. Bianka was nursing Muho the whole time so he wouldn't cry. But it was so dark and stuffy. He started crying." Mijda was wracked with sobs. Raif waited for her to calm down. "They dragged us out of the cupboard. They raped us both. On the table, the two of us, face down, from behind. They pinned down our arms and legs. And raped us, one after another. The pain... Raif..."

Mijda was too choked to speak. Raif noticed for the first time that her skirt was caked with dried blood and excrement.

"And Bianka? What happened to her?"

"Muho was bawling and screaming so loud. One of Arkan's Tigers grabbed him and threw him out the window."

A strangled growl rose from Raif's throat.

"That's when Bianka freed her hands and feet and rushed over to the window. She was cursing the Serbs. One of them grabbed her, pushed her down to the floor and stuck his rifle between her legs...Raif, he stuck it way in... And I heard a gunshot... I must have passed out."

Raziyanım was tired of waiting in the car. She slowly opened the door and got out. It was a mild day. Spring had come early to the Balkans. She breathed in the smell of fresh grass and began walking toward the milling crowd.

As she'd waited in the car she'd made up her mind: if her children were really that fed up with her and she could only do wrong in their eyes, she'd move in with her widowed sister-in-law. They were the same age. She would live in Zvornik from now on, for as long as God gave her sister-in-law a healthy life.

April 10, 1992

Bijelina was no more. Zvornik was no more. Raif's young wife, Nimeta's sister-in-law, was no more. His baby boy was no more. Hundreds and thousands of young men were no more. Hundreds and thousands of young women and children were no more. Those who remained behind would lead poisoned lives, forever. The women with torn sexual organs and anuses, the children who would never speak again, the old people who'd suffered strokes and heart attacks, and were ashamed to be alive, were all that remained behind. Ethnic cleansing had been completed. Emboldened by Belgrade -that is, by Milosevic- under the orders of Radovan Karadzic, deployed and commanded by the radical nationalist Seselj, Arkan's Tigers had "liberated" Zvornik.

And just whom had Zvornik been liberated from?

It had been liberated from people who spoke the same language, shared the same culture, thrilled to the same events, joined in the celebrations of their neighbor's feast days and Christmases, presented gifts on others' holy days, and sympathized and grieved with them when times were bad.

The only thing different about these people in Zvornik, the ones who'd been plundered, cut down, clubbed, skinned alive and raped, all in the name of liberating Zvornik, was that they fasted one month a year, performed special prayers on the first day of two of their own religious festivals, and had their sons circumcised.

And because of this difference they had lost their lives, their families, their livelihoods, their possessions and their land: five thousand people turned destitute overnight!

Nimeta listened to the afternoon news on the radio, stock-still, her face a blank, her eyes glassy. Ivan brought her a cup of hot coffee and said, "Drink it, Nimeta. It'll do you good."

"Are you asking me to just give up hope on all those people?" Nimeta asked.

"We have a list of the names of the survivors. There's no hope for those who were rounded up outside the valley. Say a prayer for the dead and save your strength for the living."

"Mother's been in the hospital since yesterday. They keep giving her sedatives," Nimeta said. "My brother's been kept asleep."

Ivan had remembered Nimeta's earlier breakdown and been afraid she'd have another one. But Nimeta had turned out to be stronger than he'd imagined possible.

She didn't seem at all surprised, as though she'd been expecting this all along. There was a heavy dullness to her, that was all. And she kept repeating the same thing:

"Can you believe it, Ivan? Aliya Izetbegovic asked for help from the Serbian army, the same army that was behind this massacre. How could anyone be so blind? Tell me, what on earth was he thinking? When the Serbs filled Zvornik with their paramilitary forces, their arms, their wireless phones and jeeps, Izetbegovic actually extended an official invitation to the Yugoslav National Army to come and stop the slaughter."

"Don't get yourself worked up for nothing," Ivan said. "If he hadn't asked the army for help would that have stopped them? Even if İzetbegovic had demanded the federal army not set foot in Zvornik they still would have come and slaughtered everyone. The Serbs are engaged in ethnic cleansing. You've got to understand that."

"What are we going to do now, Ivan?"

"Either we find a way to flee or we stay and wait our turn. They'll come for us, be sure of it."

"Stop it! You're demoralizing me!" Sonya shouted. "The world would never allow it. The whole world's watching and they'd never turn a blind eye to another genocide. Even if nobody else cares, the Jews with ties to the Balkans would never let it happen. I haven't given up hope. The madness will stop."

"They're waiting for the Bosniaks to be wiped out before they put a stop to the madness. My neighbor, Azra, has been right all along," Nimeta said.

"Who do you mean by 'they'?" Sonya asked.

"Those who don't want a Bosniak presence in the Balkans." Nimeta's voice was dry and flat, like it was coming not from her throat but from a metallic pipe.

"Well, we are here," Sonya said. "And we're staying here. We Bosniaks will be here to end!"

May 2-3, 1992

Nimeta was trying to make lunch for Hana before she left for work. With power cut after power cut, it seemed the meal would never finish cooking. It hadn't taken long for her to start missing the days when her mother was responsible for the housework and shopping, and for keeping everyone fed. Working part-time hadn't freed her up; it had made her a slave to her household. Her only luxury was the hour she had to herself after everyone left in the morning, those blissful moments stretched out in an armchair with a cup of coffee and a cigarette, just listening to her own thoughts. She still had to get up early to get the kids ready for school but at least she had that one precious hour before she moved on to housework and cooking. For years, she'd complained about never having enough time. Now, in a with an entire morning stretching out before her, the early still punctuated by gunshots, there was nothing for her to do but light a cigarette and scan the newspaper. There was nothing else to do in Sarajevo. Going to the marketplace was out of the question, let alone visiting a couple of galleries, taking in a film or stopping by a friend's for coffee.

The war had swept into their lives like a tornado. It all seemed so sudden, even though the events in Kosovo way back in May of '89 had all but made the outbreak of war inevitable. The Bosniaks had been sleeping while the Serbs, under the leader of Milosevic, had gradually been realizing their ambitions. It had been a deep sleep, a sweet dream of peace shared by President Aliya Izetbegovic. It had been the dream that in this day and age the countries of the West would never allow a war of this kind to rage right under their noses. The dream that they would never permit a bully to use brute force to deprive people of their homes, their homelands and their lives, would never permit genocide and torture. It was a sweet dream, very naive and very human.

The schools had officially been closed since the events of the 6th of April, but a few enterprising teachers had decided to continue giving lessons in underground shelters. Pantries and storerooms were being used for this purpose on virtually every street so that the children wouldn't have to walk through sniper fire. Children of mixed ages attended these makeshift classes. Most of Hana's group was the same age, but a few of her classmates were ten or eleven. Fiko's education continued in a different cellar with students his own age.

The Bosniaks of Sarajevo had two choices: They could either completely bow to a war with an unpredictable outcome, with the survivors of that war left to pick up whatever pieces of their shattered lives remained once it was over, or they could continue to go about their daily lives as best they could. Those able to keep alive even the slightest hope for the future would choose the latter, which meant continuing to educate their children at all costs.

For people like Burhan and Nimeta, life had gone underground. Families joined with teachers to help educate their children. In dank cellars illuminated by kerosene lanterns and candles during the frequent power cuts, life went on. Women facing death daily on the streets above found that they no longer feared the rats in their cellars. Rats, bugs, darkness, mildew, cobwebs, gunfire and the fear of the death had all become a part of daily life.

Raziyanım had moved into her own flat in Kraya Tomislav, not far from her daughter's. Raif, who was now living with his mother, hadn't spoken a word since the Zvornik massacre.

Nimeta checked the pot on the stove; it wouldn't be done until the afternoon. She considered leaving a note telling Hana to have lunch at her grandmother's. There would always be something to eat there.

Raziyanım was convinced that any and all of the children's problems could be solved through food. If one of the kids looks upset or sad, out of the oven would come some freshly baked *börek* or custard.

"Have some of this and you'll be fine. I made it myself just for you," she'd say, placing before them a steaming plate or a tray heaped with dates.

Nimeta had once remarked to her brother, "If Mother had been as generous with a sympathetic ear as she was with her food, you and I would have turned out completely different."

"She's a talker not a listener," Raif had said. "But give credit where it's due, she's a great cook."

Unfortunately, Raziyanım was rapidly running out of ingredients with which to treat her son. It had become next to impossible to find provisions in Sarajevo. The butchers and grocers had closed up shop after they were looted. New deliveries had failed to arrive. Karadzic had thrown up barricades as part of his plan to partition the city into Serbian, Croatian and Muslim districts. Serbian commanders were in charge of the city's checkpoints and they were doing everything in their power to starve the Bosniaks.

Even so, nobody, including the local Serbs, could imagine Sarajevo being permanently divided into ethnic enclaves.

Their homes, workplaces, shops, schools -in short, their lives- had been side-by-side and intertwined for centuries. They couldn't imagine it being otherwise.

But others could.

At his military headquarters in Pale, Karadzic was spreading maps of the city across tables and drawing lines with a red pen. The old Ottoman neighborhood of narrow lanes centered on the Bashcarsi bazaar in the east of the city would be left to the Bosniaks, while the wide boulevards built at the time of the Habsburgs would go to the Croatians.

The modern business and industrial district built mainly in the 20th century in the west of the city was to be allocated in its entirety to the Serbs, thereby cramming most of the population into the eastern districts while the Serbs enjoyed plenty of space in the west.

Nimeta was horrified by the signs of intolerance and racism spreading around her. Something had begun happening to her neighbors, the people she'd grown up with, gone to university with, had fun with, made love with, gone through good and bad times with.

Over the ages, mankind might have grown increasingly sophisticated and technologically adept but certain primitive instincts had obviously remained unchanged since the day he first stood erect on two feet.

Nimeta checked the time. She'd better not be late to work today. Aliya İzetbegovic was returning in the afternoon from a three-day visit to Lisbon. Even though she knew he'd emerged from meetings empty-handed she'd still have to meet him at the airport to get a firsthand account.

I hope Ivan sends someone else, she thought to herself. She was in no shape to do anything today, having spent the better part of the previous night quarreling with Burhan. She'd told him she'd be home late the following day and asked him to come home early. Burhan had exploded. "If you expect me to be the lady of the house, you can go work on construction sites," he'd said.

"Can't we share the responsibility for bringing up the children?"

"We already do. But you've started working into the night more and more often."

"There's a war on, Burhan. I'm a journalist. That's just about the only job available in Sarajevo these days. If I quit, how do you think we'd make ends meet?"

The moment the words left her mouth she realized she'd gone too far. Burhan's work had mainly been in Knin and ever since he'd signed over the business there he'd barely earned any money. He'd actually been lucky: many of the Bosniaks working in Croatia had lost their jobs and businesses much earlier, when the Croats first began discriminating against Muslims. Watching the contracts of his fellow engineers and friends cancelled one by one as he kept his own job had made Burhan uncomfortable.

Then the Serbs had come. They'd been focused on getting rid of the Croats, but he'd terminated his contract before the Serbs could, since he knew he'd be next. Experienced engineers were quickly snatched up and he'd had a number of contracts elsewhere. But then, across all the republics of Yugoslavia, the Serbs began terminating any work with non-Serbs. Burhan was left with a single contract in Sarajevo before the outbreak of war soon shut down the construction sector entirely. If he'd continued to drop by his office in the twin towers of Momo and Üzeyir, the symbol of modern Sarajevo, it was only to keep himself busy.

Burhan and Nimeta had laughed so hard when Raziyanım said, "Silly goose, why'd you open an office in Momo when you could have worked in the Üzeyir tower?" that she felt she had to explain herself by adding, "You can't expect any good to come of places named after giaours." Her words turned out to have been prophetic: the offices in Momo were being closed one after another, not that office blocks with good Muslim names weren't facing the same fate all across the city.

His pride stung by having to depend on his wife financially, Burhan had grown increasingly irritable. For quite some time, he'd been grumbling and scowling at the most trivial things. Nimeta knew why and did her best to humor him.

Another economic victim of the Serbs was Mirsada. She'd called Nimeta a few months ago, sounding distraught. "They've fired me for no reason," she'd said. They'd talked it over and decided not to tell Ivan what had happened. Mirsada had quit her job as their Belgrade correspondent to work at the same Serbian news agency as Petar. He'd arranged the whole thing, foolishly imagining that they could keep her Bosniak identity a secret. Nimeta and the others had begged her to reconsider and now they'd all been proven right. Mirsada was far too proud to ask Ivan for her old job back and didn't want any of her old colleagues to know that she was unemployed. Nimeta had had to swear repeatedly that she wouldn't say anything.

"Come home," Nimeta had said. "You can find work anywhere in Sarajevo. How many journalists have your kind of experience?"

"I don't want to leave Petar," Mirsada had said. "It took me all these years for me to finally believe in true love. How can I walk away from him now, especially at my age?"

Nimeta knew all too well what it meant to walk out on love, but she bit her lip and held her tongue. Fortunately, Petar had managed to find Mirsada another job, where she was known by the Serbian nickname “Miza”.

After speaking with Mirsada, Nimeta had said to Burhan, “If you weren't such a well-known engineer you'd have hid your identity too. But all the construction firms know you.”

“I've had this name for centuries and I'm keeping it for as long as the world keeps turning,” he'd said. It was the first time Nimeta had ever heard her husband pride himself on his name, and it surprised her. Unemployment and despair can do things to a person's character, she thought to herself.

Nimeta considered herself to be a fairly unlucky person and accepted that fortune would rarely smile on her; even so, the minor irritations of life infuriated her, such as a power cut while she was cooking lunch, on a day she absolutely couldn't go in late to the office.

She quickly jotted, “Hana, sweetie, have lunch at your grandmother's and call me when you get home,” on a slip of paper and stuck it in the corner of the mirror opposite the front door. Just as she was walking out the front door it occurred to her that she'd better let her mother know that Hana was coming. She picked up the receiver and waited for a dial tone. There was a strange clicking sound, and she couldn't decide if the line was dead or the phone itself was broken.

She stepped out into the corridor and knocked on her neighbor's door. Azra opened it in her nightgown.

“Excuse the outfit, Nimeta,” she said. “I have trouble telling if it's day or night anymore. We can't go out on the street so what's the point in getting dressed?”

“You have a point. It seemed like the gunfire was heavier today than ever.”

"I turn the radio up full blast so I don't hear it."

"But the power's out."

"Mine's battery operated."

"Good idea. I'll get some batteries on the way home."

"If you can find any, grab them quick. I'm glad I always kept extra ones around the house."

Not for the first time, Nimeta realized what a strain the minutiae of everyday life had become. From coffee to medication, basic foodstuffs to batteries, everything had disappeared. Gas, electricity and water outages were frequent. They'd gone back to living in the middle ages.

"Azra, is your phone working?"

"It hasn't rung since morning." Azra walked over and picked up the receiver. "It's dead."

"So it's not just my line," Nimeta said. "I was going to phone my mother. Oh well, I'll stop by the post office and give her a call."

They both jumped at what sounded like a clap of thunder. They could hear the tinkle of shattered glass.

"Shall we go down to the cellar?" Nimeta asked.

"Let's not bother," Azra said. "It'll be over soon." She seemed inured to the sounds of gunfire and bombs. They'd been shelling the city every day for a month. The people of Sarajevo were constantly being bombarded from Serbian positions on the mountaintops. "Have you got enough time to have some tea?"

"I'm afraid not. İzetbegovic is returning today. I've got a lot of work to do and I'm already late."

"Is Izetbegovic crazy or what?" Azra asked. "He keeps knocking on door after door, trying to solve this mess. Does he really expect the giaour countries to help Muslims?"

"This isn't about Muslims and non-Muslims, it's a human rights issue. Karadzic has laid siege to areas where the Muslims are the majority. He's forcing people out of their homes at gunpoint, and killing them. Just like the poor Bosniaks in Dobrinya, who've been there practically forever, woke up one day to find that some madman had declared their town to be in the so-called Republic of Serbia. The countries of the west care too much about human rights to let his continue..."

Azra cut her off before she was finished. "Look, Nimeta, I haven't got your education or brains, but I can tell you and Izetbegovic both that if you're waiting the West to save the day you're waiting for nothing. People in the West will start remembering human rights once the last Muslim is dead."

"How can you say that?"

"I'm more of a realist than you. Go ask Izetbegovic what he managed to wheedle out of the West in Lisbon. I can tell you right now: nothing!"

Nimeta decided there was no point in arguing with Azra and changed the subject by asking, "Do you want me to get you anything on the way home?"

"Just get home safely through the whizzing bombs," Azra said.

Nimeta headed down from Gorica and began walking briskly. She knew fresh fighting was likely to break out soon. The commander of the Bosnian units, Sefer Halilovic, had surrounded the barracks housing the YNA units under the command of Kukanjak and given them an ultimatum: surrender your arms and withdraw from all Bosniak-majority areas. Nobody expected the Serbs to sit on their hands and watch how things panned out.

As Nimeta walked along thinking about this latest development, the city was shaken by another explosion and all the pedestrians darted for safety into doorways and under eaves. When it was clear that the bomb had landed somewhere far away, they started walking again. Bosniaks had learned to hug the doorways as they made their way down the sidewalk. Nimeta turned into a street intersecting Marshall Tito street and began running towards the post office. The sound of gunshots was getting closer. All of a sudden she was enveloped in smoke and a red glow, the sky scarlet, the clouds tinged red. There must be a fire, a terrible fire somewhere, was her first thought. She kept moving, sprinting past the top of the street leading to Kulin Ban Avenue, turning left, and rounding the bend, where, abruptly, she froze in her tracks, horrified by what she saw.

Shards of glass were pouring down from the skies, a crystal waterfall, crunching under the feet of the people dashing left and right as flames burst forth, licking and swallowing everything in their path. Everything. The newly renovated post office had been smashed into a heap of glass and stone, and was ablaze.

Nimeta stood knee-deep in broken glass, straight-backed and spellbound, watching Sarajevo burn: the post office, the national theater, the law school... then new explosions and fresh flames, fanned by the wind, an inferno spreading across the city.

"Now this, this is hell!" Nimeta said to herself. "I've lived to see hell on earth. God must be making us pay for our sins here and now, in this world."

When the Serbs were fighting in Croatia they'd used the JNA units to reduce cities to rubble, leveling buildings and eradicating centuries of history before they moved in to capture it. They'd gained expertise in this strategy of total destruction, and now they were using it against Sarajevo.

"Hey, Nimeta! Are you in shock, sweetie?"

"Mate! What are you doing here?"

"I was wondering the same about you. You looked like you'd been hypnotized. Come on, let's get out of here before something lands on our heads."

Mate had materialized like a guardian angel. Oblivious to the heavy camera resting on his shoulder, he began dragging Nimeta away from the flames.

"Mate, I have to call my mother."

"Forget about it, Nimeta. The post office is gone and the lines are all down anyway. They haven't been working since morning. Didn't you notice?"

They crunched through the broken glass.

"The car's over here," Mate said.

The car windows and windshield were shattered. Nimeta's legs were a bloody mess from the knee down. She winced in pain as Mate helped her pull out dozens of slivers of glass.

"There's a a pharmacy over there," Nimeta said, pointing to right.

"They just bombed it."

"What about the obstetrics clinic a little further along?"

"It was on fire. Let's go to the TV station, we can sort you out there."

"But Mate, the kids! My kids…"

"Where are they?"

"They went to class in a cellar a couple streets from our house."

"We can't go back, Nimeta. There hasn't been any fighting or bombs in your neighborhood. In any case, their teachers wouldn't let them leave class if it was dangerous."

"But Mate…"

"No buts about it. Are you coming with me?"

Nimeta got into the car. The seats were covered in glass. They brushed away the glass with Nimeta's scarf and sat down. Nimeta told herself that Mate was right: the safest place in the city was probably her own neighborhood. And she was absolutely certain Burhan would come home early as she'd asked, despite their quarrel.

Mate drove at breakneck speed all the way to the television station, in the western part of the city. When they got there, still reeling from the fire, they were told the shocking news: President Aliya Izetbegovic was missing. He'd flown out of Lisbon the previous night but hadn't yet landed. His plane had either crashed or been hijacked.

With 40,000 phone lines out of order across the city since morning, it had been extremely difficult to conduct a thorough investigation. The television building had a direct working line to the presidential residence, but the line had been busy all day.

Nimeta had intended to make an appearance at work and then get straight home at the first opportunity, but Ivan ordered everyone to stay put until the "Izetbegovic Incident" was resolved. When some of colleagues started grumbling, he bellowed, "We're in the middle of a war. Your jobs demand total commitment. If necessary, you'll stay on the job 24 hours straight – or even 48 hours. If you're not up to it, the door's right over there!"

Nimeta sank into her chair with a curse. Azra had been right about one thing: Izetbegovic hadn't simply returned empty-handed from his meeting with the giaours, he hadn't even managed to return.

Sonya told the others about a rumor that was making the rounds. Fikret Abdic, the president's political rival, had supposedly plotted with the Serbs to kill Izetbegovic, upon which Abdic would become the leader of the Bosniaks.

"Isn't that the same guy who opposed independence for Bosnia?" Nimeta shouted. "Mirsada sent us some confidential information from Belgrade. If Abdic had taken the reins of government the war would have ended and we would have joined the rump state of Yugoslavia."

"We'd have spent our lives as a minority under the Serbian fist. That's not my idea of peace," Mate said.

Musta poked his head through the door: "Ivan wants everybody in his room, on the double! With the phones down, he's probably going to send us all out to gather information."

At the meeting, the team ironed out the final details of that evening's broadcast. Their direct line to the president was still busy and there had been no reports about him. Everyone was tense, Nimeta even more so because she kept thinking about her argument with Burhan the previous night. She was anxious to get home and make peace but, as usual, everything had gone wrong. She was always tied up at work when Burhan managed to come home early, but whenever he left the city on business there wouldn't be a single newsworthy incident in the country. Izetbegovic had chosen a fine day to go missing!

"Stop looking at me with those pitiful eyes," Ivan told her when the meeting ended. "If there are no more developments after the evening news you're free to go home, Nimeta."

The anchorman was presenting the news. Mate's footage of the fire had just been aired. The entire team was watching the live broadcast together when the phone rang. Ivan reached over and answered it. His face went chalk white.

"What? What are you saying?"

Ivan cleared his throat and relayed instructions via the ear piece of the news presenter: "We've got the president on the line," he said. "Start doing a live interview. Now!"

The presenter managed to conceal his astonishment. They'd decided not to cover the president's disappearance on the news that evening, so the presenter asked a couple of routine questions about the talks in Lisbon before Ivan prompted him to ask the question they'd been wondering all night.

"Where are you right now, Mr. President?"

"I'm in Lukavika," Izetbegovic replied.

There was a collective gasp in the conference room. Every Bosniak living in Sarajevo knew that the Serbs' most important military headquarters, the place where they planned all their attacks, was in Lukavika. The President had fallen into enemy hands. In a voice that trembled slightly, the speaker asked a follow-up question.

"In what capacity are you there, Mr. President?"

"It would appear that I have been kidnapped."

When Nimeta finally stumbled home some time near dawn, she was greeted by her husband's ghostly white face.

"Do you have any idea what time it is?" Burhan asked.

"Do you have any idea what's been going on? Haven't you seen the news? Izetbegovic was kidnapped. I was just on my way home and–"

"Is Izetbegovic more important to you than Fiko and Hana, than your husband, your mother and your brother? You couldn't care less about any of us. Did a bomb fall on our heads, did the kids get home in one piece? Are they hungry or ill? You couldn't care less."

"How can you say that?" Nimeta shouted. "I started working part-time just for them."

"Is this what you call working part-time? It's nearly five o'clock in the morning."

"What would we do if I lost my job? You haven't been bringing home enough for us to get by. Don't you realize that, Burhan?"

"When did you become so money hungry, Nimeta?"

"We're in the middle of a war, and I'm doing all I can to make sure we don't go hungry, even if it means working all night. When I do finally get home, this is what you say to me?"

"Working all night, where?" Burhan asked, eyes blazing in his ashen face. His hands were trembling and his voice shook.

"What's that supposed to mean?"

"Tell me where you've been working all night. At the TV station, or in that Croat's bed?"

Nimeta clutched at the wall for support. Her heart was pounding in her ears. She could hear her blood pulsing, it was deafening.

"I asked you a question," Burhan said in a menacing whistle.

"What's the meaning of this?" Nimeta managed to whisper.

"The meaning is this," Burhan said, coming right up to his wife, their faces now inches apart. She could feel his breath, could smell the brandy on his breath.

"The meaning is that you've been sleeping with that Croatian dog for years. You've cheated on your husband and betrayed your family, and you've been shameless. You had a breakdown because of him but you made it look like it was my fault, which is another kind of betrayal. Did you think I'd never find out, Nimeta? Well I have! And if you only knew how I found out."

He went quiet, breathing hard; one of his bloodshot eyes began twitching. Nimeta was glued to the wall, pressing her back as hard as she could against the hard concrete, wanting nothing more than to somehow push her way through and lose herself in the wall. But she was still there in the hall, unable to speak, her heart bleeding and hurting more than her legs had all during that terrible day. It's not like that, she wanted to say. It's not at all what you think. I fell in love, that's all. I couldn't help it but I couldn't leave you and the kids, either, Burhan. I could never leave you.

"Speak!" Burhan shouted. "Tell me how you could do this to me. Tell me what I've done to deserve such a terrible punishment. I don't remember doing anything bad to you. Am I paying for the sins of my ancestors, is that it?"

Nimeta felt like she was shouting at the top of her lungs but not a sound left her throat.

"You don't even bother to deny it." Burhan's right hand sliced through the air and landed on Nimeta's face. For a moment, she thought she really had gone through the wall, was inside the wall. She felt like she had a mouthful of broken teeth and saw flashes of light. When she came to, Burhan was gone. Bending over her as she lay stretched out on the floor at the end of the hallway was Fiko, and the wounded look in his eyes, the pain and the fear in her son's eyes, was unspeakable.

May-June 1992

Nimeta set the table for dinner as though nothing had happened. Burhan would soon be home. She decided to act normally and wait until the children were in bed before she talked things over with her husband. She had nothing to hide. Burhan now knew all about her affair. He also needed to know that the affair had finished a long time ago. She had to tell him that she'd been unable to leave him, that her family meant more to her than anything else in the world. She would ask Burhan to understand her and to forgive her. She was only human. At a difficult time in their relationship, when they'd drifted apart and she was feeling particularly lonely, another man had appeared and she'd been carried away. Except she hadn't gone anywhere. She'd stayed. She'd stayed with her husband and children, and she'd promised herself that she'd never see Stefan again. Never again would they meet, talk, kiss and make love. Stefan had left Yugoslavia and gone to London out of respect for her decision. Would Burhan ever be able to appreciate how difficult it had been for her to separate from Stefan?

A tear ran down her cheek and plopped onto the freshly laid tablecloth. No, nobody would ever understand what a struggle it had been, not Burhan, not the kids, not her mother, nobody. In everyone else's eyes, she and Stefan were nothing but a pair of impulsive adulterers.

She'd fallen hard for him, but even when her heart was soaring above the clouds she'd never forgotten that she was a married woman with two children, even when their love had been at its most ecstatic she'd felt cursed. Guilt and a sense of impending doom lurked always in the background. She knew, for example, that her mother would never forgive her if she found out. She doubted that even her own children could forgive her. Perhaps when Hana grew into a young woman, but only if the same thing happened to her. If she learned through her own experience that a married woman with children might still have a heart and body open to love and feelings she couldn't control. It was something she'd never want to happen to her daughter, even it helped her to understand her mother. It was better that Hana never forgive her than that she suffer the same pain and shame.

She brought in a stack of dishes and set the table. A plate on each side!

She set the table just as she had all those years ago, when she'd made her final decision to separate from Stefan. She'd been bracing herself to tell Burhan that she loved another man. She'd imagined the table the following day, one plate short. A missing plate, Burhan's plate. Her hand had shaken so badly that the plate slipped through her fingers and broke. A broken plate and the shattered heart of her husband when he heard what she had to tell him.

She'd fetched the broom, swept the broken pieces into the dustpan and dumped them in the trash. Later, after she'd finished setting the table and heated up the food, she'd inexplicably dashed into the kitchen and retrieved the broken pieces from the trash. She'd washed the pieces of porcelain and set them aside. When Burhan saw them he's said, "Why don't you throw them away, darling. We can always get new plates."

"I want to glue them together," she'd said.

"That plate will never be any good, not after it's been broken. Just throw it away."

Nimeta had phoned Stefan the following day and said, "I couldn't tell Burhan. I won't be able to leave him. Forgive me, Stefan."

If she told him about that plate tonight, would he understand? Would Fiko, who'd stared at her last night with horrified, accusing eyes? Would her son ever understand how she'd battled with herself not to abandon her family?

She hadn't even tried to explain.

"Son, sometimes husbands and wives fight like this. The war's making us all a bit jumpy. Go get me some ice. And don't say a word to Hana," she'd told her son.

"Mom, why did dad hit you?"

"We were arguing."

"Why'd he hit you?"

"He didn't hit me. I fell. I slipped and fell.

"Why'd he hit you, Mom?"

Nimeta tried to get up off the floor. "Fiko, why don't you help me instead of asking silly questions. What did I tell you? Get me some ice, quick."

"Mom, I heard what he said. Dad said something about paying for his sins. What did he mean?"

"Fiko, do what I say. Get me some ice. I'll explain everything later," she'd said. She needed to buy a little time and to stop her face from going purple and swollen. When Fiko went into the kitchen she somehow managed to get herself up off the floor and into the bathroom. She was afraid to look at the mirror. She locked the door, buried her face in a thick towel and began to sob.

It had taken all her powers of persuasion to convince Fiko that the altercation had been a typical marital dispute that simply got a little out of hand. Nimeta hadn't gone to work that morning. The only thing she'd wanted that day was to talk to Mirsada, so she'd gone to her mother's house to use the phone. Thank God her mother was out. Turning her back to Raif, she'd dialed her friend's number. But there was no answer. She'd have said, "It turned out just as you feared, Mirsada. Burhan knows." She'd have unburdened herself to her best friend, and probably sobbed. But Mirsada wasn't at home, yet again. There hadn't been any news from her for the longest time. Nimeta knew she'd been planning to leave the city with Petar, and tried not to fear the worst.

Raif had frowned at her black eye and swollen face, but hadn't said a word.

"Raif, aren't you going to ask me what happened?" she'd asked.

There was no reaction from her brother.

"Have you been taking your medication?"

Raif didn't so much as blink.

"Not talking won't solve anything. Do you think I don't know it's a form of escape? While everyone else is facing up to the painful realities of war you just go right ahead and clam up. Raif, you were always doing that as a boy, too. When something bad happened you'd stay under your blanket for hours. You've grown up. Come out from under your blanket."

She kept an eye on the door as she talked to her brother. Raziyanım would never let her talk to her brother like this. Her son had been babied and coddled and loved most of all, always. Sometimes Nimeta suspected she'd been adopted; it was the only explanation for how differently she treated her children. Her mother had been scolding her, criticizing her and butting into her business ever since she was a little girl. Raif could do no wrong. He was mama's little pasha.

"Raif, I know you're blaming yourself for not being at home that terrible day. I'm not stupid. Nothing would have happened any differently, except you'd be a corpse today instead of a deaf-mute, that's all! You wouldn't have been able to save your wife and son. Nobody could have saved them. They'd have killed you to get you out of the way. Get that through your head, and start speaking again. Talk to me!"

Nimeta realized there was no point in trying to get Raif to talk. She walked over to the phone and picked up the receiver. This time, her mother's phone was dead. Cursing, she stormed out of her mother's house and went back home, where she spent the entire morning in bed, sleeping and crying. She was in no state to do anything else. Only one thing mattered: saving her marriage. She had to explain everything to her husband and tell him how sorry she was. Neither of them had the right to turn their home into a second warzone; it wouldn't be fair to the kids. Even if Burhan was unable to forgive her, they should at least continue living together until the war was over.

What would Burhan do if she said, "I gave of myself by walking away from Stefan; now it's your turn to give of yourself by forgiving me." Do men realize that some things are more important than their pride and their egos? Like the ability to forgive, devotion to one's children or being able to view a woman as a person and a friend? She'd give it a try.

In order to make Burhan's favorite dish, she'd waited for an hour at the supermarket meat counter and paid five times the normal price for 600 grams of lamb. She was wearing the green blouse he always complimented. She'd concealed the black eye with some heavy makeup and pushed any more thoughts of the fight early that morning out of her mind. Finally, everything was ready and she and the children waited for Burhan to come home.

But he never did.

Nimeta didn't serve dinner and asked the children to wait, like she always did when Burhan was late. They waited. The clock ticked from eight to nine, and she let Hana eat. Fiko was hungry, so she dished out his dinner when the clock struck ten. The phone was dead, so she couldn't call his office.

"Do you think something bad might have happened to dad," Fiko asked.

"He's often late, you know that," she said, but she was getting worried. What if he'd left her?

She gathered up the dishes she'd so carefully laid out. Alone in the kitchen, she had a few forkfuls of cold food. The leftovers went into the cat's dish. Bozo took a couple of sniffs, turned her back and curled up under the chair. Even the cat seemed affected by the mournful atmosphere. Fiko tiptoed around Nimeta for a while before he finally confronted her: "Maybe dad's not coming home because he's angry with you."

"Don't be ridiculous."

"You two were fighting this morning. He was furious, I heard the way he was shouting."

"Husbands and wives fight sometimes. It's normal."

"I'd never seen you and dad fight like that, Mother."

He was right. They never fought. Perhaps that's why she'd fallen in love with another man, perhaps she'd bottled up her desires, her disappointments and her anger. Burhan was as still as a pool of water, unruffled, unquestioning and placid. The only outward sign of distress he permitted himself was to compress his lips and put on a long face.

"It's time you went to bed, Fiko."

"I wish we could call him, Mom."

"Well, we can't. This damn war! Go on, off to bed. You've got school tomorrow morning."

It was only Fiko had gone to her room that it occurred to her to try and phone from her mother's, completely forgetting that Raziyanım's phone had also gone dead that morning. She woke Fiko up and told him she was going to his grandmother's house to call his father.

"You can't go out alone at this hour. I'm coming with you," he said, pulling on a pair of trousers.

"I'll be fine, Fiko. Stay here with Hana. I'll be back in no time."

"I won't let you go out alone, Mom. Dad will get mad at me if I do."

When had Fiko grown big enough to look after his mother? Nimeta couldn't believe it. There he was, fully dressed and standing right across from her. She gave him an appraising look, and what she saw was a tall, well-built, handsome boy of sixteen, the spitting image of Burhan in his teens.

"Alright then. We'll tell Azra we're going out so she can keep an eye on Hana," Nimeta said.

"Don't wake Azra at this hour, Mom," Fiko said. "We can leave a note for Dad, so he doesn't get worried if he comes home."

Nimeta was just about to step out the door when she remembered that her mother's phone had also gone dead. "I've changed my mind," she said to Fiko. "We'll leave things until the morning."

"What happened, Mom?"

Nimeta didn't want to appear to be a scatterbrained fool in front of her son, so she said, "We don't want to worry your grandmother this late at night. We've done everything we can. Let's not leave Hana alone at home."

Fiko didn't press her. After he went back to bed she pulled a chair over to the window and sat down. She wanted a cigarette but there weren't any in the house. Cigarettes, like coffee, had become impossible to find. She stood up, got her handbag and returned to her seat, rummaging through the various pockets on the odd chance that she'd find a stray cigarette. Nothing! She flung the handbag to the floor. Mate had rolled cigarettes from strips of paper and loose tea. Her grandmother had told her about the fine paper they'd used in the old days, and what a ceremony they'd made of rolling cigarettes. So, history was repeating itself, yet again. She'd be taking up the practice soon enough, provided she could find some tea.

For some months now, the people of Sarajevo had been growing various herbs on their balconies and window ledges for that very reason. Nimeta spent a lot of time with foreign journalists, and had been able to keep herself and her friends supplied with tea, coffee and cigarettes. On those occasions when Nimeta had been able to share her coffee with Azra, the next door neighbour had done what so many others were doing: pounding lentils with a mortar and pestle, roasting the powder and using it as coffee grounds. Nimeta had tried a swallow once and nearly spit it out.

"Drink it up," Raziyanım had immediately said. "In the days ahead we'll be missing even lentil coffee. You'll never know what people resort to in times of war until you've been through war yourself."

But you know, mother, don't you, Nimeta had said to herself. Is there anything you don't know?

She was getting drowsy. It's good she hadn't gone to her mother's. She was terrified of worrying her or arousing her curiosity. Raziyanım would have asked how she got a black eye. If Fiko let anything slip about what happened that morning, she'd be interrogated until dawn, and then face a flood of accusations. She tried to shake off her drowsiness; she was feeling too lethargic to get up and go to bed. In the chair by the window, waiting for Burhan, Nimeta nodded off and jerked awake until dawn.

Burhan didn't come that day, or the next. Or ever.

Nimeta went to Burhan's office early the next morning. He hadn't come to work and nobody knew where he was. When got to the TV station she called her husband's relatives in Travnik. She was unable to get through to his relatives or to anyone else in Travnik. On the spur of the moment she called his old office and the construction site in Knin. Nobody knew anything. Finally, she turned to her boss.

"Ivan, I'm terrified something's happened to my husband. What if he's been shot or stabbed in a dark street?"

She started to cry.

"It's easy enough to find out, Nimeta. I'll have them call the hospitals and police stations. We'll find out everything we need to know by this evening," Ivan said. "Stay calm and get to work on the interview you're doing with MacKenzie. I want you to fire off some tough questions. He's the person most to blame for not lifting the arms embargo."

"Ivan, I'm sorry, could you give that assignment to someone else?"

"We can't allow personal issues to affect our work, and that's that."

Nimeta slammed the door on her way out. She felt sleep-deprived, exhausted and guilt-ridden. She shuffled over to her desk and pulled out the file on MacKenzie. She didn't think she could think straight without a coffee, but knew that the store in her locked drawer was gone. At least she had a couple of packs of cigarettes left over from a carton an English colleague had given her. She lit a cigarette. When these two packs were done, what on earth would she do?

Lewis Mackenzie, a Canadian, commanded the UN's peacekeeping force in Sarajevo. Even during the bloodiest days of war he'd failed to grasp the severity of the situation in which the Bosniaks found themselves. In his eyes, Izzetbegovic was an unreasonable politician who sought to get the UN forces embroiled in a hot war and who was paranoid enough to believe that the Serbs and Croats planned nothing less than wiping Bosnia from the map. Trained for war, Mackenzie was inept when it came to political maneuvering. He'd badly botched things when Izzetbegovic was kidnapped, wasn't particularly fond of either the Muslim Bosniaks or their Muslim president, and was known to rue the day he'd been posted to Sarajevo. There were also reports that MacKenzie had been receiving funds from Serbian-American lobbyists.

Nimeta had been jumping through hoops to land an interview with MacKenzie. Now she had to prepare a series of pointed questions that would lead to other, more penetrating, questions.

It always happened. Every time God presented her with a spoonful of benevolence she'd get poked in the eye with the handle. She started working simultaneously on her questions and on a list of places Burhan could be. He didn't have that many close friends. Her mind elsewhere, slumped across from an ashtray now brimming with butts and ashes, Nimeta completed the rough outline of the interview questions. She hadn't even gone for lunch. The latest round of reports had arrived from the police stations and hospitals. Burhan had not been wounded or killed within the municipal lines of Sarajevo.

When Sonya screamed, Nimeta was translating an article from a British newspaper. She sprang up and ran over to Sonya's desk. Mate had grabbed Sonya by the waist. Musa tried to hold her wrists and ankles as she kicked and punched. She was crying and screaming as they tried to restrain her, but nobody could understand what she was saying.

Some more people came running in from another department. Nimeta leaned against the wall for support.

"Has she gone mad?" Ibo asked.

"She's about to," someone said. "Snipers just opened fire on a busload of children in front of the *Oslobodenje* newspaper offices. They're all dead."

Nimeta sank to the floor and began vomiting. Sonya fainted. They laid her out on a desk and Ivan administered short, sharp slaps to her cheeks.

From where she lay in her own puddle of vomit on the floor, Nimeta could hear Ibo say, "Sonya, the bus belonged to an orphanage. The children were all preschoolers. Nothing's happened to your child. Do you hear me? Hey, Sonya..."

The next day, Nimeta took a few photographs of Burhan with her and went to visit hospitals and police stations. She was unable to find out anything. When she got home that evening Fiko was waiting for her in the window.

"I was unable to find him, Fiko," she said.

"Look harder; you're the one who lost him," he said.

"What's that supposed to mean?"

"I know what happened. Dad left because of you!"

Nimeta's hand rose in the air to strike her son, but she was able to restrain herself. They stared at each other for a moment. Nimeta lowered her hand and Fiko stalked off to his room, slamming the door behind him.

Nimeta was able to keep Burhan's disappearance from Raziyanım for only a week. Fiko had told his grandmother all about the fight, as well.

"Be grateful your husband didn't kill you," she said. "There's no use in being sorry now. You should have thought about it earlier."

"But mother, we're not the first couple to have a fight."

"Your father and I never argued."

"That's because nobody dares pick a fight with you. You're always right."

"And furthermore, I never deceived my husband, never had to hang my head in front of him out of my own shame."

"What are you talking about? Anyone listening to you would think I'd cheated on Burhan."

"I can look right inside my children's hearts and minds, Nimeta. I've always been able to," she said, fixing her hard hazel eyes on Nimeta.

She truly could. But for some reason, she always did it to Nimeta, not to Raif. Whenever Nimeta had done anything wrong, her mother had always found out. Whenever she had a crush on a boy, her mother sensed it. She'd been questioned and cornered and badgered all her life.

Nimeta didn't respond to her mother. She was exhausted; she was upset; she was distraught. Burhan had been missing for a week. She'd begun accusing herself and thinking that it really was all her fault. She needed a sympathetic ear and missed Mirsada more than ever. If she could just talk to her childhood friend, the only person who would understand her right now. But Mirsada had disappeared, just like her husband. Private lives were not immune from the destruction of war.

Day after day, Nimeta stopped by Burhan's office, hoping he'd gone in to work. Every night, she set the table and waited. But Burhan never came.

Could God have given her a harsher punishment? Fiko wouldn't talk to her. Hana had soon picked up on the tension between mother and son. Thank goodness Hana had befriended a girl named Zlata at school. Zlata was a bit older than Hana, an intelligent girl and a good influence. Even Raziyanım had approved of her. Zlata was keeping a diary chronicling daily life in Sarajevo, and Hana was one of her faithful readers. On some days, Hana would even join in with some of her own experiences. She asked to visit Zlata every day after school. Normally, Nimeta would have insisted that the kids come straight home after school, but she was pleased that Hana had interests outside the home during these difficult days.

Having tried everything else, Nimeta decided one day to put a missing person ad in the paper. She included her name and those of her children. The tiny ad began running in *Oslobodenje* every day.

When she got home a few days later she found an envelope stuck in the front door. Her name was written on the envelope, but there was no stamp. She tore it open before entering the house and, with trembling fingers, unfolded the sheet of paper inside. Written on it was: Burhan is alive. He's fighting up on the mountain behind the Jewish Cemetery. There was no signature and the writing wasn't in her husband's hand.

At work the next day she tried in vain to find someone who could take her up to the Jewish Cemetery. Nobody wanted to travel through the wide open streets, facing Serbian bullets and bombs in the line of fire. They looked at her like she was crazy. Ivan was no different from the others. Ah, Mirsada, everything would be different if you were here, she sighed to herself. Where, oh where, was Mirsada?

If Mirsada were in her shoes, she'd go up the Jewish Cemetery all alone if she had to. Nimeta made up her mind. She'd go tonight. She'd do whatever it took to find Burhan. She couldn't take the accusatory look in her son's eyes and the nagging voice of her own conscience, not now that she knew where Burhan was.

Nimeta waited for nightfall. Once the children were in bed she exchanged her skirt for a pair of jeans. She left a note on the table by the front door and made sure she had her papers allowing her to break the nighttime curfew. The nights were cold in Sarajevo; she pulled on a sweater and slipped into her son's basketball shoes. She was just stepping out the door when she turned back to get a flashlight. As she rummaged through the drawers, she turned up toys, envelopes, letters and pictures. There was a photo of Hana, her first, in her father's arms in the delivery room. She put it in her pocket for some reason. She found the flashlight at last, made sure it was working, and stuffed the contents of the drawers back inside. It had been drizzling since morning. She stuck Fiko's cap on her head, pushed her hair up under it and left the house.

The city was deathly quiet at night. She walked down Ciglane. The streets were deserted. Winding back behind the church, she emerged in front of the parliament building and huddled into the doorway of an apartment building when she spotted a group of men further along. When she could no longer hear their voices, she started scurrying toward Suada Bridge, which had been renamed after the young medical student who was the first victim of the Bosnian war. She'd just begun crossing the bridge when someone shouted, "Halt!" She wasn't sure whether to make a run for it or not. Then she heard a round being loaded. I'm about to become the second victim on this bridge, was the thought that flashed through her mind. She stopped in her tracks.

"Don't move. Turn around and put your hands on your head."

She did as she was told. The sound of approaching footsteps. The night was so quiet that she could hear the wheezing breath of the person coming up behind her. The barrel of a gun poked her in the back. A pair of hands patted her down from her underarms to her heels. When the hands were done with her back, they moved to her front, hesitating a moment on her breasts.

"It's a woman," a man's voice said. The hands kept patting. The flashlight was pulled out of her pocket and examined.

"Turn around!" the voice said. She was now facing two armed men.

"Who are you? What are you looking for out here at night?"

"I'm a broadcast journalist. I need to get to the station immediately." She made to reach into her pocket for her ID card. One of the men pointed his gun at her chest.

"Move again and I'll shoot."

"I was going to show you my ID card."

"Shut up!"

The first man kept a gun pointed at her chest while the other one thrust his hand into her pockets. He found and examined her ID card and curfew permit, using her flashlight.

"OK, put the gun down," he told the first man. "Nimeta Hanım, were you looking to meet your maker out on the streets like this tonight?"

"People die during the daytime too," Nimeta said.

"We'll take you as far as the TV station," the other one said. "The streets are dangerous after dark."

"I think they're safer. At least snipers can't see us," Nimeta said. "Don't worry, I can go alone. I'm used to it."

The TV station was far away from where she actually wanted to go. She'd have to give these guys the slip.

"Do what you want," the first man said, "but I'd use the backstreets and stay away from the riverbank."

Nimeta thanked them, followed a street to a boulevard and waited for a few minutes, Then she turned heel and didn't stop running until she'd crossed the bridge. On the opposite riverbank she crept along, staying close to the buildings. She'd just reached a down-at-heels neighbourhood when it started drizzling. As she was walking up the hill towards some two-storey homes, the rain grew heavier, until it was a torrent. She thanked God for sending everyone on balconies and in courtyards back into the shelter of their homes. Plowing through the mud, she started climbing a steep incline. There wasn't a soul around. She crawled under fences on all fours or clambered over them, from garden to garden, going higher and higher. When her feet slipped in the mud she grabbed hold of bushes and branches, pulling herself onwards and up. The gurgling water and pouring rain kept anyone from hearing her as she trekked through the gardens and backyards. When she finally reached the Jewish Cemetery, her sweater and jeans were torn, her nails broken and her hands black. She looked as though she'd been dipped in mud.

Located exactly halfway between the Serbian and Bosniak military positions, the Jewish Cemetery was a woeful place of huddled ancient tombstones, many of them crazily aslant. Nimeta couldn't help feeling that the tombstones were gazing at the ground, ashamed perhaps that the revealed truths of the holy books of the three Abrahamic faiths had so often been misinterpreted to inspire bloodshed where by Jew, Christian or Muslim. She sank down onto a stone. The rain was letting up, allowing the moonlight to filter through the ragged clouds and illuminate the freshly washed city below. Nimeta could see the Miljacka river, glistening here and there as it snaked through the heart of Sarajevo. She gazed a little further to the right and made out the ruins of the post office, the theater, the Law School… then along the School of Engineering… and now images she saw were of her youth… her youth, a thousand years ago.

She saw herself emerging through the gate of the Law School and walking at a brisk pace along the river bank on

Kulin Ban Avenue before she broke into a run, her long blonde hair trailing behind her. She crossed Cumuriye Bridge and entered the old town. She was on her way to meet Burhan. First, they went fishing a little further along the river. Then, arms holding each other close, they walked to Alifakorac, where they kissed for hours in the open air, along with dozens of other young couples. It was a kind of lover's lane, a place where nobody leered or disturbed anyone else; a place where couples touched lips, and were warm and secure in their love, just like Nimeta and Burhan.

In this city nestled at the foot of the mountains she and her husband had spent a lifetime together. She had never upset him, never hurt him. She'd always loved her husband, the husband she'd finally pushed towards his death.

If Burhan was shot before she had a chance to talk to him she would never forgive herself. She wouldn't be able to bear the condemnation in her son's eyes and the insinuating tone in her mother's voice. The raindrops wetting her cheeks were replaced by the teardrops welling from her eyes.

She turned her back on the city and her face towards the military position pointing its guns at the city, and began shouting, "Burhan! Burhan! It's me, Nimeta. Come out. If you can hear me, come out from wherever you're hiding!" Her voice was growing choked, but she kept shouting.

She was making so much noise that she didn't hear the bullet whizzing above her head, but she felt the muscular arm grabbing her round the waist and the hand clapping her mouth. She resisted at first, but then, too weak to put up much of a fight, allowed herself to be dragged off like a sack of potatoes.

"Are you out of your mind? You were shrieking like a madwoman. You almost got a bullet in your head." It didn't sound like Burhan, but she was still full of hope as she turned to look him in the face. It was too dark to see his face clearly. Could he be the one who sent the letter?

"What are you doing here at this time of night? How'd you get here? Who sent you?"

"Nobody sent me. I came here to find my husband. Burhan Kulinovic. They said he was fighting here."

She pulled out the photo of Burhan holding Hana. He took it and studied it with her flashlight.

"Commander Burhan went to Stup this morning. He's not here anymore. You risked death for nothing," the man said. "Now how do you expect to get back down?"

"I'm begging you, help me find a way to get to my husband. Please!"

"Everyone's got a husband or a son or a brother fighting somewhere, but nobody else has come up here and started screaming in the middle of the night," he said.

"This is a special situation. I absolutely must see my husband. I need to see him, even if it's only for ten minutes."

"Why's it so urgent?"

"That's private. There's something I have to tell him."

"Are you pregnant?"

Nimeta couldn't believe her ears. "What?" she said.

"What else could make you do something like this."

"Just get me to him, for five minutes."

They heard a rustling sound somewhere behind them. The man pulled Nimeta behind a tombstone and crouched over her.

"This is supposed to be a neutral zone, but you never know with the Serbs," he said. They waited a moment, and then they sat down across from each other, backs resting against tombstones.

"If I could see him... for just a second."

"You've gone from ten minutes to five to a second," he laughed. Nimeta rested her head on her knees and began weeping softly. She made a pitiful sight, this middle-aged woman, soaked to the skin, covered in mud, and apparently on the verge of a nervous breakdown in a cemetery in the middle of the night.

"What's your name?"

"Nimeta."

"Look, Nimeta, I'm sure you've got a good reason to want to see your husband or you wouldn't have put yourself through all this. We're going to be making some deliveries to the area where your husband's stationed. I don't know the exact day, but it should happen sometime next week. How can I find you?"

"I'm always at the TV station. I work there," Nimeta said.

"Ah, I thought I recognized you," the man said. "I'll get word to you a day early. You can go and see your husband. If you hit a mine or get bombed on the way, don't blame me."

Nimeta seized the man's hands. "Thank you, thank you so much. I didn't catch your name." He hesitated for a moment and said: "Esat."

"Esat, I'll never forget your kindness."

"Wait here and I'll get someone to escort you down the mountain. You'd better clear before dawn. And don't ever do anything like this again. You're lucky to be alive, the odds were against you."

"I can go back down on own, just like I climbed up on my own."

"No, you can't. The rain's stopped. They'll shoot at the slightest sound. Wait here," Esat said. Nimeta crouched even lower as she looked up at the Esat. He was young, and good-looking if rail-thin. They all were these days; man or woman, all the Bosniaks living in Bosnia had shed ten or fifteen kilos since the war started. Nimeta couldn't tell what color his hair or his eyes were. He was wearing dark clothing. She wondered if Burhan was wearing something similar, or if he was fighting in the trousers and shirt he had on when he left home.

"Don't go anywhere and don't move," Esat cautioned her as he walked off.

Fiko stared in shock at his mother when she arrived that morning.

"Where were you?" he asked in an icy voice. "The TV station?"

"Didn't you read my note?"

"It said you'd gone to work."

"Why are you up so early? It's not even six o'clock."

"Mother, where were you?" he demanded, raising his voice this time.

"I was out looking for your father," Nimeta said. She took off her mud-caked sweater and shoes. Fiko forgot how upset he was with her. "What did you just say, Mother?" he yelled.

"Your father's joined the volunteer forces. He's gone up to the mountains to fight. He's alive. He's not dead. He's not dead, Fiko."

Fiko found himself in his mother's arms. Tears were streaming from his eyes too. He felt incredibly guilty about the way he'd been treating his mother. He'd been upset with her for some time, for reasons he didn't fully understand. Then when his father disappeared he'd sensed that she was responsible in some way, and he'd blamed her. Even so, he'd missed her terribly when they weren't speaking. He missed her hugs, missed resting his head in her lap as he stretched out his legs on the sofa, missed being spoiled.

"How'd you find out, Mother? Who told you?"

"I got a response to my missing person ad. Not from him, but from someone who knows him."

"Did you get to see him tonight?"

"No, but I found someone who's going to arrange it."

"So you haven't found him or seen him?"

"No, not yet. But I know where he is, Fiko. I'll be able to go and see him."

"When?"

"Within a week."

"He might be somewhere top secret. That's why he didn't tell us himself where he was going."

"I don't care where he is. I have to see him," Nimeta said.

"I'm coming with you."

Nimeta was about to say no... but then she considered the advantages of having Fiko at her side. Burhan might refuse to see her if she went on her own, but he'd be careful not to upset Fiko. She could always arrange for a word or two alone with her husband, even if their son came along.

"Alright, Fiko. We'll visit your father together," she said. "I'll soon find out where we're going, and how. Don't tell anyone about this. Even Hana."

They rattled along in a jeep sending up clouds of dust. Two soldiers in yellow and green uniforms the color of a spinach omelet sat up in front while Nimeta and Fiko sat in back with among boxes of provisions. It was hot outside; it was even hotter inside the jeep. From time to time, Nimeta fanned Fiko with her straw hat.

"Stop it, mother," he said. He was tired of his mother hovering over him all the time and treating him like a child, especially in front of these soldiers. Neither of the soldiers ever said anything. The occasional breeze would carry the acrid stench of their stale sweat to Nimeta's nose. They obviously hadn't been near any water for days or weeks. Their cracked skin had been blackened by the sun, as well.

"How much further is it?" Nimeta asked. Fiko squirmed in his seat in embarrassment, but he didn't say anything. Who knows how many times his father had traveled up and down this same dirt road. Women were so impatient. They loved complaining. His grandmother, his mother, Hana; they were all the same.

"We've got another half hour or so to go," one of the soldiers said.

"We've already climbed up quite a way."

"The higher we go the safer it is."

A few minutes later Fiko suddenly asked, "Do you know my father, Burhan Kulinovic?"

"The tall engineer?" a soldier asked.

"Yes, that's him."

"The engineer commander. I know him. He designs underground tunnels, secret shelters and bridges."

"Does he ever fight?" Fiko asked.

"Of course he does. We all do. But everyone's got other duties as well."

"Like what?"

"There are doctors, engineers, tailors, drivers, cooks, laborers… Everyone does what they do best, and fights as well."

"How many of you are there?" Nimeta asked.

"That's confidential, sister," one of the soldiers said.

"Do you need more soldiers?" Fiko asked.

"Why? You plan on joining us?" the soldier driving the jeep asked.

"He's still a boy. He'll join later when he's grown up," Nimeta said. Fiko bridled with resentment.

"There are a lot of guys his age up in the mountains," the soldier said.

"Fiko's tall for his age. He's only–"

Fiko couldn't stand it anymore. He cut his mother off with, "The women in our house all think their boys never grow up. My grandmother's the same."

"Mothers are all like that," the driver said.

They all fell silent. The closer they got to their destination the more scared Nimeta felt. What would Burhan do when he saw her? As they rounded a bend, she saw a makeshift shelter in the distance. A rope of smoke curled up from the chimney.

The moment the jeep stopped Fiko leapt out and began running toward the shelter.

"Wait for us!" one of the soldiers shouted. "They don't know you. Don't get us in trouble."

Nimeta watched as Fiko waited for one of the soldiers to catch up, then walked off toward the shelter with him. She was staying put. Fiko would surely mention that she was outside. It was better she waited for Burhan to come to her. She got out of the jeep and sat down in the shade of a tree, her back resting against the trunk.

"Aren't you coming?" asked the driver. He was unloading something from the jeep.

"I'll let Fiko catch up with his father first. They can have a man-to-man chat. Then I'll go in," she said. Now, after all those days of desperately trying to see Burhan, of wanting to touch him and hold him, of doing everything in her power to find him, including risking her own life, she felt a strong urge to run off before his eyes met hers. Her desire to see him had been waning ever since she'd learned he was alive and healthy.

It was all she could do to keep herself from bolting headlong down the mountainside.

Time had slowed to a crawl. Nimeta slumped back against the tree trunk; then she stretched out on the ground. She put her hands under her head and looked up through the green foliage at the blue sky. It was such a peaceful powder blue, as though a sky that belonged not to a country torn by war but to a happy country where everyone was on holiday all the time had decided to take Bosnia under its protection. Would Bosnia ever know peace and family holidays again?

She was so engrossed in her musings on the sky that she lost track of how long she'd been lying on her back. She got up and brushed bits of grass and dirt off her clothes. Her limbs and back were stiff. She started walking toward the shelter. It was time to put an end to this torture. Whatever happens, happens. Several armed young men stood guard at the entrance of the shelter. One of them was the soldier who'd driven the jeep.

He pointed to the back of the shelter. She walked over to it.

Burhan and Fiko were sitting at a wooden table in the shade. Nimeta couldn't hear what they were saying, but she could tell that they were deep in conversation.

Burhan had his back to her. When she got a little closer, Fiko spotted her, pointed and shouted: "Mom's coming!"

Burhan got up and turned around. Nimeta's heart sank; his arms were stick-thin, his face gaunt, his cheeks sunken. He'd grown a beard and was wearing one of those omelet-colored shirts over a pair of his own trousers, which he kept up with a thick piece of twine knotted around his waist. He looked so different she might not have noticed him on the street. But those dark blue eyes she knew so well were exactly the same. She raced into his arms. He didn't recoil, and he kissed her on the cheeks.

"How are you doing, Nimeta," he asked in a flat voice.

"Burhan! We looked everywhere for you. You didn't even tell us you were leaving. The children were worried sick. Why didn't you call us?"

"You've got every right to be upset with me. I realized I'd made a mistake when I was talking to Fiko. I should have called and let you know where I was."

"Burhan, I need to talk to you. Can we take a little walk?"

"Nimeta, it's better we don't talk."

"No, Burhan. There are some things you need to know. I want you to understand me."

Fiko got up and walked over toward the soldiers guarding the shelter. Nimeta inwardly thanked him for realizing that he needed to be alone with Burhan.

"Look, we're on our own. Now listen to me."

"You listen to me first," Burhan said. He didn't sound at all angry or hurt. In fact, he sounded as calm and collected as he always. "Nimeta, my priorities have changed since I arrived here. I've come to realize just how unimportant some things are."

"Let me explain," Nimeta interrupted.

"You might have the chance to explain one day. If this war ever ends and we're still alive, we'll talk things over. Right now, only one thing matters to me: the liberation of Bosnia. I've completely devoted myself to the cause, Nimeta. I'm not the man I was. Something's happened to me up here in this pine forest. The things that used to bring me joy or make me angry just don't matter anymore. It all seems so trivial. I'm sorry I hit you. I wish I hadn't. But if that hadn't happened, I wouldn't have had a reason to come here and I would have spent the rest of my life designing stone buildings. I'd never had known the rage, the hatred, the passion that's driving me to be a Bosniak and stay a Bosniak at whatever cost."

"Aren't you going to come home, Burhan?"

"My home is here, and it will be for a long time to come. They need me here. I'm helping the people fighting for us all. I'm helping to build bridges, shelters and tunnels. When it's necessary, I'm fighting too, fighting for my country."

"One day, when this is all over–"

"When that day comes, we'll talk again."

"I've always loved you and I never dreamed of leaving you–"

"None of that matters now, Nimeta," Burhan said. "It's all in the past. You lived on your own from time to time. I never realized how lonely you got when I was out working in the field. But you managed on your own. You're stronger; stronger than me, maybe. You've got a career, friends, business trips." He paused for a moment so he wouldn't add, you even found yourself a lover. "You were always a great mother. I know you can get along without me."

"I want you to come home."

"If we're both alive when the war ends we'll talk about it."

Nimeta's tears trickled round the corner of her mouth, down her throat and onto her blouse.

"Don't you ever come down from the mountain?" she asked.

"We put ourselves and our friends at risk every time we leave. None of us are allowed to go anywhere without a good reason. There's a team that goes out to get weapons and supplies, but the rest of us always stay here. I'm amazed they let you come."

"I found a young fighter by the name of Esat in the Jewish Cemetery. He felt sorry for me and arranged for me to come here," she said.

"What were you doing up there? Are you crazy?" Burhan reached over and put his hand on his wife's.

"I had to find you. I must have seemed pitiable. Burhan, I think you're the only person who doesn't take pity on me."

"There's never been anything pitiable about you. I always knew how strong you were. I tried to give you plenty of space because you were always complaining about how domineering your mother was when you were growing up. Perhaps I overdid it and left you on your own too often. Anyway, that's all in the past. Our lives have taken a completely different course."

Nimeta decided to change the subject. "Some things are getting better," she said. "They put a lot of pressure on Milosevic at the London Conference. You must have heard about the promises Milan Panic made. I'm glad he's been appointed prime minister of Yugoslovia. He's been living in the West for a long time and seems to know what human rights are."

"He's a puppet," Burhan said. "Milosevic is still the one holding the strings."

"Haven't you heard about the way Panic publicly humiliated Milosevic, and told him to shut up?"

"I've heard," Burhan said, "and I wouldn't be surprised if Panic got fired or killed. Let's see how many of his promises he keeps. Will the Serbs turn over their weapons? Will their troops withdraw from the territories they've occupied? Will they make reparations for all their looting and killing?"

Nimeta couldn't believe it. Her husband had never the slightest interest in politics. Now his eyes were flashing as he spoke.

"They haven't got any choice, Burhan," she said, her voice weary. "The London Conference decided to impose heavy sanctions for non-compliance. Belgrade would starve."

"Nothing will ever happen to those demons," Burhan snorted.

"Well, what about you? How long do you think you can stand life up here in the mountains? Won't you miss your home?"

"I'm fine here. I'm better than I've ever been. Take good care of yourself and the kids. Thank you for going through so much trouble to find me," Burhan said. He got up. Fiko, who'd been watching them, immediately came over, but he didn't sit down. Nimeta was the only person seated.

"You'd better get going," Burhan said. He squeezed his son's shoulder.

Nimeta couldn't bring herself to stand up.

"Don't ever come here again," Burhan told her. "You took a terrible risk. You could have come under enemy fire on the way."

"Come on, Mom," Fiko said. "Get up and let's go."

Clutching the edge of table, Nimeta pulled herself to her feet. None of her fears had materialized. Burhan hadn't ignored her or treated her harshly. Even so, she felt completely drained. She realized for the first time that her husband no longer belonged to her, but to something intangible that had no place for her. Burhan appeared to be his usual mild self, but something was raging behind the placid exterior and Nimeta blamed herself for her husband's dangerous transformation. She went over and embraced him.

As he kissed her on the cheeks tears welled in her eyes. She threw her arms around his neck and stayed like that for a moment. Then her arms helplessly fell to her side. He seemed to give her son a more enthusiastic send-off, repeatedly kissing his cheeks, his forehead and the top of his head. The three of them walked over to the front of the shelter together. The soldiers who had brought them were waiting in the jeep. Burhan helped his wife into the vehicle.

"Godspeed," he said.

"Dad, take care and don't get hurt," Fiko called out.

"Look after your mother and Hana," Burhan said.

The jeep jumped and jolted to a start. Fiko leaned out and waved to his father. They were able to see his receding until they rounded the bend, and he was gone. Nimeta knew she'd lost her husband and knew that she was partly responsible. But she also knew that he'd done his part to build a wall between them.

A few days later, in honor of their meeting with Burhan and his good health, they went to Raziyanım's for a celebratory dinner. Even in that time of wartime privation Raziyanım had managed to produce dish after dish. Hana was as fidgety as ever, darting around the room and picking out a tune on her grandmother's piano. Fiko was beaming, still thrilled that they'd found his father. But Nimeta's listlessness didn't escape her mother's notice. Raziyanım kept pressing Fiko for more details about their meeting.

"When did your father say he was coming home?"

"When the war's over. They're all going to fight until the war's over or they're dead. That's what the soldiers who took us there told me," Fiko said. Raziyanım glanced over at Raif to make sure he wasn't listening. He was staring at the wall, oblivious to their conversation. She still thought it best to change the conversation. She tried not to use words like "war," "gun" and "blood" when he was in the same room.

"Burhan loved this type of *börek*. That's why I made it today," she told her grandson. "Be sure to have an extra serving since he's not here to eat it himself."

Fiko looked at his plate piled high with the savory pastry. "I wish he was here to eat it. He's so skinny," he said.

"This *börek* doesn't have any cheese," Hana said. "Whatever's inside it doesn't have any taste."

"How do you expect grandma to find cheese these days?" Fiko asked his sister.

"What do you mean it hasn't got any cheese? I made some cheese myself right here at home," Raziyanım said. She'd cooked up a pot of mushy rice and added salt and yeast to it. It was one of the many culinary tricks the women of Bosnia had mastered. Grown-ups had learned to accept these bland substitutions, but children were brutally honest.

"It doesn't taste at all like the cheese we used to eat," Hana said.

"I still don't understand why you didn't bring Burhan home with you," Raziyanım said, hoping to change the subject again, this time to avert a quarrel between her grandchildren. "You went all the way up there for nothing. If I'd come along I'd have persuaded him to come home."

"Mother, Burhan isn't a child. He wants to stay there and fight. He's got a mission and a duty."

"He also has a family. How can he walk out on his wife and kids in the middle of a war?" Raziyanım asked.

"We're fine," Fiko said.

Raif hadn't touched his food. As the man of the house he sat at the head of the table, in his own little world, as always.

"We know you won't talk, but you could at least eat," his mother said. Nimeta could not help giggling.

"It's not funny. Not eating is his latest thing. It's one thing not to talk, but if you don't eat, you die," Raziyanım said.

Maybe that's what he wants, Nimeta thought to herself. So many people seemed eager to die these days. She kept her thought to herself.

When Raziyanım was absolutely certain Raif wasn't following the conversation, she repeated the question that had been nagging at her: "Fiko, did your father tell you why he went up to the mountains?"

"I told you what he said, grandma."

"Tell me again."

"Mother, what kind of a question is that? Why do people fight for their homeland? Isn't that what you're really asking?" Nimeta said. She'd had it with her mother's cross-examination of Fiko.

"I just asked a simple question," Raziyanım said. "Why are you interrupting us?"

"Dad said he was doing his duty," Fiko said. "He thinks everyone able to carry a gun should be fighting for Bosnia."

Raif took his eyes off the wall and looked at Fiko for the first time that night.

"Is that all he said? Duty?" Raziyanım persisted.

Hana jumped in with, "Mother, Zlata asked whether or not I'm going to have a birthday party. I told her I would."

"That's all we need right now," Raziyanım said.

"Didn't anyone ever tell you not to speak with your mouth full," Fiko said to his sister.

Deliberately flashing a mouthful of mashed potatoes, Hana said, "Her mother had a party for her on her birthday."

"We'll have one for you too, dear," Nimeta said. She was happy to be talking about something other than her husband's sudden disappearance.

"Who would throw a party in wartime?" Raziyanım said.

"We should do whatever we can to make sure our children have normal lives. And anyway, it would be the perfect opportunity for you to show off your cooking. You might make a cake out of potatoes or some such thing," Nimeta said.

"You've always been envious of my cooking, Nimeta," Raziyanım said. "If you'd spent more time in the kitchen and less time tapping away at a typewriter your husband would still be at home with you today." She snatched away the untouched plate in front of Raif and flounced off to the kitchen.

Nimeta leaned over and remarked to her brother, "This has been quite a celebration, Raif. Like I always say, somehow the handle of the spoon always ends up poking me in the eyes." She gathered up the other plates and headed for the kitchen. Not wanting to be alone with her mother, she called out to the kids, "Bring in some of those things."

"I'm going to do a puzzle," Hana said. Fiko didn't even bother to respond.

Nimeta decided to confront her mother in the kitchen. "Listen to me, Mother," she began, "Burhan's decision has nothing to do with me. Stop blaming everything on me. I've really had it with you."

"I'm not happy about the way you've suddenly found yourself all alone in the middle of war with no man around the house and two kids to look after."

"We don't always get we want out of life," Nimeta said. "Besides, aren't you all alone as well?"

Raziyanım opened her mouth to speak before thinking better of it.

"Don't tell me you've got Raif," Nimeta said.

When Nimeta and her mother went back to the dining room together they were in for a shock. Raif and Fiko were huddled in a corner whispering about something. Raziyanım clutched her daughter's arm, afraid for a moment that she was seeing things. Nimeta reached out and clapped a hand over her mother's mouth. With the other hand, she tugged her mother back into the hall. The two women tiptoed backwards into the kitchen. Nimeta closed the door.

"Mother, don't do anything to agitate Raif and don't let on how excited you are." Raziyanım was trembling.

"Did I see right? Was he really talking? You saw it too, didn't you Nimeta?" she asked.

"I saw it too, Mother. He was definitely talking," Nimeta assured her.

"Come on, let's go back in."

"No, Mother. Let's not frighten him. Just wait a little longer here with me."

"There's a miracle going on out there and you won't let me see it."

"Please. Just wait here for fifteen or twenty minutes. It's not like I'm asking you to stay in the kitchen all night."

"He spoke! My son spoke!" Raziyanım sobbed.

"Mother, don't get so excited. When we go back out there you've got to act like nothing out of the ordinary has happened. OK?"

"What?"

"Remember: act like nothing's happened," Nimeta said. She was surprised by how firm she sounded, almost as though she were ordering her mother around. Perhaps Burhan was right, and she really was stronger than she'd ever imagined.

A short time later, mother and daughter tiptoed back to the dining room. Fiko and Raif were still sitting at the table, but this time Fiko was telling his uncle something. When they walked into the room, Fiko looked up and, as if it were the natural thing in the world, announced: "Uncle Raif wants to go up into the mountains and fight with Dad."

Nimeta spoke before her mother could. "In that case, I'd better find Esat," she said. "He's the one who arranged everything before. Fiko, remind me to put a another ad in the paper tomorrow so he calls me."

"I'll remind you," Raif said. His voice sounded perfectly normal for someone who hadn't uttered a word for all those months. If anything, Nimeta's voice sounded slightly choked when she replied, "OK." Then she turned her attention to her mother.

"Why don't you go peep into your room to make sure Hana's not getting up to any mischief there?" Raziyanım didn't move a muscle. "Come on, mother. We can continue our chat in the other room while we keep an eye on Hana."

Nimeta ended up propelling her mother down the hall by the elbow. She sat Raziyanım on the bed and rubbed some cologne onto her temples and wrists.

"You always talk about blessings in disguise," Nimeta said. "Burhan's being up in the mountains has given Raif a reason to live. Nothing concentrates a man's mind like a thirst for revenge."

On the way home, Nimeta tried to learn every last detail of how Raif started talking again, but Fiko would only say, "He asked how we got up to the mountains."

Nimeta probed him for more information.

"Who talked first, Fiko?"

"He did."

"Well what did he say? Did he just ask you out of the blue?"

"I've told you a hundred times. You were in the kitchen and I was clearing the table. Then all of a sudden he asked how we'd found dad and how we'd got up to the mountains."

"Well what did you say?"

"I told him you'd organized everything. He also asked about the camp. He must have been listening the whole time."

"Do you think he really wants to go up there?"

"Of course he does. And so do I."

Nimeta recoiled. "You're too young. Wait a few years."

"There are a lot of guys my age fighting."

"Is that what your father told you?"

"No. A soldier told me up in the camp."

"You can't go, Fiko. You've got school. You're too young. Your father and I would never allow it."

He didn't say a word, but as soon as they got home Fiko slipped into his room, silent as a shadow.

The following day, Nimeta set about organizing things for her brother. She placed an ad addressed to Esat. They'd had a long chat when he'd called her at work to tell her how to get to Burhan's camp. He knew that she had two children and a brother who hadn't spoken since his wife and son were killed in the Zvornik massacre. Even so, Esat refused to give her his address. She'd wanted to thank him with a gift of coffee, cigarettes or some other luxury, but he'd turned down her offer. When she pressed him, he said that if there was ever an emergency she should put an ad in the paper and he'd call.

Nimeta placed the ad and waited. She'd been visiting her brother every day after work. Raif had seemed fine ever since he decided to fight, but she worried that a long wait would push him into depression again.

When several days passed and there was still no call from Esat, she even considered taking her brother up the mountains herself. Then she thought about the sniper fire and mines. It wasn't death she feared, it was leaving Hana and Fiko orphaned.

Esat finally contacted Nimeta one thursday just as she was giving up hope. A note promising to take Raif up to the mountain a week later, when a food and medicine delivery was scheduled, arrived at the TV station. She was to be informed at the very last minute of the exact time and place they'd meet.

Nimeta dropped everything and raced to her mother's house.

"Where's Raif?" she asked, the moment Raziyanım opened the door.

"Where would he be? In his room staring at the wall."

She burst into his bedroom. He was sitting on the bed and, yes, he was staring at the wall.

"It's finally happened, Raif. Esat sent word. You'll be leaving next week."

"You came into my room without knocking," Raif said. They'd been squabbling over this since childhood. Nimeta was always complaining about her mother walking in on her; Raif would complain about his big sister for the same reason. Nimeta started laughing.

"I'm sorry. At least you weren't up to anything top secret when I came in. You weren't even picking your nose."

"I was thinking private thoughts," Raif said.

"Aren't you excited about the news I brought you?"

"I'm not excited about anything, anymore. We're all like zombies these days: the living dead."

"I thought the idea of fighting in the mountains had brought you back to life."

"Nothing's changed. Before, I was dead and didn't talk; now I'm dead, but I talk. I hope that I'll be dead at the hands of the Serbs when I go up to the mountains next week."

Nimeta sat down on the bed and put her arm around her brother.

"It'll pass. It'll all pass, Raif," she said. "One day, we'll have grown into old people who've known real pain. We'll have happy memories too, of course. Don't give up on life. It's always worth living."

Raziyanım had managed to cram a life's worth of underwear and socks into her son's duffel bag.

"Mother, where did you find all this underwear?" Nimeta asked.

"Some of it belonged to your father," Raziyanım said, "back when we got married."

"Mother, do you expect Raif to run around in forty-year-old underpants?"

"If he doesn't want them he give them to someone else. Waste not want not," Raziyanım said.

The Bosniaks had always been a thrifty people, storing away everything in wooden chests and never throwing anything out. It was the tribal mentality of a people accustomed to displacement and forced migration, to the ever present fear of finding themselves destitute and dependent on others. Since Ottoman times, their homeland had seen a succession of wars and occupations: The Austro-Hungarian Empire, the Kingdom of Serbia, the Balkan Wars, World War I and World War II. The Bosniaks had good reason to keep everything they owned in wooden chests.

"What's in there, Mother," Raif asked, pointing to a second bag.

"Don't open that until you get there."

"What's in it?" Raziyanım seemed not to hear. "Is there food in there?"

"I made you some zucchini *börek*, son."

"Do you think I'm going off to a picnic?" Raif reached inside and tried to unknot a plastic bag.

"Stop it, Raif," Nimeta said. "Once you're up in the mountains you'll appreciate whatever's in there."

"Do you want to turn me into a laughingstock, Nimeta? She's done everything but pack me lunch."

"Nobody will be laughing at you," Nimeta said. "They'll be thrilled you've joined them and, believe me, they'll be even more thrilled when you share your *börek* with them. They're even worse off than we are, Raif. I can only imagine how much Burhan has missed Mother's cooking."

Raziyanım shot Nimeta a look of appreciation. The shops were empty, but everyone with a patch of soil was growing tomatoes, zucchini and potatoes, and selling whatever extra they had. A friend with a backyard vegetable patch had been providing Raziyanım with her pick of produce at a reasonable price before they were sent off to market. This was only the latest example of her mother's resourcefulness that had amazed Nimeta. Twice a week, Raziyanım would push a handcart all the way to the brewery in Ciglane to get fresh water from the spring there. The mains, electrical grid and gas networks were being bombed on a regular basis, and they would sometimes go up to two weeks without a single drop of water from their taps. Electricity and gas they could do without, but life was impossible without water.

"Mother, don't get yourself killed chasing after water," Nimeta had said.

"It would be quicker and more painless than dying from not having water," her mother had retorted. And she was right.

"Raif, don't forget my letter," Nimeta said. "Make sure Burhan gets it. I'm counting on you."

"Look, I've already tucked it away in my pocket," Raif said, showing her the inner pocket of his jacket.

"They'll pick you up at five in the morning. Have you set your alarm clock?" Nimeta asked.

"I'll be up all night in any case," Raziyanım said. She had mixed feelings about Raif's decision. No mother is happy about sending her son off to war, but she had to accept that it was war that had brought him back to life.

"Mother, don't try to stop him," Nimeta had told her. "Just for once, put your own feelings aside and support him when he goes up to the mountains. I know how much you want to keep your children tied to your apron strings, but, just this once, let him go."

She's never forgiven me, Raziyanım thought to herself. She's still blaming me for something that happened twenty years ago, and she'll keep blaming me for not sending her to Istanbul until the day she dies. Actually, she deeply regretted not having allowed her daughter to marry that Turkish boy. If Nimeta had settled in Istanbul she and the rest of the family could have gone and lived with her when the war started. Her daughter-in-law, grandson and sister-in-law might have been alive today. Raif wouldn't have been forced to choose between a life staring at walls and probable death up in the mountains.

Nimeta threw her arms around her brother.

"Be careful, Raif," she said. "Don't take any foolish risks. Stay healthy, and come home with Burhan one day. We've still got some good days ahead of us. Believe me, we'll forget about all we've suffered."

"God tests us in this world," Raziyanım told her son. "None of his servants can escape the trials of this world. Nimeta's right. Stay safe and don't cause me any grief."

Here we go again, Nimeta thought to herself, emotional blackmail from mother.

"Come here my little nephew," Raif said to Fiko. "You and I are going have a private man-to-man talk before I leave."

"Keep it short," Nimeta said. "I've left Hana with Azra."

Raif went off to his room with Fiko, leaving the women in the living room.

"You see that," Nimeta remarked to her mother, "Raif's being a good uncle to Fiko again. It's a good sign. Once he comes face-to-face with death up in the mountains he'll forget about his pain and the past. He'll realize that life is all that matters."

"Is that what you think, that life's all that matters?" Raziyanım asked.

"Don't you?"

"When you reach my age you'll think again about what is and isn't important," Raziyanım said.

Fiko appeared at the end of the hall with his Uncle. Nimeta hugged her brother one last time. She gritted her teeth to keep from sobbing. At the front door, Raif kissed Fiko and his sister again.

Hand on the doorknob, Nimeta said, "I'll pick you up after work tomorrow, Mother. You can stay with us for as long as you want."

"Come stay with me here," Raziyanım said.

"But Mother, there's not enough room for the four of us. And it's too far from the kids' school."

"Can't you talk about this tomorrow," Fiko said. He seemed impatient to get home.

"May God's blessings be with you, dear," Nimeta said on the way out the door, the tears she'd suppressed running her down her cheeks as soon as Raif couldn't see her anymore. Raziyanım stood at the window and watched as Nimeta and Fiko raced across the green lawn of the park next door. In a few hours, she'd watch from the same window as her only son went off to war in the chill of early dawn, perhaps never to return.

Hana was waiting on the neighbour's balcony when Nimeta and Fiko got home.

"I tried to put her bed but she wouldn't listen," Azra said. "She's been scribbling in a notebook all night."

"She's followed Zlata's lead," Nimeta said. "You know the girl I told you about, the one who's keeping a journal. Hana's taken to writing every night as well."

"Has Raif gone?" Azra asked.

"He's leaving early in the morning," Nimeta said. "May God watch over him and shield Mother from the kind of pain he's suffered."

They all said good night to Azra and went home.

A few minutes later Nimeta tapped on Fiko's door. He'd gone straight to his room. "Have you gone to bed, son?" she asked.

"I'm just about to."

She pushed open the door a crack, just enough to see that her son was putting something under his pillow. She pretended not have seen. He looked mortified.

"I know how upsetting it must have been to say goodbye to your uncle," Nimeta said. "And I know how much you'll miss him. But he's doing the right thing. Your father will keep an eye on him. This meaningless war will come to an end one day, and they'll come home together."

Fiko got out of bed and hugged his mother tight.

"Good night, son," she said, closing the door behind her. When she got to her own room she found Hana in her bed, the sheet pulled up to her chin.

"What are you doing in my bed?" she asked.

"Can I sleep with you tonight?"

"Ok," Nimeta said, "but I'm not letting Bozo into my room! "She crawled into bed, gave Hana a hug and fell into a deep, but troubled, sleep.

When she woke up it was nearly nine o'clock and Hana was still sound asleep. She must have forgotten to set the alarm; it hadn't rung. She jumped out of bed, ran to the kitchen and sawed a few slices from a loaf of stale bed. Then she took the tea kettle and the bread down to the entrance to the apartment building, where her neighbours had long since finished their morning cooking. The wood-burning stove they'd set up there was one of many dotting the streets of the city. The trees that once provided shade were now used as fuel. She went back home without waiting for the kettle to come to a boil. She'd gone through hall to get some milk for Hana, but the fridge wasn't working and it had curdled. She made a face at the smell, and dumped it down the drain. She splashed some water onto her face from a bottle lugged home by her mother from the brewery and walked down the hall to wake Fiko.

"The alarm didn't go off this morning," she shouted through the door. "You got an extra half hour of sleep." He probably needed it as much as she had, she thought to herself. First his father, now his uncle... he was losing the men in his family, one by one, just at the age when he needed them most. Would she be able to act as both mother and father to him?

She went into the kitchen and set the table. They had some olives and some gooey butter to go with their bread. She shook her head at the sight of the pitiful breakfast spread out on the table. Is this what they'd slaved away for all these years, she and Burhan doing everything they could to make sure their kids enjoyed a better life than they had. Nutritious meals, good schools, new clothing... she tried to swallow the lump in the throat.

There was still no sign of her son. "Fiko! Don't make me come and get you! You know what I'll do," she shouted down the hall.

There was nothing like tickling to get her son out of bed. He was so ticklish, and would laugh so hard when he was little, that Raziyanım would come to the rescue, afraid he'd choke to death. That's what it had been like living with her mother: she couldn't even tickle her own son.

She grabbed a pinch of mint, put some tea in a small cup and ran down to the stove. She'd brew the brownish liquid that passed for tea these days right in the kettle, a hot concoction that tasted and smelled of absolutely nothing. It was the lack of coffee that got to her, but how were regular tea drinkers managing, she wondered.

Moving the tea kettle aside, she arranged the slices of bread on top of the stove.

She started thinking about Burhan. What did he have for breakfast? How many people would get shot to death today? She read the daily lists at work first thing every day and counted herself lucky on the days she didn't find the names of her husband and friends. Now her heart would be beating twice as fast as she scanned the lists for Raif's name as well.

She carried the kettle and the bread up to the kitchen. Bozo kept rubbing against her leg. She opened the balcony door so he could get to his litter box.

"Fiko!" she shouted. "If you're not out of bed by the time I'm through with the bathroom I'm coming in to get you. Don't say you weren't warned." She went into the bathroom and locked the door. Out of habit, she turned the faucet in the shower, which produced a mocking "tisss". She poured a cold, thin stream of water over her body, watching the droplets roll across her skin. Had Raif got there safely? It was normally about a two-hour drive but could take up to four hours. That's what Esat had told her. When she's gone up with Fiko it had taken them three hours because they kept stopping to check for mines.

She'd expected to find Fiko eating his breakfast when she stepped into the kitchen in her bathrobe. The little rat was still in bed! She marched down the hall and knocked on his door as she threw it open. Fiko wasn't there. She went back to the kitchen, then she quickly checked the living room, the dining room and Hana's bedroom. When she went to her own bedroom Hana was still sound asleep. She checked the kitchen again, then the bedroom, tearing the pocket of her robe when it got caught on the doorknob. She turned on the light without pulling open the curtains. There was an envelope on the nightstand. Heart sinking, weak at the knees, she sank onto the bed and tore open the envelope addressed to "Mom". On a sheet of lined paper torn from her son's notebook she read the words:

> Dear Mom,
>
> I wanted to tell you earlier but I was afraid you'd try to stop me. I'm going up to the mountains with Uncle Raif

and dad to fight for Bosnia because a lot of guys as young as me are fighting and I should be up there too. I've wanted to do this ever since we visited that day. I can't think about anything else. I know you'll understand and that you'll forgive me. Kiss Hana and my grandmother for me. Don't let this upset you and try not to worry about me. I'll be with dad and my uncle. See you one day soon in free Bosnia.

All my love,
Fiko

ETHNIC CLEANSING

Summer, 1992

When Stefan Stefanoviç first told the management of his newspaper that he wanted to do an investigative piece on the Bosniaks forced to flee to Croatia, and that he hoped his research would influence international opinion, the reaction was lukewarm at best. Thousands of ethnic Croatians fleeing Serbian atrocities had been inundating Croatia for the past year. Nobody would want to read about Bosniak refugees, they told Stefan. Then, starting in april, tens of thousands of Bosniaks forced out of their homes at gunpoint, many of them tortured as well, began massing in camps on the Croatian border. Europe could no longer ignore this humanitarian crisis and the plight of refugees would have to be addressed on an international platform.

Stefan pitched his project to management again.

"Unfortunately, print media doesn't influence people the way television does," he said. "So if we want to draw attention to the thousands of people massed on our border, and the torture they've suffered, we need a piece that is absolutely riveting. Otherwise nobody will care about the ethnic cleansing perpetrated against the Muslims by Karadzic."

"Frankly, I don't care all that much myself," Boris said, "but if you're determined to write this thing up, knock yourself out."

"Boris, do you have any idea how many people have been killed or displaced since april, when Karadzic declared the Serbian Republic of Bosnia?" Stefan asked.

"About 300,000."

"That was the figure back in april. Now, at the end of june, it's risen to 1.1 million."

"Holy shit!" exclaimed Boris.

"Have I managed to prick your conscience a little, Boris?"

"Look Stefan, I'm never going to get worked up over Bosniaks the way you do. And speaking of pricks, I believe yours is what led you to feel such sympathy for the Bosniaks in the first place."

"That's got nothing to do with it!"

"I approved your piece. What more do you want? Now get to work, and leave me and my conscience alone."

Stefan was out of the office like a shot. Boris was right, he'd need to get down to work immediately. He'd need a Serbian ID card so he could easily cross into Karadzic's Serbian enclave and he'd need a list of camps so he could arrange interviews.

When he was quoted a price for a fake ID the following day, he said, "Fine, I'll give them whatever they want. Just get me the ID right away."

As Stefan waited for his ID, Croatia kept its borders closed to a new wave of refugees, the tens of thousands of Bosniaks trapped in the mountains of northern Bosnia began falling victim to Serbian torture, rape and execution, and the people of Sarajevo, along with their president, Aliya Izetbegovic, shook themselves awake from the dream that the West would come riding in to rescue them. Human rights organizations wouldn't save them. The UN wouldn't save them. They were on their own, completely on their own. They were being left to the tender mercies of the very enemies that had been plotting against them for years. Izetbegovic no longer had a choice: He'd have to stop the Bosniaks from fleeing their country or see Bosnia erased from the map.

Jovan Plavic

Stefan Stefanoviç stared wide-eyed at his reflection in the mirror. His chestnut hair was a few shades lighter and the mustache he'd sported for years was gone. The space between his nose and upper lip seemed to have expanded by a few inches. Strangest of all, he looked about fifteen years younger. He'd have barely recognized himself if it hadn't been for those familiar eyes, the lines of his chin, the shape of his nose. Had the bottle of hair dye, now empty and resting on the back of the sink, caused this transformation, or was it the whiskers he's washed down the drain?

He combed his hair back without parting it, as always. Then he remembered the warning the ID card man had given him: If he was found out as an imposter, the consequences would be dire. He tried parting on the right, but the resemblance to Hitler was unsettling. When he parted on the left, his hair stuck up like a rooster's tail. He smoothed it down with some hair gel; now he looked like an Italian rake straight out of a '30s flick. He washed off the gel and pushed his hair back with his fingers. It would have to do. He studied his new face for a few minutes, then he threw on some clothes, ran down the stairs to his car and drove until he found a barber's shop somewhere in north Zagreb.

"Give me a number 2," he told the barber once he was settled in the chair.

Clean shaven and with a buzz cut, the face looking back at him from the mirror now looked like it belonged to a soldier.

"You looked better with long hair," the barber said, with a sad shake of his head.

"I've got a long journey ahead of me," Stefan said. "This is more practical."

"If it's grown out by the time you get back to Zagreb, look me up. We'll pick out a more flattering style."

"Insha'Allah," Stefan said, an expression he'd picked up from Nimeta and his old Muslim colleagues. The barber narrowed his eyes.

He'd agreed to leave Nimeta, but that didn't mean he never thought about her, sometimes with longing. He was also honest enough to admit to himself that the possibility of seeing her again was one of the reasons he'd wanted to do the story on Bosniak refugees. Nimeta still had a place in his heart, even if it was mostly scar tissue. The pain was gone but something of her would stay with him forever, that much he knew.

He paid the cashier and went back over to tip the barber, who pushed his hand away.

"Anything the matter?" Stefan asked.

"No," the barber said.

"Are you refusing a tip because I said 'insha'Allah?'"

"Yes."

"Why?" Stefan was furious. He was determined to have it out with the racist barber.

"My grandmother was a Muslim. I haven't heard anyone use that expression since she died. Thank you for reminding me of her.

"So you're half Muslim then," Stefan said, feeling a little sheepish.

"One-quarter. But you know what it's like in the Balkans, nobody can be sure exactly what they are. We've been mingling for centuries. I'll never understand what all this fighting is about."

"It's about a power grab by a bunch of madmen," Stefan said. "Isn't that always the way? A mad scramble for power, and the rest of us pay for it."

"Some of the rest of us follow along like a bunch of sheep," the barber said.

"I'll stop in again on my way back," Stefan said. "My hair will have grown out by then and we can continue our chat – insha'Allah," he added with a smile. "Oh, by the way, is there anywhere around here where I can get a mug shot taken?"

"There's a shop on the opposite side of the street, about two hundred meters to the right. Are you a Muslim?"

"A quarter."

"Mother's side or father's side?"

"A woman's side."

When Stefan stepped out of the shop he glanced up at the sign so he'd remember it. The man waved a chubby hand at him through the window. He found the photographer's in no time and asked for two snapshots.

"There's a minimum of eight," he was told, "and it'll only take ten minutes." He waited patiently as the photographer carefully cut and trimmed the photos with a pair of scissors. The photos paid for, he walked out of the shop without even looking at them, got into his car in front of the barber's, sped home and dialed the ID man's number.

"The mug shots are ready. You can pick them up."

At nine the next morning he was holding his new ID card. He studied the face of the man with a light brown buzz cut, a bit too much space between his nose and his upper lip, and a trace of sadness in his eyes. His name was Jovan Plavic, born in Yayce.

Jovan Plavic though it prudent to avoid the northern border crossing into Bosnia that Stefan Stefanovic had passed through so many times. Instead, he travelled the length of his country to reach the southern border. If he hadn't chosen that alternative route, he would never have seen the refugees forced out of Foca and Visgrad, some of them later picked off by Arkan's Tigers as they crossed the mountains on foot.

They'd been walking for days under a blistering sun to get to Split. Those lucky enough to be on buses were sometimes forced out onto the road, robbed and beaten. Many had died on the way.

Stefan should have known better than to approach a group of dusty travelers near the border and to ask a young woman, "Where are all your men?"

"No men under seventy escaped. Either they were killed or they were taken away to camps."

These were the camps Jovan Plavic intended to visit. He was going to see them, talk to them and write about them for an international audience. And he might run into Nimeta while he doing it.

An elderly woman came over to him. "You're not a Serb, are you?" she asked.

"No."

"I could tell," she said.

Stefan didn't say another word. He'd changed his name and his face but there must have been something that gave him away. The guy who had brought him his ID card had told him to "think like a Serb" if wanted to pass as one. Now, even a weary old woman had been able to tell with a glance what he was and what he wasn't. That was bad.

"You shouldn't go up to strangers," he advised the elderly woman. "And be careful what questions you ask. You could get yourself killed."

"Ah, I've got no reason to be careful about anything anymore. I can't wait to die. If I was dead I wouldn't have seen them skin our men alive, wouldn't have seen them chop off the hands and feet of our husbands and sons so they couldn't kill themselves when they were left to die, covered in flies, some of them out of their minds from the pain, some dying right away, but others..."

"Hey! What are you doing talking to those women?" A Serbian policeman shouted as he came marching over.

"I was asking about the roads," Stefan said.

Stefan hadn't expected any problems from the Serbian policeman at the border, but he'd been mistaken.

"Why are you trying to get into Bosnia just as everyone else is trying to get out?" the policeman asked.

"I was living in Zagreb when the war started, but I'm Bosnian. I'm going to stay with my family."

"Where are you going?"

"To Sarajevo."

"How long do you plan to stay."

"For good."

"Is that all you've got with you?" the policeman asked, eying the bag and small suitcase Stefan was carrying.

"Yes."

"You're going back for good and you haven't got anything else?"

"I'm single. I don't need to travel with a suite of furniture."

"Don't get smart with me or I won't you let you cross."

"My boss wouldn't be too happy about that."

"Who's your boss?"

"Mitevic."

The policeman blanched. "Is Mitevic really your boss?"

"I work for Belgrade Television. I'm going to shoot some footage in Bosnia."

"Wait for me here," the policeman said before he disappeared into a makeshift hut, carrying Stefan's ID card.

Stefan sat down on a bench a few feet away. As he waited in the sun, another banged up bus covered with dust pulled to a stop. A group of miserable looking travelers got out of it. A small boy started crying. A policeman told his mother to shut him up. She picked up her son, rocked him, whispered in his ear and kissed him. He kept crying. The policeman snatched the boy from her arms and squeezed his nose, hard. The boy couldn't breathe. When his mother sank to the ground, the boy started crying again. The police picked up the boy and threw him against the wall. He fell to the ground and was silent. Nobody moved. Nobody intervened. They were all used to this sort of thing. The mother was still lying on the ground. Another woman ran over and made a pillow with her knees. Nobody dared to go over to the boy. Stefan got up and started walking.

"Plavic," a voice said. Stefan kept walking.

"Plavic! Jovan Plavic!"

Stefan turned and looked. It was the policeman who'd interrogated him.

"Plavic! Are you interested in crossing the border or in that Turkish brat? Why are you making me shout?"

"I was going to see if he was dead."

"If he's dead, he's dead. What's it to you."

"You're right," Stefan said. "It's none of my business." He went over to the hut to get his ID card. The policeman was grinning.

"I don't expect Mitevic would want you to trouble yourself over some Turkish brat."

"Can I have my ID? Are you done?" Stefan asked, reaching out his hand.

"In a hurry, are you?"

"Yes."

"Here you are, Jovan."

Stefan took his ID and started to walk back to the car. Then he spun round and said, "That boy, the one lying on the ground. He's not a Turk; he's a Bosniak."

When he was travelling through the parts of Bosnia that weren't under Serbian control, Stefan would pull off his left boot, take his real ID card out from its hiding place under the felt insole, replace it with Jovan's ID, push the insole into place, and put his boot back on.

Sarajevo was hellish. Stefan didn't even recognize some parts of the city. All the main roads were barricaded. There was always something burning in the middle of the streets. Corpses were strewn along the shoulders of the roads. The deathly silence was ruptured by the staccato report of machine guns, of exploding bombs, of sniper shots. The building in Ali Pasino Polye where he'd sometimes made love with Nimeta was riddled with holes. Nothing had been left unscathed. Still, life somehow went on. He saw people rushing to work, to appointments and dates, to shops with nearly empty shelves. Young people filled cafes and bars, and listened to music. Love, too, was in the air, along with death. He saw couples everywhere, embracing and walking hand in hand.

When Stefan walked inside a hotel whose facade had been sprayed with bullets, he was astonished how ordinary everything looked. There wasn't a trace of panic or fear. He could hear music somewhere, and walked toward it. In a secluded bar, a few musicians had gathered around a piano and were playing jazz. Had he ever come here with Nimeta? He couldn't remember. He went to the bar and ordered a drink. When he went to pay he couldn't believe the price, but it was too late. He took a sip of the $25 whiskey and vowed to give up drinking until the war was over.

"Haven't seen you here before," the barman said.

"No."

"Are you a reporter?"

"You guessed it."

"Who else would come here? It's not like anyone's coming here for a holiday," the barman said.

"You got a point there."

"Where are you from?"

"Zagreb."

Stefan didn't feel like talking but the barman kept peppering him with questions. Well, he wasn't going to be sweet-talked into ordering another drink. He asked where the restroom was, just to make an escape. "Over there, on the left," the barmen said.

The restroom was empty. He needed to switch identities again, so he leaned over and undid the laces to his left boot. He was just leaning over to press the felt insole into place other when he heard something directly behind him.

"Don't move. Stay where you are," a deep voice barked.

He froze.

"What have you got in your hand?"

"What does a man usually have in his hand in front of a urinal?" Stefan asked. The moment the words left his mouth he was booted in the ass. He rolled forward and bumped his head on the wall. Even as he was falling he had the presence of mind to shove his ID deep into his pocket.

"I think I'll take what you've got in your hand and feed it to you," the voice said. Stefan got to his feet and turned round, expecting to see a policeman. But the voice didn't belong to a cop, a militant or a gendarme: it belonged to a hulking brute in a black suit.

"What were you looking for inside your boot?"

Stefan didn't answer.

"You were hiding your money there, weren't you?"

They were standing across from each other and Stefan was trying to decide whether or not to jump him. He'd relaxed the moment he realized he was dealing with some punk out to rob him.

"It doesn't matter whether you stick your money in your boot or up your asshole," the man said, flicking open a switchblade. "I'll get it one way or another. Or you can just hand it over real nice."

Stefan pulled his wallet out of his front side pocket and took out all his cash.

"It's the money in the boot I'm after." The man picked up his boot and shook it. A grimy ID card fell out. The man flipped it over with the point of his shoe.

"So, you're a Croat."

"That's right. I'm not a Serb."

"It doesn't make any difference to me. Serb, Croat… you're all the same to me. Now take off your other boot."

Stefan pulled it off and handed it over. Not even an ID card fell out this time. The man grabbed the cash in Stefan's hand, jammed it into his inner jacket pocket and tossed the ID card on the floor into the toilet.

"If you try to follow me I'll kill you. Stay here for ten minutes," the brute said on his way out. Stefan ran over and fished out his ID card. He looked for some paper towel to dry it off. The dispenser was empty. There wasn't even any toilet paper. He shook the card back and forth a few times. Then he put on his boots, slipped the wet ID card into his empty wallet and walked out of the bathroom.

Jazz was still playing in the bar.

It sounded like a number he and Nimeta had particularly liked. He wondered what she was doing right now. Was she at home?

He left the hotel and wandered around through the devastated city for a while.

The Holiday Inn they'd visited so many times was a favorite with foreign journalists, so it had been protected from gunfire even if the windows got shattered from time to time. A bomb launched from the mountain hadn't landed on it either. The Bristol Hotel was another story: it had burned down. The Serbs had been unable to figure out which of the twin towers, Momo and Üzeyir, had a Muslim name, so they'd lobbed bombs at both of them. The post office, the museums, the Law School, the theater… Stefan kept walking past scene after scene of destruction. Then he decided to see if the skyscraper housing the offices of *Oslobodenje* newspaper was still standing, praying that it was. His colleagues there were lucky. The upper floors had been destroyed, but they continued to publish in the underground levels of the same building.

He told the woman at reception that he wanted to see Rasim. She sent for him. A few moments later Rasim appeared. His huge belly had melted away and his cheeks were hollow.

"Yes?" Rasim said. "What can I do for you?"

"Rasim, it's me. Stefan."

"Who?"

"Stefan Stefanovic. Stejo. Don't you remember me?"

"Oh! Stejo! My God you look different."

"So do you, Rasim."

"I've changed, but nothing like you. I've been here getting shot at and starving, and you've been somewhere getting ten years younger. How'd you manage that? Are in love?"

"I turned into a Serb," Stefan said, taking off his boot and extracting his ID card to show Rasim.

"March," Rasim said. "We can't talk about any of this here."

Stefan was in high spirits as he left the newspaper offices that evening. They'd reviewed every last detail of his plan to gain access to the concentration camps housing Muslim Bosniaks.

The timing couldn't have been any better for him to arrive in Sarajevo. *Newsweek* had sent a correspondent to interview some of the camps' inmates, but they'd been unable to get permission. *The Guardian* had also sent a correspondent.

UN Secretary-General Boutros Boutros-Ghali was being pressured by the United States, and had increased pressure on the Serbs. It would soon be impossible to deny monitors permission to enter the camps. Foreign correspondents would find it easier to get into the camps if they applied jointly with a Serbian journalist/translator. Rasim promised to pull strings to make sure Stefan was that Serbian journalist.

"Do you really think you can make it happen?" Stefan kept asking Rasim.

"Yes," Rasim said. "I'll introduce you to Zlatko."

"Who's that?"

"An attorney here in Sarajevo. He'll be a great help to you. He's been gathering evidence and information about the camps for months now. If we combine his documentation with your Serbian credentials, we'll have an unbeatable team. Just be certain you don't do anything idiotic, like let your real identity slip. Whatever it takes, we've got to get you into at least a couple of camps."

The best way for Stefan to forget he was Stefan Stefanovic was to stay far away from Nimeta. He was determined not to call her.

Stefan moved to a Serbian-controlled zone of the city, settling into a room in a flat left behind by a Muslim family. Rasim had said his "boot operation" was too dangerous, and confiscated his real ID card. "If they found a Croatian ID card on your person or in your room, you'd be dead," Rasim had said. "Go live in the Serbian zone and I'll get word to you when we're ready for you to make your application."

He'd been waiting for ten days. Finally, word arrived in a bakery of all places. He'd gone to his usual baker and picked up a loaf of bread. The baker had taken it, saying it was stale, and given him a different loaf. When he got home, he found a note on the sheet of newspaper wrapped around the bread: "Apply for July 10."

He shaved and showered as he got ready to go to the Press Office. When looking in the mirror he noticed that his hair was growing out and he had dark roots. It hadn't occurred to him that that would happen; he'd imagined that once you'd dyed your hair you were done with it for good. How could he get a bottle of hair dye at the pharmacy? If he asked for one himself, what would they think of him? No, it didn't matter what they thought of him; what mattered was that a man buying hair dye would arouse suspicion. Why hadn't he thought to bring a couple of extra bottles with him from Zagreb? But then what if they'd searched his bags at customs?

"I'm losing it," he said to his reflection. "I'm turning into a paranoiac. Nobody suspects me and nobody cares if I dye my hair. Anyway, how do I expect to find hair dye in a city where most people can't find bread? I've got to sort out my hair first, and then go and fill out my application."

He snipped at his hair with a pair of scissors, lathered up what left of it with a bar of soap, and shaved it clean with a straight razor. This time, it was a youthful version of Yul Bryner that greeted him in the mirror. He winked and said, "Now that's more like it, Jovan Bryner Plavic."

Rasim had kept his word; Zlatko had done all the groundwork. A group of foreign correspondents was expecting him to accompany them to the Manyaka Camp on the 10th of July.

The inmates of the camp had their hands chained behind their backs. Their heads were shorn clean, their eyes full of fear and horror, their bodies so emaciated that their ribs stuck out. The wardens kept waving their clubs at their intimidated and defeated-looking charges. The guards allowed Stefan, a fellow Serb, to wander freely, but they kept following the American and British journalists.

Stefan set about learning as much as he could as quickly as possible. The problem was, the inmates were too terrified to trust him, probably fearing reprisals if they attempted to complain. Then one of them called out to him: "I don't care if you're a spy. We'll never get out of here alive. If you want the truth about this place, I'll tell you!" Stefan raced over.

He'd been driven out of Banya Luka. Men, women and children, they'd all been crammed onto the manure-covered bed of a cattle truck and brought here, with no food and water during the journey. He didn't know what had happened to the women and children. The men's hands were kept chained day and night. They slept one atop another on a concrete floor. The healthier inmates let the ones with rheumatism and heart problems sleep on top, so they wouldn't catch a chill. They were all skin and bones.

Stefan was also able to visit Omarska Camp and Keratern Camp.

The Serbs were using Omarska Camp to intern all the leading academics, intellectuals and artists they'd rounded up in Priyedor, a city east of Banya Luka. The camp was situated in a disused mine. The Bosniaks were kept caged behind bars, with no latrines provided, so they had to urinate and defecate on the floor. Anyone approaching the camp could smell the stench well before they arrived.

Keratern Camp was in an old ceramics plant. The inmates there had suffered every conceivable type of torture designed to extract information. Those who supported the Bosniak militia or had served with the defense forces were executed after they were tortured.

Stefan barely slept the three days and two nights after they visited the camps. Once the interviews were translated, and the footage they'd shot edited and narrated, everything was sent to various news agencies.

When footage of the camps was aired internationally, the first stirrings of outrage began. It was as though the only way to appeal to the consciences of global leader was via the television screen. Men and women who had closed their ears and eyes to months of warnings, pleading, documentation and evidence watched TV and feigned shock as they learned what they'd already known.

"Television has achieved what presidents and ambassadors couldn't, Stefan. Many thanks to everyone involved for a job well done," Rasim said. "Mitterrand is planning a visit to the Bosnian president. The Serbs will have to lift their blockade of the airport, whether they like it or not."

Stefan kept his promise and didn't call Nimeta. He was busy all through the winter in any case, acting as a sort of spy with his fake identity. He'd never expected to find himself in this situation. His only intention had been to infiltrate the camps so he could expose the atrocious conditions. But to the foreign correspondent he was worth his weight in gold and he started earning huge sums for his services. And it was all because he was able to visit places and get footage available only to Serbs.

As spring approached, he decided to return to Zagreb. He'd made enough money and he was tired of shaving his head and living like a mole. He missed his home and his friends. Rasim also thought it advisable that he return home before his luck ran out. He would pack his bags and go once he'd completed his final assignment, in Gorazde.

Two days before he was scheduled to leave the city Stefan decided to call Nimeta just to see how she was. He'd be leaving soon, and they wouldn't be able to see each other for long, even if they both wanted to, he reasoned. He just thought it would be nice to see her face and hear her voice. Or he might have secretly wanted her to know about all the work he'd done on behalf of the Bosniaks. He'd promised not to call, but surely she could spare five minutes.

The phone lines were down that day, so he went to Nimeta's house. Nobody was home. When he kept banging on the door a woman poked her head out her front door and told him that Nimeta had moved to her mother's house.

"Why?" Stefan asked. The woman shut the door without answering him.

He considered stopping by her workplace, but then he remembered how much that had bothered her.

The following day he went to see Rasim.

"Are you still here? I thought you were going home last night. The longer your stay in Sarajevo the more dangerous it's going to get for you," Rasim.

"There's something I've got to sort out before I go. Are the phones still out?"

"Stefan, you know the phones don't work. Who do you need to call, anyway?"

"It's personal. There's someone I've got to talk to. Say, aren't the phones are working at the television station?"

"That's a separate network. It's the only place where the phones work. Oh, and there's the president's office. You could pay a visit to Izetbegovic and ask to call your girlfriend. I'm sure he'd understand."

"That's enough out of you," Stefan said. He knew he wouldn't be able to leave Sarajevo until he found out why Nimeta had moved to her mother's. Had she lost her husband? Was she hurt? How could he find her? He couldn't go to the television station, not after all the times she'd asked him not to call her there.

When Rasim saw how upset his friend looked, he said, "Why don't you visit this person, whoever she is, instead of trying to call?"

"I did. Nobody was at home."

"She might have been out. She'll be back."

"She's moved."

"Then find out the address of her new house."

"Rasim, do you think I haven't been able to figure that out on my own? I can't find her new address."

"There's a war on, remember? The person you're looking for might be dead."

Stefan went pale. "Damn you," he said on his way out. He began running up the stairs two at a time.

When he got outside he crossed the street and began walking toward the city center, not caring whether or not he came under sniper fire. It wasn't long before he'd reached the television station. He asked the man at reception to get Nimeta.

"Haso, can you go and have a look?" the man asked a boy.

"She's not there," the boy said.

"What time will she be there?" Stefan asked.

"I don't know."

"Then go and find out."

The boy went back upstairs muttering under his breath. This time he shouted down from the top of the stairs: "They don't know."

Stefan hesitated for a moment.

"Then ask if Mirsada is there… or Sonya!"

"Who's asking for me?" Sonya voice echoed in the stairwell.

"Sonya! I finally found one of you," Stefan cried out. "It's Stefan… from Zagreb. Doesn't Nimeta work here anymore?"

"Ah, Stefan. What a surprise. I can't talk right now, but we can meet this evening when I finish work. You've got a lot to catch up on," Sonya said.

"A lot to catch up on? What happened?" He pulled out a cigarette. "Sonya, I can't wait until evening. Don't you have a lunch break? I'll be at the front entrance at twelve sharp."

"Don't come before 12:30," Sonya called out.

Stefan ran all the way back to Rasim's office.

"You're taking a terrible risk," Rasim said. "It wouldn't matter who stopped and searched you. You've got two different ID cards. How would you get out of that one? Go home. Stop chasing after women."

"I'm going to find out what I need to know this afternoon. Then I'll go. Now get me a Turkish coffee, Rasim," Stefan said.

"A Turkish coffee? You'd be lucky to get tea brewed from grass. If I were you I'd find a church, light a candle and ask God to help you get home in one piece."

"Seriously, do you think God is watching over me?" Stefan asked.

"I'm a Muslim. Of course I do. Don't you believe in God? What kind of Catholic are you?"

"You can't really call me a Catholic, Rasim. I never go to church."

"What! Are you an atheist? I always thought you were a Catholic."

"I'm not an atheist, but I have seen enough of war to know that more blood is shed in the name of religion than anything else."

"You're the first Croat I've met who isn't religious. Your mother must have miserable when she found out."

"My whole family's like this."

"Why?"

"It's a long story."

"Everybody needs religion," Rasim said. "We all need to take refuge in God and pray for divine intervention."

"Maybe we do," Stefan smiled.

He was waiting in front of the TV station at ten past twelve. Sonya appeared at half past and started looking for Stefan.

"Pssst! Sonya!"

Sonya turned and looked at the man who'd shouted her name. "What is it? Who are you?"

"Sonya, it's me. Stefan. Don't you recognize me?"

"Ah, it really is you. Stefan, what happened to you? You look like you just got out of a camp."

"I've been in and out of more camps than you'd believe," he laughed, "but never as an inmate."

"Why'd you shave off your hair and your mustache? Are you hiding from someone?"

"You could say that. It's a long story. I'll tell you all about it. Sonya, why did Nimeta move? Has something happened?"

"That's a long story too. Let's go and sit down somewhere."

"It's nice outside. Let's go to the park."

"Are you crazy?" Sonya asked. "Do you want to get shot? Let's go to my place. I moved nearby. It's easier to get to work and back."

"Nimeta?"

"I'll tell you everything."

"Tell me now."

"Stefan, don't be so impatient."

All of sudden, Stefan was afraid.

"Is Nimeta alive?"

"Of course she is."

"Hold on a second," Stefan said. He took a deep breath and felt the pain in his heart fade. Then he pulled a cigarette out of his pocket.

"Where you'd find that," Sonya asked. "Do you mind if I have one? We're almost there. See those green buildings up ahead. That's where I live."

Stefan wasn't listening anymore. They walked up two flights up stairs. Sonya unlocked the door and they passed through a dim hall and into a small but well-lit room containing a bed, a card table and two chairs.

"Have a seat," Sonya said. Stefan perched on the edge of one of the chairs.

"I'd like to offer you something but I haven't got anything but water. Can I get you a glass?"

"No, thank you."

"The war's been terrible for us all. I had to send my mother and daughter to Istanbul. We let our house to an American general. We send part of the monthly rent to a fund for homeless Bosniaks. It was mom's idea. I've moved here temporarily..."

Stefan wanted nothing more than to steer the conversation to Nimeta, but Sonya banging on about things that didn't interest him in the slightest. Finally, he couldn't stand it anymore. "Please, Sonya," he said. "Tell me where Nimeta is. Why wasn't she at home?"

"She's moved. She doesn't live there anymore. Her family's been broken up, Stefano."

"What do you mean?"

"Burhan joined the volunteer force up in the mountains. Her son followed his father. Nimeta and her daughter are staying at her mother's."

"Does she still go to work?"

"Yes. But only three days a week. She should be getting back from Tuzla today."

"Let's go. Maybe she's back."

"Where are we going?" Sonya asked.

"To her mother's house."

"I'll give you the address. You can go on your own," Sonya said.

"Sonya, I want to ask you a favor," Stefan said. "I can't just show up on her mother's doorstep. Could you go and tell her I'm going. I'm returning to Zagreb tomorrow. I'd love to see her before I go."

"I can go after work," Sonya said. "This not being able to phone anyone is driving me crazy. If you need to talk to someone you've got to go all the way to their front door. That's why it took so long to find out what had happened to Mirsada."

"What happened to Mirsada?" Stefan asked.

"You haven't heard?"

"I know she moved to Belgrade. Didn't she come back to Sarajevo when the war started?"

"So you don't know."

"What happened? Tell me," Stefan said.

"Mirsada's dead."

Stefan swallowed hard. First, he thought how terrible it was that a woman who'd always been so full of life could die at such a young age. Then he thought of Nimeta. She'd lost her best friend. It must have been devastating. "How'd she die?" he asked, in a near whisper.

Sonya didn't answer.

"A bomb?"

"No, Stefan. Stop asking. I haven't got the strength to tell you. She's dead. Killed. The Serbs killed her." Sonya got quieter and quieter until Stefan had to read her lips to understand her last few words.

"They killed her... They shot her in the back of the head... They broke her backbone...They sliced her to pieces, Stefan... to pieces."

March, 1993

Nimeta had been jolted, bumped and shaken all during the jeep ride from Sarajevo to Tuzla. There wasn't a decent stretch of road left in all of Bosnia. Her eyebrows and lashes were coated in dust; her lower back was so stiff she thought she'd never stand up straight again. But every time her thoughts traveled to her husband, brother and son, she forgot all her discomfort.

They were somewhere up in the mountains, living in far worse conditions than hers. They didn't even have a seat to sit on or to lean back against. These thoughts of her husband, brother and son also made her a little angry.

They'd all abandoned her. They hadn't considered what it would be like for her to be left alone and completely responsible for a young daughter and an elderly mother. More than any one, she was cross with her son. Raif hadn't had his wits fully about him when he left. He'd run off to an honorable death to end his pain. Burhan had found out his wife had deceived him, and was heartbroken. But Fiko, what excuse did Fiko have for running off without even saying goodbye? She'd never wronged him in any way. One of the main reasons she'd broken away from Stefan was to protect her son, who doted on her, from dishonor.

"We'll be there in an hour," the driver said.

Nimeta wiped away her tears with the back of her hand. Life went on. Her heart had been broken, too, but she hadn't been able to flee to the mountains. She earned enough to keep her mother and Hana fed, even if that meant a slice of stale bread and a tin of sardines bought on the black market.

Penny Mcguire, an English journalist, was sleeping in the seat next to hers, head resting against a bag used as a pillow. Penny was going to Tuzla to visit a four-year-old rape victim who was being treated in a shelter there. Nimeta felt a little ashamed of herself for having cursed giaours so often over the past two years.

Serbian women had gathered in their windows to throw stones and buckets of boiling water at Bosniak women and children in the beds of trucks taking them away from their homes and homeland. Nimeta had seen it with her own eyes and praised God she was a Muslim. She truly believed that no Muslim would ever treat even her worst enemy with such cruelty. Once she'd said to Azra, "Can you believe the way Christians pride themselves on being the religion of peace, of turning the other cheek?"

"Don't believe it for a minute," Azra had said. "For all their talk of human rights, Europeans have no mercy for anyone but their own."

She'd reproached Azra. They both counted Croats and Serbs among their close friends. And hadn't she once been madly in love with a Christian?

Less than a week had passed before Azra seemed to prove the truth of her words by getting killed in Ferhadiya, waiting in line for bread. Nimeta was working that day, so Azra had also been waiting in line for her neighbor's monthly ration of half a kilo of sugar and three kilos of flour, when a mortar attack had ended her life and those of twenty other women. Body parts were scattered, heads were severed. Nimeta hadn't even been able to find a corpse to bury. When she got home that evening she'd collapsed in front of Azra's door, not crying, not talking...

"Please, Mother," Hana had pleaded, "come home."

Did Hana remember that day years earlier when her mother had been unable to move? Nimeta had seen the fear in her daughter's eyes. She'd shaken herself and stood up.

"Come on, Hana," she'd said. "Let's go inside and pack our bags. We're taking the cat and moving to mother's. Azra's gone now. Let's get out of here, too."

"Who killed her, Mother?"

"The giaours."

Now, the gaiour woman sleeping next to her was risking death to talk to a Muslim girl who'd been raped by Serbs, so the world would learn the girl's story. For years, Nimeta had loved a giaour, one she knew wouldn't harm so much as an ant. Her husband, who she also knew would never harm so much as an ant, had gone up to the mountains, to kill. So had her innocent fifteen-year-old son! It was a funny old world.

She hadn't wanted to worry her mother or agitate her daughter, so she hadn't told anyone at home where she was going today. She'd let them know she'd be away for two nights, saying she had to work until dawn. Raziyanım had been having anxiety attacks ever since Raif left, and was distraught whenever Nimeta had to leave Sarajevo.

The English journalist stirred in her sleep.

"We're almost there, Penny. Time to wake up," Nimeta said. Penny opened her eyes and rubbed her neck. The feeble sun was no match for the march chill. They'd both been shivering. Nimeta pulled the dirty, torn blanket back up over legs. Up ahead, she say a road sign for Tuzla. Both women said a silent prayer of thanks for having made the journey safely, neither of them aware that they were doing it in unison.

The two-storey house had a red tile roof and was painted white. From the outside, it looked like it contained a happy family. Who knows, before the war a husband and wife who loved each other, and their children, might have lived here. There was probably room for grandparents, too, in this cheerful home.

These days, the house sheltered women and children who'd survived the massacres in the area... Woman and children scarred by war. Outwardly, they looked healthy, all their limbs in place. But they suffered from what was called "war syndrome": persistent insomnia and recurring nightmares, headaches and backaches. They had amnesia, or remembered too much. They couldn't concentrate or carry on a conversation. The house was full of them.

A girl sat on a table, sweat plastering her yellow ringlets to her forehead, wide blue eyes staring at something visible only to her. She sat and stared, always. Without speaking, without getting hungry, without getting thirsty or tired. She had another affliction: she couldn't swallow. The doctors and nurses did everything they could to get food in her stomach, but she was getting thinner day by day. She'd cough up the watered-down food they spoon-fed her. But there was nothing wrong with her throat, her esophagus or her windpipe.

In a few days, they'd have to move her to the hospital and hook her up to an IV drip. The doctors had delayed it as long as possible, knowing what the girl had been through and hoping against hope she'd begin eating.

Her mother, who had crawled from room to room on all fours, two weak too stand after being raped by ten or fifteen Serbs, had found her daughter lying motionless on the wooden table in the kitchen, white foam frothing from her mouth, blood flowing from between her legs. The girl's torn underwear was resting on the table next to her. She hadn't been able to swallow since that day.

The girl was sitting motionless on a table right now, being fed gruel by a nurse. The doctors had no way of knowing when or even if she would recover from the shock. Her vagina and bladder had been damaged, but would heal with time. Her spirit, however, seemed broken beyond repair. She was four, old enough to remember the events of that day for the rest of her life.

The boy in the playroom on the floor above was six. His head was swathed in gauze. He couldn't talk either. He stood in front of table covered with sand, playing with tin soldiers. From time to time he's race to the other side of the room, crashing into the wall, and then return to his spot at the table. His forehead was dark purple. "My God, why are you letting him bang his head against the wall like?" Nimeta cried. The nurse explained that it was the only way he could vent his rage.

When Nimeta got back home, she rang the doorbell and acted as though nothing had happened.

"Mother," she said, "I need to be alone for a while. I can't even talk you to you or Hana right now. Let me stay in my room and don't send in any food or ask my any questions until I'm ready to come out." She locked the bedroom door behind her, buried her face in her pillow, and was wracked with sobs. She forgot why she was crying, or for whom.

The light tapping on the door entered her dreams. She'd been having a nightmare. A bunch of men with horns and ram's heads had been trying to force Hana into a chicken coop. Hana was screaming, but no sound come out of her mouth. White foam trickled from the corner of her mouth. Nimeta sat up in bed. For a moment she didn't know where she was. The room was dark. Was it morning, was her mother trying to wake her up?

"What is it?" she croaked. "Is it morning?" She fumbled for the nightstand lamp and switched it on. Then she jumped out of bed and threw open the curtains. It was pitch dark outside. She was fully dressed. She panicked. She ran to the door, but she couldn't open it.

"Mother," she screamed. She could hear feet running down the hall.

"What is it?" Raziyanım called out in an alarmed voice.

"Help me! I can't get out."

"What are you talking about? She could hear her mother fiddling with the handle of the door. Then she noticed that she'd locked the door herself, from the inside. She turned the key, and the door swung open.

Her eyes met those of her mother.

"What is it? What happened?"

"Nothing, Mother. I must have drifted to sleep, and I woke up in a panic," she said. She was beginning to breathe normally. "Was that you knocking on the door?"

"Oh, Nimeta. You know I wouldn't knock on the door after you said you didn't want to be disturbed. Your friend wouldn't listen to me. She insisted she had to see you. I told her you'd come home exhausted, and that we shouldn't wake you if you'd fallen asleep."

"What friend? What are you talking about, Mother?"

"Your friend from work. Sonya."

"Sonya? Is Sonya here?

"She's in the living room," Raziyanım said, pointing with her chin. "Get undressed and go to bed. I'll tell her you can't see any visitors right now. Go on, get to bed."

Nimeta gently pushed her mother aside and ran down the hall.

"Sonya, is anything the matter? What are you doing here at this time of night?"

"Is anything the matter with *you*, Nimeta?" Sonya asked. "What were you doing in bed so early? Your mother wouldn't even let me come in and see you."

"The trip to Tuzla was exhausting. I saw and heard such horrific things. I lay down when I got home and next thing I knew I was waking up in bed," Nimeta said. "Anyway, enough about me. Tell me what brings you here."

"There's someone who needs to see you."

"Who?"

"Stefan."

Nimeta's breath caught in her throat for a moment. Then she calmly asked, "When did he come?"

"Today."

"What does he want?"

"Ask him yourself," Sonya said. "He says he doesn't want to leave Sarajevo without seeing you. He's going back to Zagreb tomorrow."

"Where is he right now?"

"He's waiting at the bar at the Holiday Inn."

"Tell him to come into the office tomorrow. That way he'll be able to see his other friends, too."

"He's already been to the office and seen his friends. He wants to see you, Nimeta."

"I can't go out this late," Nimeta said. "I'm exhausted."

"He's going back tomorrow."

Nimeta shrugged. "I haven't offered you anything. Can I get you a bowl of mother's stewed apples?"

Raziyanım came over to the them the moment she heard her name.

"Has anything happened, Nimeta?"

"Sonya just wanted to know how my trip to Tuzla went."

"You went to Tuzla?" Raziyanım asked. "Didn't you promise me you wouldn't leave Sarajevo?"

"I'd better get going," Sonya said. Nimeta walked her to the door.

"What am I supposed to tell Stefan?"

"Tell her I was asleep and you couldn't wake me up," Nimeta said. "You've come all this way. Thank you, Sonya. I'll see you at work tomorrow." She shut the door and went into the living room to smoke a cigarette.

"So you went to Tuzla," Raziyanım said.

"Mother, please," Nimeta said.

She decided she didn't need a cigarette after all and headed for her room. As she was passing the door to Hana's room, she opened it a little, glanced inside at her sleeping daughter and gently closed it. She changed into her nightgown and stretched out on the bed with her hands laced under her head. Eyes on the ceiling, the lay there like that for quite a long time, not thinking about anything in particular. Then she got up, changed out of her nightgown and into a skirt, ran a comb through her hair, and put on some lipstick. When she left her room the living room was still. Her mother must have gone to bed. Just to be on the safe side, she tiptoed to the front door and quietly slipped outside. The cool night air struck her like a slap to the face. She began running down the hill toward the Holiday Inn.

Nimeta was stopped at three different checkpoints. She showed them her press card. They asked where she was going in the middle of the night. When she insisted that she had a critical meeting at the Holiday Inn, they let her through.

She was finally there. She went in through a back door: the front entrance had been closed ever since the war started. She went straight to the bar, but nobody was there and the lights had been turned off. She glanced over at the magenta arm chairs and sofas. Nobody. She woke up the receptionist.

"Stefanovic," she said.

He blinked at her several times.

"Stefanovic. Could you tell me Stefan Stefanovic's room number?"

The man glanced at the registry in front of him and then at his watch.

"I'm a journalist," Nimeta said, pulling out her press card.

"I recognize you. I've seen you on television," he said. "Stefanovic. Room number 500."

"Call him, please."

"At this hour?"

"Tell him it's urgent."

The receptionist dialed the number and waited.

"There's no answer. He must be sound asleep."

"Call him again."

He dialed the number again and handed the receiver to Nimeta. She waited until the twentieth ring and handed it back.

"Might he have checked out?"

"No. He's still registered."

Nimeta searched the lobby again and even pushed open the door to the men's restroom. Even there, the lights were off. Some of the buildings in the city were being provided with emergency power sufficient only to generate twenty watts worth of light. Everyone looked jaundiced and weak when she visited the Holiday Inn, the hospitals and the presidential residence.

"Aren't you going to leave a note," the receptionist asked her as she walked toward the closed front entrance by mistake.

"No," Nimeta said. She went out the back door and trudged along the same street where she'd been running a half hour earlier. Later, as she walked past her husband's old office, she asked herself why she'd ever come to the hotel in the first place. Why had she told Sonya she couldn't go out, only to jump out of bed and rush to the hotel? Why? What was she expecting?"

For all she knew, Stefan was sleeping in Sonya's bed right now. She felt a pang in her heart, and her throat and eyes stung. She had no rights over Stefan. He was someone she'd once loved very much, a long time ago. That was all. He could sleep with whomever he wanted. She started walking faster. It was getting chilly. As she marched along, head bowed, a man cut her off. She gasped in fear. He'd opened his arms wide, as though he was determined to block her path.

"Please get out of my way," Nimeta said.

"Nimeta!"

Nimeta stared blankly. "Do I know you?"

He was tall, and wearing a woolen beret. He pulled off the beret, and she saw he had a bald head.

"I... I'm sorry. It's dark," she said.

"It's me, Nimeta. Stefan. Stefan!"

"Stefan! What happened to your hair? And your mustache?"

"I'll explain everything. What are you doing out here? Do you know what time it is?"

"I could ask you the same question."

"I was heading back to my hotel."

"I went there to see you," Nimeta said. Stefan clasped her hands.

"Sonya said you couldn't come. Why did you come so late?" he asked. He was rubbing her hands, trying to warm them. "Let's go to my hotel."

"No, Stefan. Let's not go to the hotel."

"Don't worry, I'm not going to make you..."

"I don't want to go to the hotel."

"But weren't you just there?"

"I was going to meet you and suggest we go somewhere else."

"Alright, let's go the park then. When I couldn't sleep I went out for a walk in Veliki Park. We'll sit down on bench," Stefan said. "You can tell me everything that's happened since I last saw you. It's been ages, hasn't it?" He pushed a lock of hair back from her forehead, cupped her face in his hands and softly kissed her on both cheeks. Arms linked, they walked to the park through the darkness.

It was getting light by the time Nimeta got home, but Raziyanım and Hana were still in bed. She pushed the cat away with her foot and went to her room. She was about to get undressed when she decided it would be better not to go to bed. She heated some water on the grill her mother had put in the kitchen, squeezed in some lemon juice and drank it steaming hot. It was the closest thing to tea they'd had for weeks.

Her nose was running, her throat hurt and she kept sneezing. Even so, she hadn't felt this good for such a long time. A great weight seemed to have rolled off her shoulders. She realized how much she'd bottled up and how desperate she'd been for a sympathetic ear and a kind word. If only Mirsada had never gone to Belgrade. If only!

She's told Stefan everything, starting with the massacre in Zvornik, then moved on to Burhan going up the mountains, followed by Raif and Fiko, Azra getting killed in a bread line, the decision to move in with her mother, word of Mirsada's death… every last detail of everything but her last night with Burhan.

"He went off to fight and left you on your own here in the city?" Stefan asked.

"I'm used to being on my own, Stefan. You know that."

"But the war hadn't started back then," he said. She'd never tell him the reason Burhan had left her.

She'd broken down completely when she told him about Mirsada, sobbing on his shoulder as he held her tight and waited for her tears to subside, and she felt, for a moment, like she was safe in the arms of the only real friend she had left. Then they'd walked around the park for a time.

They were sitting on some tombstones, still talking about Mirsada, when a couple of militiamen approached. She showed them her press card and her papers.

"Haven't you got a home somewhere?" one of them asked.

"Don't you realize how many people don't have homes anymore?" Nimeta asked. The men had walked away.

Along with the weathered tombstones in the cemetery were newer ones, the white markers of young lives lost in the war. There had been so many deaths across the city that they'd started burying the war's victims in parks, the gardens of mosques and the courtyards of their homes. Sarajevo was turning into an open cemetery.

"We didn't know what happened until much later, Stefan. She never answered the phone and she'd quit her job. We couldn't get hold of Petar, either. Even so, it never occurred to me that she might be dead. Like I'd forgotten we were in the middle of a war. Why, when even my three-year-old nephew was killed in the war, did it never occur to me that Mirsada could be another of its victims? She'd told me in one of our last conversations that she wanted to take a week off from work and get away from Belgrade. Petar had relatives in Nis she thought they could visit together. I told everyone she must be all right and away on holiday. I've always hated having my every movement tracked and wanted her to be free to go wherever she wanted, without anyone asking questions and pestering her. Sometimes I feel like it's all my fault."

"What could you have done? You couldn't have saved her."

"We might have found her in time and taken her to a hospital."

"Nimeta, the Serbs wouldn't leave anyone alive. Especially if they're Bosnian and a journalist. They would have stayed in her house until they were certain she was dead."

"They didn't just leave her for dead. They tortured her."

"I wish she'd come back to Bosnia."

"We all do! But Petar wouldn't let her go."

"Mirsada is resting in peace now. She's saved. Perhaps she's luckier than us, the living," Stefan said softly.

Neither Nimeta, Stefan nor anyone else realized what had really happened to Mirsada. Other than four Serbian commandos, nobody would ever know the events that took place in her house the day she died.

Petar was away on a long trip. Since long absences were routine for journalists, Mirsada didn't expect anything. Later events, however, aroused her suspicions. A letter informing her that her position was to be terminated at the end of the months was placed on her desk when Petar was away. When she got home that evening she called Petar repeatedly until late at night, but never got an answer. She'd hope to consult with him before making a move.

The next day, having been unable to speak to her lover, she was feeling extremely tense as she confronted her manager. Why had she been fired? Had she done anything wrong? She'd been working longer hours than anyone, scanning publications in English and German and translating them. Had she ever delivered her research late? Hadn't the interview she'd conducted two weeks earlier generated a strong positive reaction? Why had she been fired?

We're downsizing the labor force, the manager told her. Well there are other people who should be let go before me, she'd insisted, like that girl with an MP for an uncle and that pudding-faced stutterer said to be close to Mitovic. Everyone had laughed at the thought of a reporter stammering his way through an interview, but Georg had said, "He's not a correspondent, he's an informant."

"What do you mean?" Mirsada had asked.

"We're a police state, Miza."

Miza! Just as she was getting used to that name, which she used to hate, she found herself getting the boot. Petar needn't have bothered to find her a new identity. Nimeta was right, she'd have to return to Bosnia if she expected to find work. But Petar came first, and she'd stay in Belgrade for him no matter what.

There was a knock on the door at about eight that night. Mirsada was in the bathroom, so she didn't hear it at first. At the thudding sound of boots, she raced to the door. She got there before they managed to kick it down.

"Your name?" one of the men asked.

"Miza."

"Your real name?"

"I told you," Mirsada said. A towel was wrapped turban-like around her wet hair.

"Is that the name your lover gave you?"

Mirsada didn't answer.

"Surname?"

"Efendic."

"Efendic, is it?" one of them said. "And the whore of that traitor, Petar Miragoslav."

"Efendic is the surname of my ex-husband. Petar is no traitor. He's every bit as patriotic as you," Mirsada said.

"Don't try to lecture us on patriotism. Tell us your real name, your Bosnian slut."

"I was born in Bosnia."

Mirsada remained composed.

"You mean, you're a Muslim."

"I'm not. But so what if I was. Since I'm Bosnian I could just as easily have been born Muslim."

She felt the heat rise to her cheeks as she lied. This was the first time she'd renounced her identity and she bitterly regretted having gone along with Petar. One of the men waited with her while the three others went to the rooms in back. They'd turned the house upside down in minutes. Every drawer and cupboard had been ransacked for documents and papers.

"Show us your ID card."

"It was stolen. I was mugged about ten days ago on the way home. I haven't had a chance to get new one issued."

"Your dark eyes tell us exactly who and what you are: a Musim whore," the tall one said. "Have you ever seen a Serb with those big dark eyes?"

"I've seen hundreds. I can tell you their names if you like."

A fist crashed into her face. The sash to her robe was tugged off and her robe fell open. Her breasts were showing. She tried to pull her robe close but the tall one grabbed her wrists from behind. Her dark breasts were now completely exposed.

"That's not what your boyfriend told us. He said you were a Muslim Bosnak whore."

"He didn't, because it's not true."

"Maybe he lied on purpose," the weasel-faced one said, "because, as he was dying, he thought he'd want you with him in hell."

"Did you kill him!" She hadn't expected her voice to thunder like that.

"Traitors who cooperate with Muslim dogs don't live long!"

Mirsada sank to her knees.

"Bosnak whore, what's your real name?"

Mirsada gave up without a fight. The person who gave her life meaning was gone, and weasel-face was right about one thing: she'd rather be with Petar than alive and alone.

"My name is Mirsada Efendic."

The tall one ripped the towel off her head, grabbed her by the hair and pulled her to her feet.

"Now you'll give us the names of all your friends. All your media colleagues and neighbours who make friends with traitorous dogs. You'll provide every last name."

"I'm not giving you anything," Mirsada said as she instantly received another blow to the face. Blood was trickling from the corner of her mouth.

"Oh, yes you will. But first there's something else we want, all four of us. We wonder what Muslim whores taste like. Once we make you happy you'll be ready to answer our questions."

Weasel-face unbuckled his belt while the others fondled and pinched Mirsada's breasts.

"I'm first," the tall one said. He pulled down his trousers and stood in front of Mirsada.

"Down on your knees!"

When she didn't move the others forced her down, her wrists still seized from behind, blood still trickling from the corner of her mouth.

"Her tits aren't bad."

The tall Serbian's erection was moving toward Mirsada's breasts. He grabbed her by the hair and roughly pulled her up against his crotch. Mirsada closed her eyes.

"Come on! Open your mouth, now!"

Mirsada opened her eyes. First, she glanced at the organ being rubbed against chin and cheeks; then, she opened her mouth as wide as she could, took it in as far as she could and chomped down.

The man bellowed like a crazed beast. Weasel-face was so stunned he let go of Mirsada's wrists. Mirsada grabbed her tormenter's testicles, sank in her nails and squeezed with all her might. The tall Serb bent double and bellowing so loud that his companions, whose trousers were around their ankles as they awaited their turn, didn't realize for a moment what was happening. As two of them grabbed Mirsada by the hair and tried to jerk her head back. Weasel-face grabbed the tall Serb by the hips to pull him away from Mirsada's nails and teeth. The man was stretched out on the floor, Mirsada right beside him, her teeth still sunk into his member, her nails piercing his testicles. The others pulled at Mirsada, but her jaw seemed to have locked onto their friend. As they tried to pull her head away he bellowed even louder. Blood started gushing from the corner of her mouth right when the bellowing stopped and at the moment she was hit by a vicious kick in the middle of her lower back. She blacked out, her ears buzzed and she suddenly felt light as a bird. She couldn't feel her hair, the pain in her back or even the man's blood in her mouth.

She couldn't even feel the muzzle of the gun pressing against the back of her neck. But her hands still clutched the testicles of the Serb on the floor, even after weasel-face ended her life with a single bullet. Try as they did, they couldn't hurt her now.

Perched on a tombstone, Nimeta luxuriated in a sense of peace and well-being. For the first time since Burhan, Raif and Fiko had left, she didn't feel at all lonely. Stefan was there, listening to her, understanding even the things she couldn't put into words. He'd always been there, and that must have been what had scared her. Their lives were intertwined. It didn't matter where she went, how far she ran: he might even appear in the middle of a dark, empty street.

Stefan told her all about his adventures, his reasons for coming to Sarajevo and for going back home to Zagreb, and how determined he'd been to see her before he left.

When they reached the door to Nimeta's house Stefan had cupped her face in his hands again.

"Nimeta," he said, "I know this isn't the time or place, but there's something I need to say. I know how devoted you are to your husband and children, and I've tried to be understanding. But if the war changed things, do you think we could try again? I don't want anything bad to happen to anyone, what I'm trying to say is... if... if..."

Nimeta put her finger to his lips. "Shhh, Stefan. Don't say it out loud," she said. "Wait for the war the end, for this cursed, senseless war to come to an end."

She embraced Stefano and went into the house. It was just getting light.

The house was dark and cold. The fire in the stove in the hallway had burned out.

"Do you know which tree this is?" her mother had asked her once as she lit the stove. "Remember that oak you could see from your bedroom?"

Trees were being chopped down across the city. She'd proposed to Ivan that they run a program protesting the deforestation of their city.

"Would you rather people froze to death in the middle of the winter," Ivan had said. "How do you expect them to cook? We're at war for God's sake!"

She could be such an idiot sometimes. Right now she was so cold she could have burned some logs from the monumental plane trees in Veliki Park. When she'd finished her lemon tea she noticed a notebook on the kitchen table. Hana sometimes left her homework on the table for her mother to check. She poured some fuel oil into a shallow bowl and lit the wick.

"Oh, it's her journal!" she cried to herself. She'd never read anything Hana had written in her famous journal. She was about to flick through the pages when she remembered what a snoop her own mother had been. The next thing she knew she was reading a page at random.

"July 2, 1992

My uncle and Fiko have gone to join my father in the army. I'm here alone with Mom and Bozo. I thought I wouldn't mind Fiko's going but I miss him so bad, as much as I miss dad... maybe even more. I'm sorry I was jealous of him because grandma and mom love him more than me. Now I wouldn't care if he pulled my hair and teased me and bossed me around. I wouldn't care if they loved him best either. Nothing's worse than being lonely! May God watch over him, and not let him get hurt or killed."

Nimeta couldn't read through her tears. She pressed the journal to her chest. Then she took the lamp with her to the armchair by the window. Hana thought her mother loved her son best, just like Nimeta had always thought Raziyanım loved Raif best. She opened the journal to another page.

"It's been many days since we lost auntie Azra in the market massacre, but I still cry at night. She was my only 'big' friend and the only adult who treated me like a grown-up. I used to tell her all my troubles and complain about mom and Fiko and grandma to her. How am I supposed to bear not being able to see her again. I never realized how important she was. I try to hide how much it bothers me from mom. The day it happened mom was so beside herself that I was afraid they'd come and take her away again. What would I do if something happened to her too? We're moving to grandma's tomorrow. Three women and a cat. Mom says Bozo will be the man of the house from now on. I'll ask grandma to treat him with respect."

Don't worry, Hana, Nimeta sighed to herself. I'm not going anywhere. I'll never leave you on your own again. As she continued skimming the diary, the words were like a stinging rebuke for her own selfishness. She'd fallen in love with Stefan when Hana was at a age where she desperately needed attention and affection. She wished she could turn back time and make things rights the next time round. If only she had another chance... if only.

"March 7, 1993

Yasna has started to look like a stork. None of her clothes fit anymore. Her trousers and sweaters and skirts look so funny on her! She says her mother wonders how she could grow so fast when there's so little to eat. I'm glad I'm not getting any taller. Mom always says she doesn't have enough money to get us new clothes.

Food's so expensive these days that we have to spend all our money to eat."

Was it true that Hana wasn't getting any taller? It was hard to tell if someone you saw every day was getting taller or older. She'd never complained that her clothes were getting too tight or too short. Had the shortage of meat and fresh fruit stunted her growth? Raziyanım had stopped going to her friend's garden in the south of the city. There were too many bombs and snipers about these days, and the Serbs had also taken to mining the roads.

Come to think of it, Raziyanım had remarked on how thin Hana was.

"This girl's not getting enough food, Nimeta. The other day, Lamia Hanım was talking about getting some pigeons and..."

"Don't even think about it, Mother," Nimeta had said. She'd heard that birds were being trapped and hunted, and she'd been certain that Raziyanım would find a way to sneak Hana some pigeon soup. Now she was sorry she'd ever opposed the idea. Nimeta decided that if she ever suspected there was pigeon meat in their soup or *börek*, she wouldn't say a word.

She heard the creak of a floorboard and lifted her eyes from Hana's journal. It was Raziyanım.

"What are you doing up so early, Nimeta?"

"I couldn't sleep."

Why'd you get dressed already? Go on back to bed. I'll fix Hana breakfast when she gets up. You had a long day yesterday. I'll wake you up at about eight o'clock."

Nimeta sneezed several times.

"Have you caught a cold?" Raziyanım placed her hand on Nimeta's forehead. "You're running a temperature. You must be coming down with something."

"It's just a cold, mother."

Raziyanım raced to her room and returned with a thermometer. "Put it in your mouth," she said.

"There's no need. I'll be fine if I get some sleep."

"Take it," Raziyanım insisted, holding the thermometer out to Nimeta, who resignedly took it and placed it under her tongue. Raziyanım stood there waiting until Nimeta checked the thermometer two minutes later.

"What does it say?" her Mother asked.

Why lie? "39 degrees," Nimeta said.

"I still don't understand what business you had going off to Tuzla," Raziyanım started in. "Now go straight to bed. I'll brew you some linden tea. I'll go to Selcukovic's house as soon as it turns eight."

Nimeta was in no state to argue. She meekly went to her room, got undressed and crawled into bed.

By the time Selcukovic paid a house call at Raziyanım's insistence it was nearly ten and Nimeta's fever had reached 40 degrees. Raziyanım had placed a vinegar compress on her forehead and was splashing cologne on her arms and temples.

When the doctor saw Nimeta moaning feverishly he felt guilty about his behavior earlier that morning.

"Raziyanım," he'd said, "the emergency rooms are overflowing with life and death cases and you come here at eight in the morning and expect me to pay a house call just because your daughter's caught a cold? Tell Nimeta to visit a hospital."

He'd relented, though, when she kept insisting. They were old friends after all. He'd grown up with Raziyanım's late husband, and couldn't easily turn down a request from his widow. The last thing he'd expected, however, was to find that Nimeta had come down with such a high fever.

He listened to her chest and heart, and examined her throat.

"You've caught a terrible chill," he said. "How did you manage that?"

Raziyanım jumped in. "She went to Tuzla. Who knows where she stayed and what she was up to for those two days. She's got no idea how to look after herself. If I'd known she was going I'd have made sure she took a heavy sweater and a woolen blanket."

Selcukovic winked at Nimeta. "Does your mother bottle feed you every morning, too?"

Nimeta managed a weak smile but she was in no condition to speak. The wheezing in her chest had gotten much worse over the last two hours.

"I'll get some antibiotics from the hospital and stop by this evening," the doctor said. "I'd write you a prescription but you wouldn't be able to fill it."

"I'll go to the hospital and get it," Raziyanım volunteered. "Let's not wait until evening."

"Stay here and nurse your daughter," Selcukovic said. "Make sure she gets plenty of fluids. If you've got any aspirin in the house, give her a couple straight away. I'll send a porter with the medicine as soon as possible and stop by later on my way home."

Raziyanım muttered and fussed for some time after the doctor went, but Nimeta was too soundly asleep to notice.

Whenever one of her children got sick, Raziyanım immediately set about identifying the cause. She'd have no peace of mind until she found out exactly where they'd caught a chill, whose hand had exposed them to germs or which particular junk food had let to a bout of diarrhea.

A few hours later, Nimeta opened her eyes to find her mother sitting next to the bed with a bowl of lemony chicken noodle soup.

"Selcukovic sent the medicine," Raziyanım said. "Finish up this soup straight away. You can't take your pills on an empty stomach. And promise me you'll never go to Tuzla again."

She'd also prepared a bowl of vinegar and water, with a length of folded muslin for a compress. Nimeta surrendered herself to her mother's capable hands for the next ten days. Just as she had when she was five or six years old, she ate what she was given and did what she was told.

During those feverish bedridden days she was vaguely aware of a visit from Sonya and of Hana tiptoeing in and out of her room.

When she was finally able to stand up, many days later, she walked as far as the living room. This time she wanted to receive her daily visitor, Sonya, not in her bedroom but in the living room. Her fever was better, but she felt weak and her head started spinning when she struggled to her feet.

"Ivan's parceled out your work to the rest of us," Sonya said. "We can't wait for you to come back. The interviews you did in Tuzla were incredible. I wish you'd been able to present them yourself."

Nimeta exploded in a fit of coughing. Her fever had broken but her ailment seemed to have settled in her chest: she'd been coughing like a goat for three days. Her mother handed her a cup of linden tea. Raziyanım had risked life and limb to travel to a friend's home on the opposite side of the city to collect the linden flowers for that tea.

Sonya wordlessly indicated to her friend that she had something important to say and wanted to talk alone. Nimeta took a sip of the linden tea and looked her mother directly in the eye.

"Can I get you anything?" Raziyanım asked.

"Mother, Sonya and I need to talk about work. Don't trouble yourself here if you have something else to do..."

Raziyanım straightened the blanket on Nimeta's knees and left the room.

"You said you were tired the night you got back from Tuzla, but I didn't realize just how exhausted you were. It turns out you were coming down with something," Sonya said. "Stefan wonders when he can visit you. What should I tell him?"

"Stefan?" Nimeta nearly choked on her tea. "Hasn't he left yet?"

"No."

"Didn't he say he was going home the next day? The day after I got back from Tuzla?"

"Some work kept him here," Sonya said. "Can he come and see you this week?"

"No," Nimeta said. "I'll be back at work in a few days. I'll call him."

"He said he needs to see you now. He's worried."

"I don't want to cause any trouble with my mother," Nimeta slowly said.

"Why would a visit from Stefan cause trouble?"

Nimeta was at a loss for words for only a moment. "Mother's not very fond of Croatians these days. She says they stabbed us in the back during the war. She's getting on in years and I hate to think what she might say to Stefan in an unguarded moment."

"Stefan wouldn't take it personally. He'd understand."

Nimeta guessed that Stefan was feeling guilty for having kept her out all through the chilly night wandering through parks. He was probably waiting for her to get better before he went home.

"I'll write a note and ask you to give it to him, Sonya," she said. "It's very kind of him to take such an interest in my health but he needn't bother coming all the way to my door."

She felt terribly weak, and the coughing persisted. The last thing she wanted was to have to defend her personal life to her mother and to get entangled in needless bickering over a relationship that had long since ended. Were Stefan to let it slip that they'd been out in the city parks until dawn she'd never hear the end of it from Raziyanım.

Sonya left her a couple of documents from work and got up to go, saying Ivan would be pleased she'd checked in on the patient, as promised. Nimeta placed the documents on her lap and tried to read them. The characters swam before her eyes.

"Is your friend gone?" Raziyanım asked. "If you've lifted the embargo I'd like to come in." She stood in the doorway bearing a tray.

Nimeta looked up at her mother. The poor woman looked as drawn and thin as though she'd been the one convalescing. Her face had a sickly, yellowish cast and there were dark circles under her eyes. Nimeta was filled with a rush of pity for her mother.

All their lives, Nimeta and Raif had been annoyed by everything their mother did and said. They'd felt suffocated by her fiercely protective love, bristled at her insistence on knowing about and keeping track of their every move, and sneered at the importance she gave to preparing their favorite dishes. No matter what she did, Raziyanım was unable to please her children, but that didn't stop her from continuing to try. Unappreciated though she was, she'd always put family first. Even now, at her advanced age, she brought drinking water home from the brewery miles away, risked death waiting in line at the market, and trundled logs home in a wheelbarrow to use as fuel. Not only that, but her beloved grandson, Fiko, and her darling boy, Raif, had gone off, leaving her behind with a witch of a daughter who begrudged her mother so much as a simple thanks.

"What are you talking about, Mother?" Nimeta said. "I wish you'd stayed if that's what you wanted. It's just I thought you'd find it a little boring..." She was wracked by coughs before she could finish.

"That friend of yours wore you out," Raziyanım said. "She really should realize that it's best to keep visits to patients short. See, you've started coughing again." She came over to put the tray and its contents on Nimeta's knees. The surge of affection Nimeta had felt for her mother was gone.

"Mother, please don't go at my friends," she said, wearily.

"Have some soup," Raziyanım said. "I made it with real broth, but don't ask how I got the 200 grams of meat, just to get you healthy again. Don't waste a single drop of this soup."

"Thank you, Mother," Nimeta said. "I'm sure it's delicious and well worth all the effort you put into it. Put some aside for Hana, would you?"

She moved the documents off her lap to make room for the tray, hoping to finish the soup before she had another coughing fit.

It's funny, she thought to herself: for as much as he loved her, Stefan caused her more harm than anyone else. This was the second time she'd fallen ill because of him. The doctor had told her that she could end up with pleurisy if she didn't take care of herself. Pleurisy could of course lead to death. Nimeta shuddered. Imagine coming down with pleurisy or pneumonia in the middle of a war, and at a time when her mother and Hana depended upon her for survival.

Burhan was off fighting because of Stefan, and so was Fiko. Their love was lethal! Cursed!

She sipped a spoonful of soup and felt warmed immediately. Then she felt guilty for blaming others for her problems and wondered if her character hadn't taken a turn for the worse. She's the one who'd wanted to wander through the city parks until dawn, and she's the one who'd fallen in love with Stefan.

Nimeta still had a prolonged convalescence ahead of her. Contrary to her expectations, it took more than a couple of days for her to make a complete recovery and return to work once her fever had broken. Raziyanım kept preparing and serving dishes designed to help her daughter mend. It wasn't until a full week later that Nimeta felt strong enough to resume her normal life.

One sunday evening, having received Dr. Selcukovic's blessing, she began preparing for work the following day.

Life was certainly strange. She'd been going to work for years. Her entire family had grumbled about her career, and so had she. Now, after a short break, everyone was thrilled she was going back, as though it had always been a source of joy. Even Hana got involved, insisting on helping her mother pick out something to wear the next day.

"I'm so pale these days, Hana, don't make me wear my beige suit," Nimeta said.

"Wear what you will, just make sure it's heavy or you'll catch your death of cold again," Raziyanım said.

Hana lay out a maroon turtleneck sweater and a navy blue skirt on the bed. She'd been taking a keen interest in clothes lately. Unfortunately, her newfound fascination with fashion had happened at a time when it was impossible to go shopping.

"That sweater's too thick," Nimeta said. "It'll make me sweat."

"But you look so good in red, Mother," Hana said. "I think you should wear it."

Nimeta held the sweater up to her chest and studied herself in the mirror. The rich color made her look even pastier. She'd lost weight, and her face was wan and drawn. Still, she was in no mood for a drawn-out debate on tomorrow's attire. Once again, she'd let a member of her family make her decision for her, even a detail as personal as this one.

She smiled to herself and said, "Alright, I'll wear it just for you. Now go to bed, it's getting late."

She took a copy of the day's newspaper into bed, without bothering to put the sweater and skirt back in the closet.

Tomorrow was a new day. She'd go to work and probably see Stefan.

She'd try to stop by the market on the way home to do the shopping. Her mother had been running herself ragged. She'd also agree to let Hana have her friend, Zlata, come over. In the name of economy, they hadn't let the poor Hana have visitors, but Nimeta decided that they needed to do more to allow the poor girl to have a normal life. She fell asleep as she was reading the paper.

First, she heard the knocking on the door in her dream, ran to open it and was met by her father. She rushed into his arms and said, "Dad, I've missed you so much. Where have you been?" Her father looked like he was in his forties, not the age he was when he died. He was young and good-looking.

When she woke with a start from the vivid dream she could hear that someone really was knocking on the door. She tried to switch on the bedside lamp, but it wouldn't turn on. She was too groggy to remember that there was a power cut.

"Who could it be at this hour? My God," she said aloud, "what could it be?" She raced out of her room barefoot. Her mother had shut the door to the hall. In the darkness, the banging seemed deafening. Cursing, she walked towards the front door and fumbled for the candle and matches they always left in the hall. "Who is it?" she called out. From below, the light of the candle illuminated her face, her eyes wide with fright and her tousled hair. Raziyanım and Hana had gathered in the front hall, their drowsy faces visibly pale, even in the faint flicker of the candle.

"Is Nimeta Hanım there?"

"Who is it?" Nimeta asked. She'd heard tales of Serbian militiamen breaking into houses and raping whole families. The example of Mirsada was still fresh in her mind. Her knees started trembling. "Who are you, what do you want?"

"We have news from commander Burhan."

Forgetting for a moment that she was dressed only in a thin nightgown, Nimeta opened the door.

Standing across from her were two men in black.

"Don't be scared. Burhan sent us."

"Go get something to wear," Raziyanım said. When she saw Nimeta was too dazed to do anything, she rushed off herself to get a bathrobe. Hana stood just behind Nimeta, clutching her mother's arm.

"What is it? Has something happened to Burhan?"

"Your son is wounded," one of the men said.

When Raziyanım came back with the robe she found her daughter collapsed on the floor. She draped the robe over Nimeta's back. The two men each took an arm, pulled Nimeta to her feet and sat her on the nearest chair.

"Burhan sent us with news. He's coming down from the mountain early tomorrow with your son. He wants you to arrange a hospital bed."

"What happened to my son? Was he shot? Was it a bomb? Is he conscious? Is it serious?"

"Don't worry," the younger of the two men said. "He's been hurt in the leg. But we can't treat the wound up in the mountains. He needs a fully equipped hospital."

"When are they coming?"

"I don't know the exact time. They were going to leave at dawn. They'll definitely reach the city in the morning. If there's a change of plan we'll let you know." The men saluted and were gone.

Nimeta, Raziyanım and Hana stood motionless and dumbstruck for a moment, until Raziyanım broke the silence:

"Let's send word to Selcukovic straight away," she managed to say. At the sound of her mother's voice, Nimeta came to her senses and raced to her bedroom, candle in hand. She threw on the clothes Hana had picked out for her, forgetting to put on stockings in her haste, slipped a coat over her shoulders and was out the door, the voice of Raziyanım echoing behind her: "Wait. For God's sake, where are you going all alone in the black of night? Wait for me!"

As Nimeta sprang down the steps two and three at a time she could hear her mother's entreaties and her daughter's sobs.

At seven in the morning, she was back home, having arranged the care Fiko would need.

"Selcukovic..."

"I found him, Mother. He's taken care of everything. What would I have done without him? The hospitals are overflowing, patients two and three to a bed. How lucky we are to have a doctor as a friend. There's a section back behind the office of the head surgeon in Kranjcevica. He's had it readied. After all his years as a professor he's able to call in favors..." There was more to tell, but she was coughing too hard to go on.

"Ah, you're not wearing stockings!" Raziyanım cried. "How could you go out like that? I'm at my wit's end with you." Raziyanım bustled off to her room to get a pair of stockings.

They waited calmly until eleven o'clock. Hana skipped school that day. Nimeta sat in front of the window, wrapped in a blanket. Just before eleven, electricians arrived to hook up their house to a 20-watt connection, which was one of the perks of being a journalist. The workers took their time, whiling away the minutes. Raziyanım served them some of the linden tea she'd made for her daughter. When they'd drained their cups, they left.

Nimeta was still sitting in front of the window, waiting.

By noon, she'd grown impatient. She didn't know who to call, or how. She started pacing and finally went to her mother's room. Raziyanım was reading the *Koran* aloud in a low voice.

"Take care not to anger Allah by reaching for your *Koran* only when you want something, Mother," she said.

"It's those who won't let a body pray in peace that anger Allah, Nimeta," Raziyanım said. "Allah asks us to turn to him in times of need. Now leave me alone and shut the door on your way out."

Feeling a bit miffed at her mother's tart response, Nimeta shut the door and returned to her post in the living room. She roughly shoved the cat off her armchair. The cat did a mid-turn tumble, landed on all fours and stared in puzzlement. Hana was trying to find a station among the crackling static of the transistor radio.

"Turn that thing off," Nimeta shouted, "and go to school."

"It's afternoon, Mom," Hana said. "School's out."

"Then go visit Zlata or Mlata or whoever!"

"I'm not going anywhere!" Hana said as she traipsed off to her room in a huff.

Stay calm, Nimeta told herself. Stay calm and be brave. And may God help me.

There was a knock on the door at about one. Nimeta sprang up out of her chair, nearly falling when the blanket got tangled around her legs. She ran to the door. Raziyanım and Hana beat her to it. Standing in the doorway was a sunburned man in a parka. Nimeta had seen him enter the apartment building but assumed he had nothing to do with Burhan.

"Any news of my son?" Nimeta asked, before he had a chance to speak.

"Yes."

"What's taking them so long?"

"The Serbs have put up barricades in two different places. We can't get through the barricades in an ambulance. I managed to get here on foot by taking a detour through the forest. But we can't carry your son through the forest on a stretcher."

"What's going to happen now?" Nimeta shrieked.

"If they head east they might be able to make it through the Croatian zone and into the city. But they'd need travel permits and other documents. Either that, or they wait until evening and try their luck with the Serbian barricades."

"Do you really think you can just crash through the barricades?"

"If that's the only choice we've got..."

"Go through the Croatian zone."

"Yes, but if they don't make it they'll have lost time and traveled over rough roads with the patient for nothing. Anyway, commander Burhan asked me to fill you in on the situation. He thought that with your connections as a journalist you might be able to get travel passes and whatever else they need... Otherwise they'll probably be unable to get through. If you could try and..."

"Please come in," Nimeta said, cutting him off.

"I'm in a hurry."

"Come in. I've thought of something. Just give me a little time."

The man reluctantly stepped inside and took a seat. Hana and Raziyanım didn't say a word. For the first time in her life, Raziyanım forgot to offer a guest refreshments. Nimeta grabbed her coat and stood at the door.

"I'm going to go find those documents. Wait for me," she said.

"I hope it doesn't take long," the man said.

She scampered down the steps and broke into a run along the back streets. She entered the back door of the Holiday Inn and went to the reception desk, out of breath and disheveled.

"Can you tell me Stefan Stefanovic's room number?"

"He checked out a week ago."

"Did he leave an address?"

The receptionist looked through the registry. "No, it seems he didn't."

Nimeta left the hotel, too tired to run, but walking as fast as her legs would carry her. She entered a back street. The buses had been avoiding the mostly barricaded main streets ever since the war began. She flagged down an approaching bus. As they approached the television building she yelled, "Stop!" at the driver and leapt off the bus.

She stormed into the building and rushed up to Sonya.

"Quick, find Stefan for me," she said.

"My God, Nimeta, you look awful. What happened?"

"I'll tell you later. It's urgent. A matter of life and death. Find him and send him to my house."

"But I thought you said you didn't want him visiting you at home. That your mother…"

"Never mind my mother. This is an emergency. Don't you understand? If it's too much trouble tell me where he is. They said he'd checked out of the hotel."

"Ivan wondered where you were. You were supposed to start work today, Nimeta."

Nimeta grabbed Sonya by the collar. "Sonya, shut up! Go find Stefan. Now! Understand?"

"Okay," Sonya said. "What should I tell him?"

"Tell him whatever you want. Tell him I'm dying. Tell him I'm taking my last breath… Just make sure he comes right away!"

Sonya grabbed the coat hanging on a hook behind her chair and asked, "Where are you going now?"

"I've got to get back home so the man there can leave."

"What man? What are you talking about?"

"Sonya, we're wasting time. Go. I'll explain later," Nimeta said. She dragged Sonya to the staircase under the bemused looks of their co-workers.

Jumping onto one of the bicycles in the courtyard, she began pedaling, shouting over her shoulder to the security guard in his hut that she had some urgent business and would bring the bike back that evening. She slipped past the checkpoint barrier without waiting for a response.

When she got home she found her mother in the kitchen, lined up in front of the window with Hana and the visitor. "We'll have to wait," Nimeta told him.

"For how long?" he asked.

"I don't know. Until we find the person I'm looking for."

"I can't stay here for hours. I've got other things to do. If you want me to come back in a few hours..."

"I can't give you an exact time. Just wait for a while longer. We might find him in a few minutes, or it might take a few hours."

"I can't wait. I'll come back later."

"Weren't you the one who said it was an emergency?"

"Yes, but you can't even tell me how long I'll need to wait."

"Just a second," Nimeta said as she ran to a back room. She returned carrying a huge rifle, her father's hunting rifle from over the years. Raziyanım, Hana and the man stared in amazement.

"You'll wait for as long as it takes. Nobody move."

The man stood. He started walking toward the door. A bullet whizzed past his right ear and opened a hole in the wall.

"Are you out of your mind?" Raziyanım shouted. Hana started to cry.

"Stop your blubbering!" Nimeta yelled.

The man hesitated for a moment. Then he slowly took his seat.

"What's your name?" Nimeta asked him.

"Nusret."

"You're not leaving here unless you kill me first," she said. "It's either you, or me: one of us dies. Or we wait here together. Do I make myself clear, Nusret?"

Nimeta pulled the nearest chair closer and sat down, the rifle trained on Nusret.

"Perhaps I'd better go inside..." Raziyanım began saying.

"Nobody move," Nimeta said.

An hour later she was still sitting on the chair with the rife pointing at Nusret.

There was a knock on the door at around two. "Go open the door, Hana," Nimeta said. Hana darted out of her grandmother's arms and over to the door. Stefan and Sonya had arrived together. When Sonya saw the scene in the living room she wondered for a moment if Nimeta had lost her mind.

"Nimeta, it'll be alright dear, everything's okay," she said in soothing tones.

"Stop talking nonsense," Nimeta snapped. "Nothing's okay." Then she turned to the man and said, "They say patience is a virtue. Thank you for waiting, Nusret."

"What are you doing here?" Raziyanım asked Stefan.

"Shut up, Mother!" Nimeta said.

"I need to go the bathroom," Nusret said. Nimeta finally lowered the rifle and pointed with her chin to the hallway. As the man trotted off, Stefan asked, "Who's he? Has he done something to you?"

"Stefan, I need you to do something for me," Nimeta said. "I'm begging you: save my son."

"Fiko?" Stefan asked, stunned.

"Fiko's hurt. He's got to get to a hospital right away. The Serbs have barricaded the roads. The ambulance can't get past. You've got both a Croatian and a Serbian ID. Find a way to get Fiko into the city through the Croatian zone. But hurry, he's seriously wounded."

"Where is he now?" Stefan asked as Nusret was coming back from the toilet.

"Nusret will take you to him," Nimeta said. "Hurry."

"I've got to stop by the place I'm staying," Stefan said. "Come on, Nusret, let's go."

"Take me with you, I want to come too. Wait just a sec," Nimeta said.

"We won't be able to bring you back," Nusret said. "And it'll be easier if there are only two of us. Don't make us waste any more time. I'm late as it is."

"I'm coming too."

The man pulled a gun out of his back pocket and said, "Look, I could have neutralized you if I'd wanted to. I understood how upset you were, so I sat and waited. Now listen to me: you're not coming. Don't make me have to stop you."

As the two men were walking out the door, Nimeta grabbed Stefan's hands. She brought his hands to her lips and kissed them. "God bless you, Stefan," she said. "God bless you."

After Stefan and Nusret left, Nimeta went to her mother's room, picked up the *Koran* on the nightstand, went over to the window and lifted her eyes to the heavens:

"Allah, save my son," she pleaded. She placed the *Koran* on the window ledge, rested her right hand on top of it and said, "Allah, I swear to you on the holy book that if you bring my son safely back to me I'll never see Stefan again. No matter what, I promise I'll never see him again."

Trebevic - March 1993

Having checked every last road, track and pass and tried everything he could to get closer to the city, Burhan returned to the spot where he'd dropped off Nusret. They'd agreed that if he failed to find a way through he'd wait at this spot for Nusret to come back.

Burhan was confident that Nimeta had left no stone unturned to get Fiko passage through the Croatian zone. If his wife had come up empty-handed, Burhan would have to come up with an alternative plan. He knew he was running out of time. If they left things too late his son would lose his leg, and maybe even his life. He'd considered slinging Fiko over his shoulder and trekking through the trees and bushes down to the city, but decided he'd be needlessly risking both their lives. The only answer was to wait a while longer. If Nimeta managed to work miracles, wonderful; if not, they'd crash through the barricades, prepared to risk death knowing that to wait any longer would mean certain death for Fiko in any case. Crashing through the barricades was a last resort for when they had nothing to lose. For now, though, he preferred to wait, calm and full of hope, praying and trying not to panic.

Burhan opened the door to the ambulance. The cool air would do Fiko good. He lifted his son's head a little higher and made sure the wounded leg, which was wrapped in layer after layer of parkas, was as high as possible. He'd recently given Fiko an injection of the morphine and the antihemorrhagic provided by the doctor. When his son grew thirsty, he gave him sips of water.

Raif, who was pacing in circles around the ambulance, watched his brother-in-law with a sense of respect and admiration.

Raif had considered his brother-in-law to be overly serious and a bit of a workaholic ever since Burhan had married his big sister, but during the time they'd spent together in the mountains he'd discovered new facets of Burhan's character. For one thing, he was stoic to a degree seen in few people, as though he had prepared himself in advance for every eventuality. He never seemed surprised, overjoyed or distraught, and never fell to pieces. He was cool-headed and farsighted. His ability to analyze a situation and ready himself for every outcome had earned him a great deal of respect among his fellow soldiers. As Raif got to know his brother-in-law better he came to understand why their command post had enjoyed greater success than those on other mountains.

Burhan hadn't panicked when Fiko was wounded either. He'd gone into the tent, rested his head on his hands and spent about five minutes weighing up their options. After speaking first to the doctor and then to his son, he'd learned that Fiko would rather die than have his leg amputated.

"But he's still a boy," Raif had said. "How can you make a decision based on what he says? Thousands of boys his age have lost arms and legs in this war. It doesn't matter if he's missing his leg as long as he stays alive."

"I'm not letting him decide. I wanted to find out how important it was to him to keep his leg," Burhan had replied. "He could have said, cut my leg off right away and save me. But he didn't."

"So what are we going to do?"

"First, we'll try to save his leg. For as long as we can. If we fail, he'll lose it."

"Will they amputate it here?"

"That's the problem, Raif. An operation in these conditions could well lead to septicemia. I'm going to do everything I can to get him to a hospital."

"I'm coming with you."

"Good," Burhan had said. Nusret drove the ambulance. When they'd spotted the barricades they'd turned back and decided to let the driver, a commando intimately familiar with the mountain paths, strike out on his own to get word to Nimeta.

Now they were waiting.

His head resting on his father's lap, Fiko gazed down at the Milacka river, which the rays of the rising sun had tinted red.

"Look over there, Dad," he said, "the Milacka's turned red."

"The Bosnaks say that the Milacka turns that color every dawn in memory of the blood they have shed over the centuries."

"I've never heard that."

Burhan caressed his son's head. "It's an old saying. As old as Kulin. You've never heard it because your generation wasn't supposed to take up arms. We thought you'd learn about warfare only in history books and didn't expect Bosnak blood to flow again. We were wrong."

Like a fiery serpent, the Milacka twisted and turned through the valley on the way to the Bosna river.

Fiko, his father and his uncle waited to be rescued... Patiently. Bosnaks were well-practiced in waiting.

TREBEVİC

March 1993

Peering through his binoculars, way down to the very bottom of the steep hillside, Burhan spotted what looked like a cloud of dust. "Please God," he prayed to himself, "may it be Nusret, may Nimeta have found a way out."

The cloud of dust grew thicker the closer it got. Burhan was feeling more hopeful with each passing second. The miracle that would save his son's life might be approaching behind that brownish cloud. The safe conduct passes, identity cards, travel papers – whatever it was that Nimeta had somehow found, was getting nearer and nearer. Burhan had to believe this. He wanted it more anything he'd ever wanted in his life, wanted the vehicle winding its way up the hill to bring hope to his son.

For many long hours he'd been cradling his son's head in his lap, with the boy's wounded leg stretched out on a stack of folded parkas. As the effect of the morphine had begun wearing off the boy had begun softly moaning. Burhan had desperately tried to find a way to distract his son from the pain in his wounded leg.

They'd begun talking about the blood-red Milacka river, and the saying about the river crying tears of blood for the Bosnaks. Fiko had said he'd never heard the saying.

"It's as old as Kulin," Burhan had told his son.

"Dad, what's all this about 'old as Kulin,'" Fiko had said. Hearing his family name used in this figure of speech had always given him the creeps. It made him feel like one of those tattered bits of hand-embroidered cloth, faded and worn with time, on sale in dusty second-hand shops, or like one of the many useless lengths of fabric laid away in one of his grandmother's mothball-scented wooden chests.

Burhan had launched into an account of the Kulins and the saying that referenced their name, mainly as a way to divert his son's attention from the wait and from the pain in his leg. Fiko began listening so attentively to this summary of Bosnak history he'd never come across in his schoolbooks that he really did seem to forget his leg for a time.

Like all boys his age, Fiko had studied the official version of history in the post-Tito era. Now, his head in his father's lap in an ambulance, his life in danger and his leg throbbing, he was suddenly eager to learn the real history of his people.

Burhan inwardly rejoiced at his son's interest. It would make the wait easier. He began relating the story of the Bosnak people, as though he was telling his son a bedtime story.

"Once upon a time, in the 6th or 7th century, no more than ten or so feudal lords shared the lands of Bosnia in peace and harmony. They were the most powerful and independent feudal lords in all of Europe. Unlike in the other feudal systems, they retained their lands even when they failed to discharge their duties to the monarchies to which they'd sworn fealty. And so the years passed. Then, in 1082, when the Hungarian King invaded Bosnia, he appointed an aristocrat named Stefan to be the "Ban", or viceroy, of Bosnia. That is, Stefan was to collect taxes and raise an army on behalf of the Kingdom of Hungary. And it was from that time onwards that the feudal lords began battling each other for the title of Ban.

"Three Ban made their mark on Bosnia in the Middle Ages. Under the rule of the first one, Ban Kulin, the Bosnaks were liberated from Serbian domination and became fully autonomous for the first time in their history in 1180. Ban Kulin later liberated the Bosnian Church and declared the Bogomil sect to be the state religion. Years later, however, he was forced to convert to Catholicism to prevent his people from being burned at the stake by the Pope's Crusaders. When he died a year later, the cause was said to be a broken heart."

"What about the other two Ban?"

"The other two important Ban were Kotromanic and Tvrtko. Prince Kotromanic ascended the throne in 1322. During his reign, Hersek became part of Bosnia. He was also a Bogomil, but was tortured by the Crusaders until he converted to Catholicism. As for Tvrtko, he ascended the throne in 1358. He extended Bosnian territory as far as the Dalmatian coast and changed his title from "Ban" to "King". Still, of the eighteen Bosnian ban and kings, Ban Kulin is the only one whose reign is legend, and spoken of as a golden age of peace and prosperity. Bosnians wrote poetry and songs in his honor, and the expression 'as old as Kulin' was coined."

Burhan saw that Fiko's eyes were shut, and decided to stop talking in case he'd fallen asleep. He himself was just nodding off, chin on his chest, when Fiko startled him with the question, "Dad, why did we become Muslims when we were already Christian?"

He wet his son's parched lips with a few drops of water from his canteen and checked the bandages on his leg. The bleeding seemed to have stopped. He'd become accustomed to the smell of blood in the ambulance.

"Do you want to sleep for a bit?" he asked his son.

"Dad, why did we become Muslims?" Fiko asked again. "Why did we convert from Christianity to Islam?"

"Do you really want me to explain all that right now?"

As the sun rose higher above the horizon it was getting hot inside the ambulance and Burhan's stomach started churning from the smell of blood. There was still no sign of Nusret. They were in a race against time and at that particular moment Burhan couldn't have cared less about the Bosnian's reasons becoming Muslims. If they'd remained Christians they might not be stuck here in the ambulance, he even thought to himself. But then again, the Serbian butchers and treacherous Croats would probably have found another excuse to expel them from their homeland.

"It wouldn't be accurate to say that the Bosnaks 'converted', Fiko," Raif said. "The Bogomil sect had a lot in common with Islam in any case. As you know, the Ottoman Empire was established in the lands of Asia Minor known as 'Anatolia'. Even as the Turks were staging incursions they'd begun trickling into the Balkans as migrants. In a sense, those first settlers from Anatolia were part of the propaganda efforts for the Ottoman conquest. Before they sent in the army they'd first send dervishes to win over the local people."

"Like a form of public relations," Burhan said.

"Exactly."

Burhan's eyes were on Fiko's leg. He'd noticed a spreading patch of fresh blood but didn't want to alarm his son. When Raif saw Burhan rummaging through the bag of medical supplies he'd taken up the thread of Burhan's story to help keep Fiko's mind off his wound.

"The Middle Ages was a dark time for Christianity. The Pope was persecuting the Bogomils on behalf of the Catholic Church while the Patriarchate did the same on behalf of the Orthodox faith of the Byzantines. The Bosnaks are a stubborn people. They clung to their faith through torture and oppression."

"But the Bogomils were Christians too, weren't they?" Fiko asked. "What was the problem?" Burhan took a syringe out of the bag.

"Dad, are you about to give me another injection?" Fiko groaned.

"Just listen to your uncle," Burhan said. "Don't worry about what I'm doing."

"Keep talking, Uncle!" I'll learn the entire history of the Bosnian people just as I'm going. Why didn't you tell me any of this earlier?"

"Going where?" Raif asked. Fiko and his father simultaneously answered, the former with, "To the other side," the latter with, "to the nearest hospital."

It took a moment for Fiko's words to register. Burhan's voice cracked as he responded.

"Fiko, you're not going to the other side. You're still so young. You've got a long, happy life ahead of you. When your mother gets here, this nightmare will be over. You've got to keep believing that everything will work out. All we have right now is hope."

Raif though it best to change the subject as quickly as possible.

"Now where were we? Ah, you're right, we never talked about any of this history. That's because we were taught that we had become a single people, and they discouraged any talk about our differences. After all, we were Yugoslavians too!" A smile twisted Raif's lips and he looked as though he didn't know whether to spit or to cry. The Bosnaks had never made a fuss over their Muslim faith, and what had that got them?

"The Bogomils were Christians, but they didn't cross themselves, get baptized or view Christ as the son of God. To them, Christ was a prophet, no more. They also preferred to perform their rituals outdoors, not in a church, and believed in the rejection of the fruits of this world. To them, the world was the work of Satan while paradise was the realm of God. Because of the similarities between their faiths, Bosnak peasants and nobility alike began taking an interest in the Bektashi Sufi Order that was spreading through the Balkans at the time. Did you know that the Muslims of Anatolia were influenced by Zoroastrians and shamans, just as the Bogomils were?"

"You're confusing me, Uncle."

"There's nothing confusing about it. The Bogomils suffered greatly at the hands of their fellow Christians, and when they found a religious order with which they had a lot in common…"

"They had no choice but to become Muslims. Is that what you're saying?"

"They did have a choice, Fiko." Raif wanted to make certain his nephew understood clearly. "If they'd chosen Catholicism it wouldn't have made any difference to the Ottomans. The Ottomans weren't interested in forcing their religion on others; their main concern was collecting taxes.

When the Bogomils were offered the opportunity to register themselves as Muslims in Ottoman ledgers, many accepted. Had they been registered as Christians they would have faced the persecution of either the Catholic or the Orthodox churches. Islam didn't take root overnight, Fiko; it spread over centuries. In the 15th century, there were about eight times as many Christians as Muslims in Bosnia. By the middle of the 16th century, half were Muslim."

Burhan prepared to give his son another injection of methergine. "Time to take a break from your history lesson," he said, as he plunged the needle into Fiko's haunch.

"Dad, when did you learn to give injections?" Fiko asked.

"War teaches you a lot of things. If only it taught us how to live in peace."

Burhan turned to Raif and said, "I had no idea you were such a history buff."

"The war's uncovered everybody's secret side. In all these years we've known each other, I never realized what a jewel of a character you've kept hidden away."

Burhan laughed. "I wish..." he began, before he fell silent. Raif tried to guess how he's have ended that sentence: "I wish there hadn't been a war and you'd never realized," or, perhaps, "I wish Nimeta had realized." Ever since he'd grown close to Burhan he'd felt a twinge of uneasiness at the mention of Nimeta's name. He turned to Fiko and resumed the history lesson.

Fiko was coming down with a fever. First, he'd started shaking. Burhan had pulled one of the parkas out from under his leg and covered him with it. Then Fiko started drifting in and out of consciousness.

When he was feeling alert, he'd say, "Go on, Uncle." Raif felt a bit like Shahrazad as he resumed his tale, dragging it out and embroidering it with details. When he grew tired, Burhan would take over, as though if they finished their story and fell silent it would be the end of Fiko. As though the history of Bosnia had cast a spell over the three of them, and the sound of their voices would keep death at bay and keep them all alive. "Tell me more, Uncle... Tell me more, Dad."

They talked and talked, with Fiko drifting in and out of sleep and the labyrinths of history.

Ottoman raiders started riding through the Balkans as of the middle of the 14th century, sweeping in across Thrace and Bulgaria, resisted by Serb, Bosnak, Hungarian and Croatian alike. The raiders would go, but they would return each spring, stronger than ever. Fiko was leading an army. Sword brandished, he led a charge through Kosovo. Ottoman cavalrymen suddenly turned into Crusaders in silver helmets and chain mail. Again, Fiko was there, this time cutting down Crusaders left and right. Never-ending war and an endless stream of blood, so much blood that the Milacka turned first pink then a bright red.

Burhan had wrapped his cigarette case in gauze and was pressing it with all his might against his son's wound. Raif had pulled his off his undershirt and was using it to mop Fiko's feverish forehead, dampening the cloth from time to time from his canteen.

Fiko was charging across the plains, sword held high. "Tell me more, Uncle... more," he whispered, the beads of sweat standing out on his forehead.

Raif kept talking, and it was only when he tasted salt that he realized tears were rolling down his cheeks. Burhan's lips trembled as he silently prayed for his son's survival.

And still Raif kept talking of Fatih Sultan Mehmet and his victorious army, of how a distinctive Bosnian culture flourished during Ottoman rule, of the Janissaries, of the waning days of the Empire…

"Raif… he's unconscious… you can stop now."

Not only was Fiko unconscious, the life was draining out of him, slowly but surely. Burhan had no idea what to do. He got out of the ambulance and emptied the contents of the medical supplies bag onto the ground, sorting through the boxes and vials of medicine, picking one up and dropping another, reading the labels and tossing them back onto the ground. Finally, he returned empty-handed to the ambulance, where he cradled his son's head in his lap once again. He leaned his head against the window, and as he stroked Fiko's burning forehead and damp hair he thought hard about life.

In a lifespan of seventy or eighty years, he thought to himself, the first and the last ten years are marked by the helplessness of childhood and old age, but are we sent to this earth to squander the remaining fifty or sixty years by constantly being at each other's throats, fighting and battling, and then suffering the losses and destruction that come from all that fighting? Whether Bogomil or Christian, Jew or Muslim, was that really mankind's fate?

Then he started thinking about something else. After a long silence, he spoke.

"You know something, Raif," he began, "I think I know a way we can solve our problem."

"Are you saying we should wait until dark and try to carry Fiko through the forest?"

"No, that's not what I'm talking about. I was thinking about our predicament and it suddenly came to me… Is there no way to get into a city under siege?"

"They're dug into positions on the mountains. They've got snipers ready to pick off anyone walking along the street."

"What if we didn't go overland but underground…"

"What are you saying?"

"A tunnel… If we dug a tunnel all the way to our only point of exit we could get shipments of food and pharmaceuticals out, and our wounded in."

"Are you saying we should start digging a tunnel?"

"Not right now, I'm not. But we should develop this idea of a tunnel."

Raif knew Burhan was prepared to die to get his son out of this hopeless situation. As long as they remained calm, they might find a way. But now the guy was starting to spout nonsense. A tunnel! He didn't even bother to respond.

The cloud of dust they'd noticed a short while ago seemed to be getting closer, seemed to be a vehicle of some kind, winding its way up the steep road.

"I think something's coming up the mountain," Raif had said. "It looks like a jeep, and it must be going fast to kick up all that dust."

They held their breaths and waited. Fiko was grimacing in pain. His head turned from side to side in his father's lap.

Raif dampened the undershirt on Fiko's forehead again and rubbed his temples.

"If we could only lower his fever…" Burhan said. He'd gone white and looked prepared to cut a deal with the devil himself if it would save his son. But even the devil hadn't visited this isolated mountain for some time; the devil was down in Sarajevo, blocking the roads into the city.

"It was more important we staunch the bleeding, and we've managed that at least," Raif said.

The growling sound of the approaching vehicle was growing louder. Burhan thought he heard a horn honk. A beep-beep-beep off in the distance, as though whoever was coming wanted to make sure they knew it. He sat stock still so he wouldn't jar his son's head.

"Raif, go have a look," he said.

Like Burhan, Raif had sat still, scared to get up and find out that the vehicle they'd pinned all their hopes on was nothing more than a mirage.

When Burhan glanced out the window he saw Raif gleefully waving his arms about in the air. It had been a jeep. So, Nimeta had come through for their son. He checked his watch and was astonished to see that they had only been waiting for a few hours. The entire history of Bosnia, from beginning to end, had been related in not much more than half an hour.

Raif was running down the hill. He shut his eyes and waited. A short time later he heard Nusret's voice. "Commander," he said. "We've succeeded. Your wife found someone who can get Fiko through the Croatian zone with no problem."

"Could you hand me that bag?" Burhan said, pointing to a spot in the front seat. He took the bag and gently slipped it under his son's head before he got out of the ambulance. The man in the jeep also got out and started walking over. A man in civilian clothes with a clean-shaven head. He seemed to recognize the face, but couldn't place it.

"I hope I'm not too late. I've come to get Fiko," the man said, holding out a hand. "Burhan, it's me, Stefan. Don't you remember me?" Stefan was left with his hand in mid-air. Stefan! It couldn't be! Stefan!

"Nimeta's friend… from Zagreb TV… She introduced us way back when, in Zagreb."

Burhan's ears were buzzing. His knees shook. So, the devil had arrived and was ready to cut a deal for his son's life. He'd wanted help to arrive even it was in the form of the devil himself; well here he was, standing right across from him. "Give me your son," he said. Burhan no longer wanted to deal with the devil: he wanted to kill him

"How do you think you've kept your job in Knin when everyone else was losing theirs," a rough voice said. "If it weren't for the connections of that Croat who's screwing your wife you'd have been fired a long time ago, just like the rest of us. Then we'd have seen what you were really made of: are you ready to fight and kill Croats, or not?"

Burhan clamped his hands over his ears but he could still hear that voice. The man had run off, cupping a broken nose, a long time again. But his voice echoed still in Burhan's ears. "That Croat who's screwing your wife… screwing your wife…"

He reached for the gun at his waist before he realized what he was doing.

"Burhan!"

Raif's voice brought him to his senses. Nusret and Raif were staring at him.

"What?" he managed to say. "What do you want?"

"I've come to get the boy. Fiko. I was going to take him to Sarajevo via Stup, but Raif tells me we don't have much time. I can get him to a fully equipped hospital in our zone. We need to hurry."

"Where did you come from? Who sent you?"

"Nimeta sent word, because I've got transit passes for both sides. Sonya was lucky to find me. If she'd called half an hour later I'd have been gone. I was planning on leaving Sarajevo a long time ago but some work came up and I stayed. Must be kismet."

Burhan heard Fiko moan in his sleep. His son was seventeen. He had to live. Nothing else mattered compared to Fiko's life. He'd sit down and deal.

"Kismet it is!" he said. There was a reason for everything. Like he'd said to Nimeta, he must be paying for some sin wrongly ascribed to him.

"How soon can we leave?" Burhan asked.

"I can't take you with me, Burhan. It would be dangerous for the boy, as well. I promise to send you word as soon as I get him to a hospital, though."

"If you can't get me across the border how are you going to get Fiko through?" Burhan asked.

"I told you, I have a transit pass. Fiko's still underage. I'll say he's my son or nephew and that he's badly hurt. It's an emergency. I'm sure I'll get him through any checkpoints."

The two men stood across from each other. "First you take my wife, and now my son," Burhan was thinking to himself. He'd compressed his lips so tightly his mouth looked like a thin scimitar. His gritted teeth ached.

Stefan guessed what was going through Burhan's mind. The expression on Burhan's face had instantly told him that he knew everything. If he drew the gun at his waist and pointed it at Stefan, he could pull the trigger. A vein throbbed in Burhan's temple. His eyes were like two dark wells, drained of color, retaining nothing but the pain he felt. He took a deep breath. The animosity that had rankled in Bosnia for centuries was searing his heart and was reflected in his eyes. He felt trapped. There was other way out. He'd have to surrender his son to Stefan and hope Fiko made it to the hospital.

In just a few seconds Burhan felt as though he'd aged at least a decade. The years rolled past. He was shaken and buffeted by memories from centuries ago. He looked at this man from a neighbouring land whose ancestors had at times lived in harmony with his, and at times had gouged their eyes out.

It was strange, the moment he'd resigned himself to saving his son at all costs, his fury started to subside, until finally the scorching rage in his heart was gone without a trace. He suddenly felt as though he'd known the man standing across from for the longest time.

Was it because Stefan was the only person able to save his son?

He spun round and walked over to the ambulance. Fiko was talking deliriously in his sleep again. He poured the last drops of water in the canteen onto the undershirt folded on his son's forehead. Then he went back to Stefan.

"I'd rather Fiko didn't have a rough ride. Could you take the ambulance?" he asked.

"Of course," Stefan replied.

"As soon as you hand Fiko over to a doctor, call the TV station. As you know, the phones work there," Burhan said. "There's not much left in the medical supply bag, but you'll find some rolls of gauze... if he bleeds on the way, press down on the wound."

"Okay. I know how to administer first-aid, but there won't be any need. I'll drive straight to a hospital and let you know how he's doing," Stefan said. "I'll look after him like my own..." He stopped himself from saying "son", and continued with... "like my own brother. Don't worry."

Burhan got back in the ambulance. He took his son's hot hand into the palm of his own hand, and pressed it to his heart.

"Have a safe journey, son. Stay safe, get well and come back to us in one piece," he said. "Godspeed." He touched his lips to his son's cheek, got out of the ambulance and stood in front of Stefan. This time, he was the one who reached out his hand. The two men clasped hands for a moment.

They were from the same race, and maybe even the same bloodline. They were roughly the same height and about the same age. They loved the same woman. Their ancestors had chosen different paths by which to get closer to God, and for that reason one of them was a Bosnak, the other a Croat. It hadn't been their own choices, any more than they'd chosen this war or their fate. There was one more thing they had in common: neither had any expectations for tomorrow.

Tomorrow would be filled with bullets, bombs and blood. Still, whether they realized it or not, each man hoped for a "brighter tomorrow". For all the pain, sorrow and violence inflicted on this magnificent world by people of different faiths for whatever misguided reason, hope springs eternal. Hope is life.

As the ambulance bounced over the rough road Fiko opened his eyes for a moment. When he saw he was headed for the Croatian zone with a stranger, his heart sank.

"I'm not really a stranger," Stefan said. "I'm a close friend of your mother's, a colleague. I'll get you to a hospital soon. Don't worry, once you've been treated and you're well again you can decide if you want to go home or to stay with your relatives in Istanbul."

"What would I do in Istanbul?" Fiko asked. "If I get better, I'm going back to Sarajevo."

"If you want to live in safety for the rest of the war... Never mind, you can make up your mind when you get out of the hospital."

"If I survive."

"You'll live," Stefan said, as though he were issuing an order.

Fiko couldn't see much more than blue sky and leafy treetops from where he was stretched out.

"Are we close to the border?" he asked.

"We'll be there in less than fifteen minutes."

They drove on a little further. When the barricades marking Croatian territory came into view Stefan slowed down. "Fiko, close your eyes and pretend to be asleep. I'll tell the police you're unconscious. Don't give me away, no matter what," he said.

Fiko glanced up one more time at the skies over his homeland. The he shut his eyes tight.

"Goodbye, beautiful Bosnia," he said to himself. "Goodbye to the land of my birth, to my country, to my family. Goodbye."

Bosnia, long-suffering Bosnia, would be waiting for yet another one of her sons to come home. Waiting with hope.